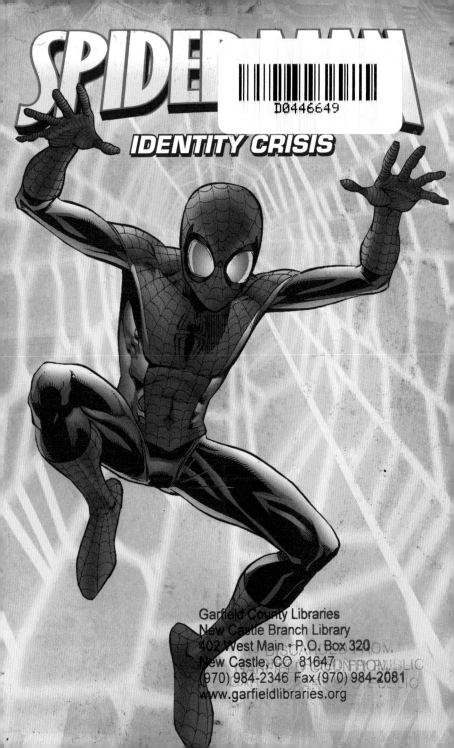

SPIDER-MAN
IDENTITY CRISIS

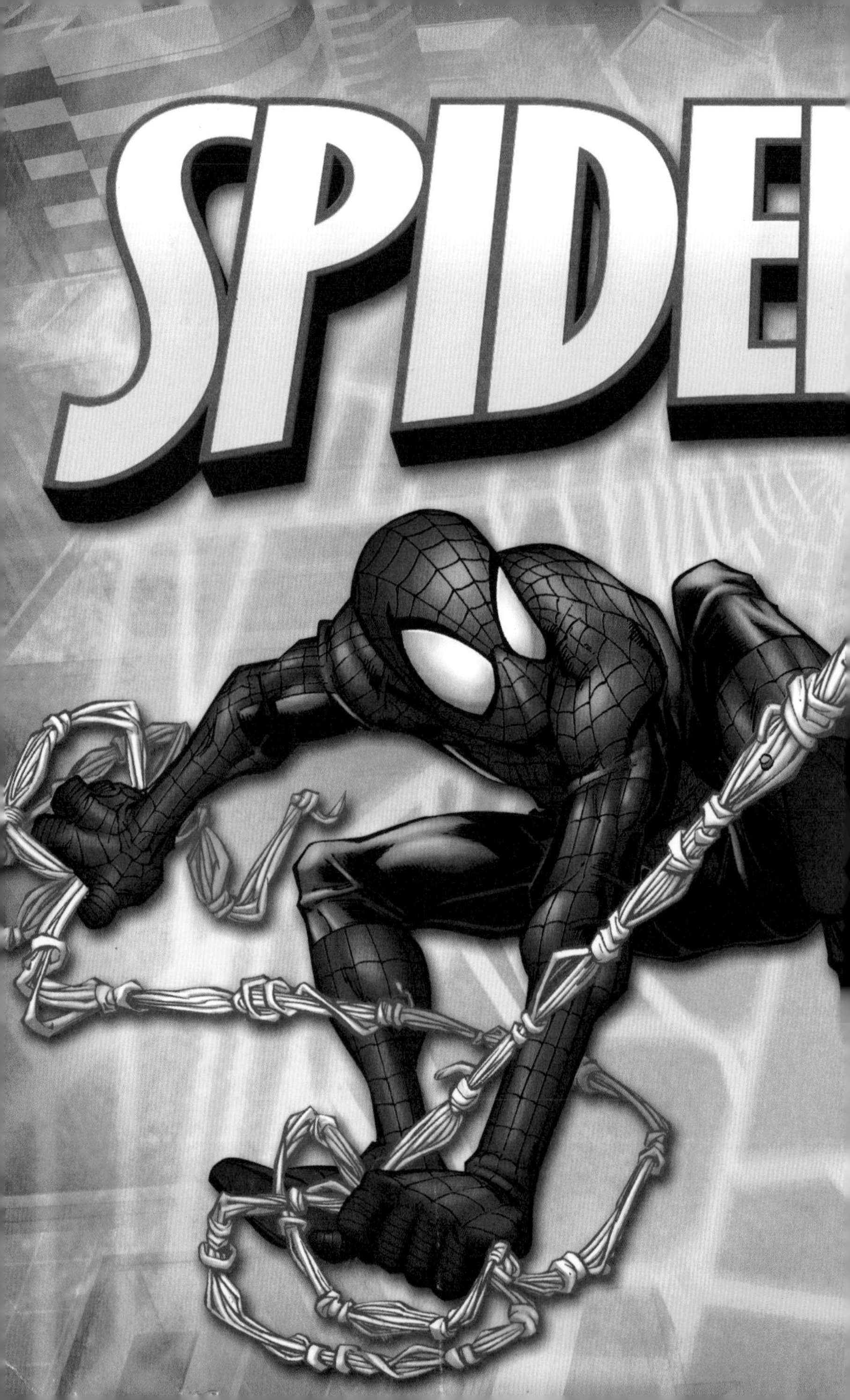
SPIDE

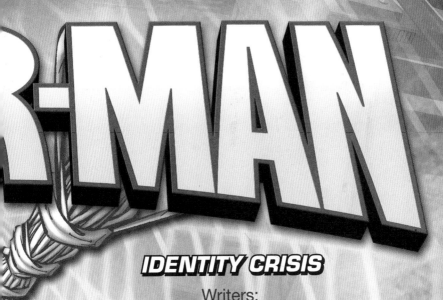

R-MAN

IDENTITY CRISIS

Writers:
Marc Sumerak & Chris Kipiniak
Pencilers:
Ale Garza, David Nakayama & Ryan Stegman
Inkers:
**Ale Garza, Gary Martin,
Ryan Stegman & Vicente Cifuentes**
Colors: **Guru eFX**
Letters: **Dave Sharpe with VC's Joe Caramagna**
Cover Artists: **Sean Murphy, Skottie Young
& Patrick Scherberger**
Assistant Editors: **Nathan Cosby & Jordan D. White**
Editor: **Mark Paniccia**

Collection Editor: **Jennifer Grünwald**
Editorial Assistant: **Alex Starbuck**
Assistant Editors: **Cory Levine & John Denning**
Editor, Special Projects: **Mark D. Beazley**
Senior Editor, Special Projects: **Jeff Youngquist**
Senior Vice President of Sales: **David Gabriel**
Vice President of Creative: **Tom Marvelli**

Editor in Chief: **Joe Quesada**
Publisher: **Dan Buckley**

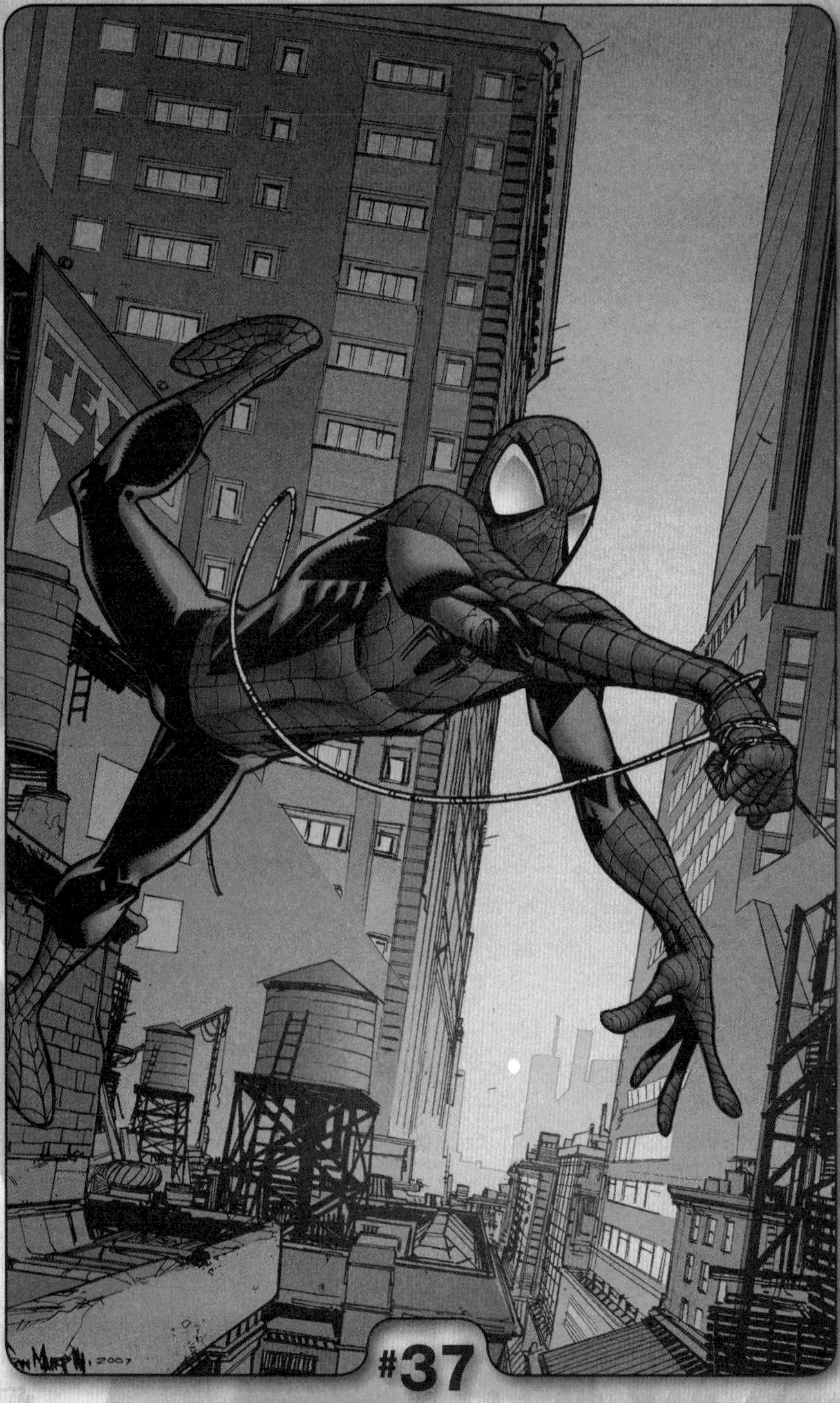

#37

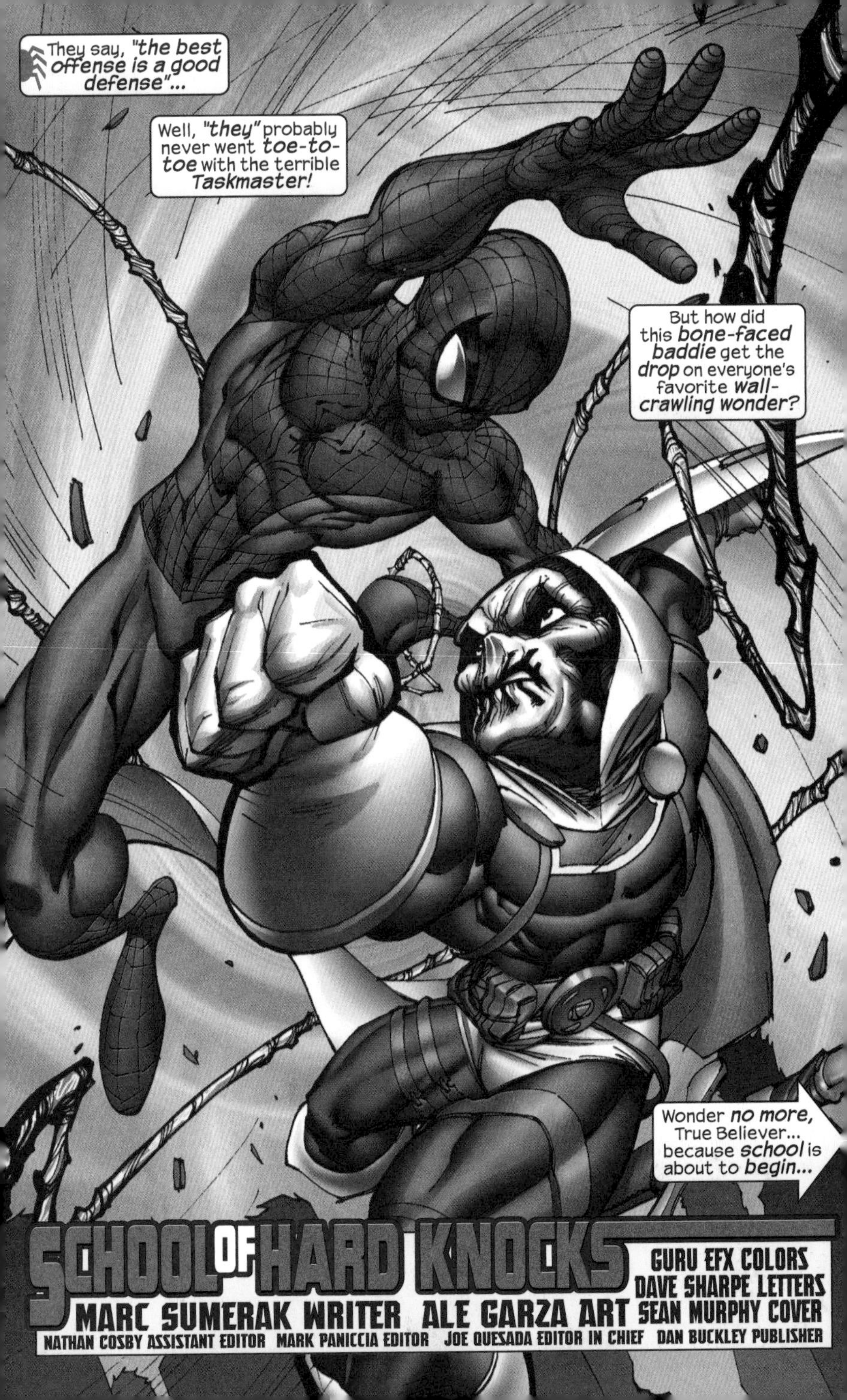
They say, "the best offense is a good defense"...
Well, "they" probably never went toe-to-toe with the terrible Taskmaster!
But how did this bone-faced baddie get the drop on everyone's favorite wall-crawling wonder?
Wonder no more, True Believer... because school is about to begin...
SCHOOL OF HARD KNOCKS
GURU EFX COLORS
DAVE SHARPE LETTERS
MARC SUMERAK WRITER
ALE GARZA ART
SEAN MURPHY COVER
NATHAN COSBY ASSISTANT EDITOR
MARK PANICCIA EDITOR
JOE QUESADA EDITOR IN CHIEF
DAN BUCKLEY PUBLISHER

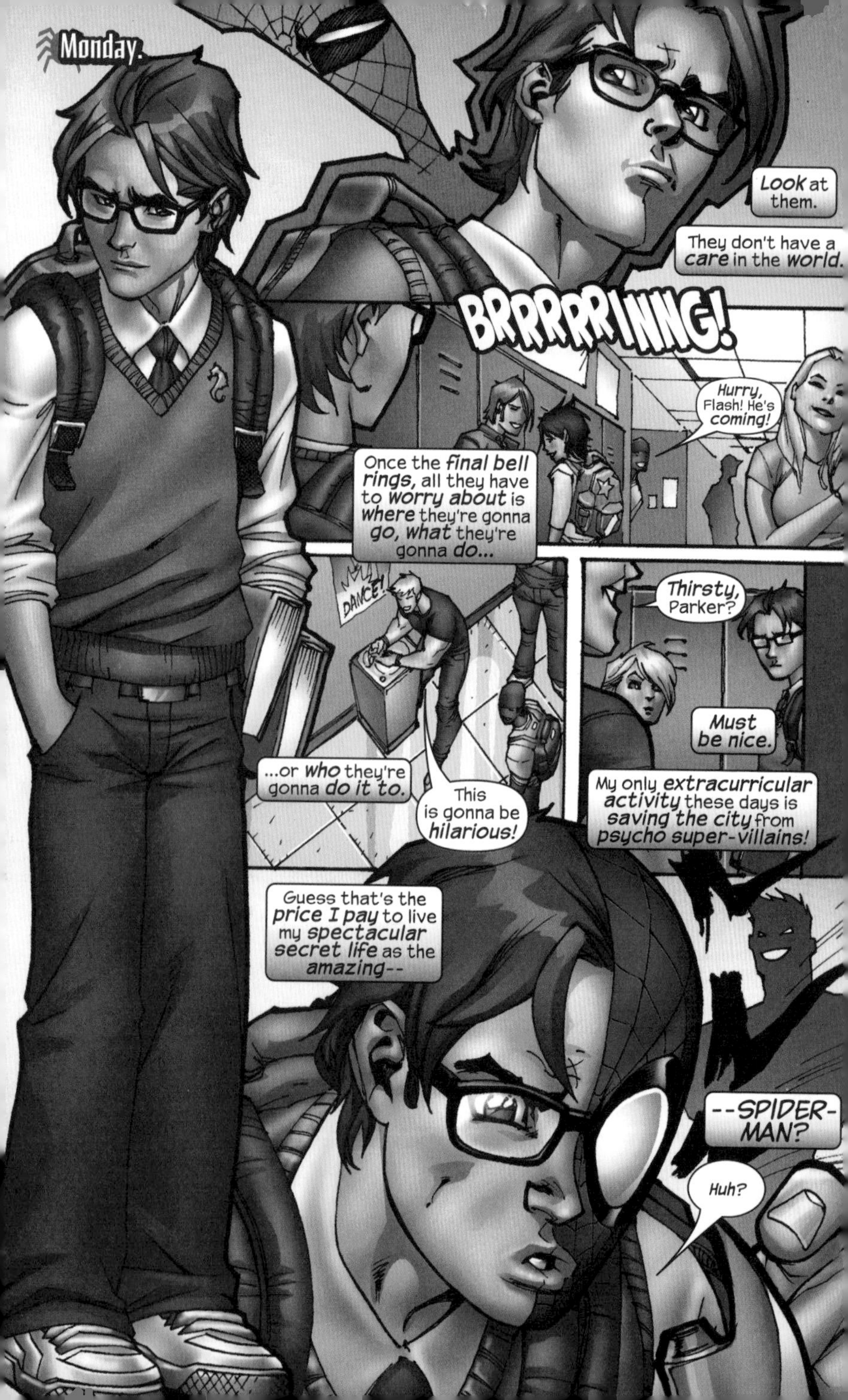
Monday.
Look at them.
They don't have a care in the world.
BRRRRRINNG!
Hurry, Flash! He's coming!
Once the final bell rings, all they have to worry about is where they're gonna go, what they're gonna do...
DANCE!
...or who they're gonna do it to.
This is gonna be hilarious!
Thirsty, Parker?
Must be nice.
My only extracurricular activity these days is saving the city from psycho super-villains!
Guess that's the price I pay to live my spectacular secret life as the amazing--
--SPIDER-MAN?
Huh?

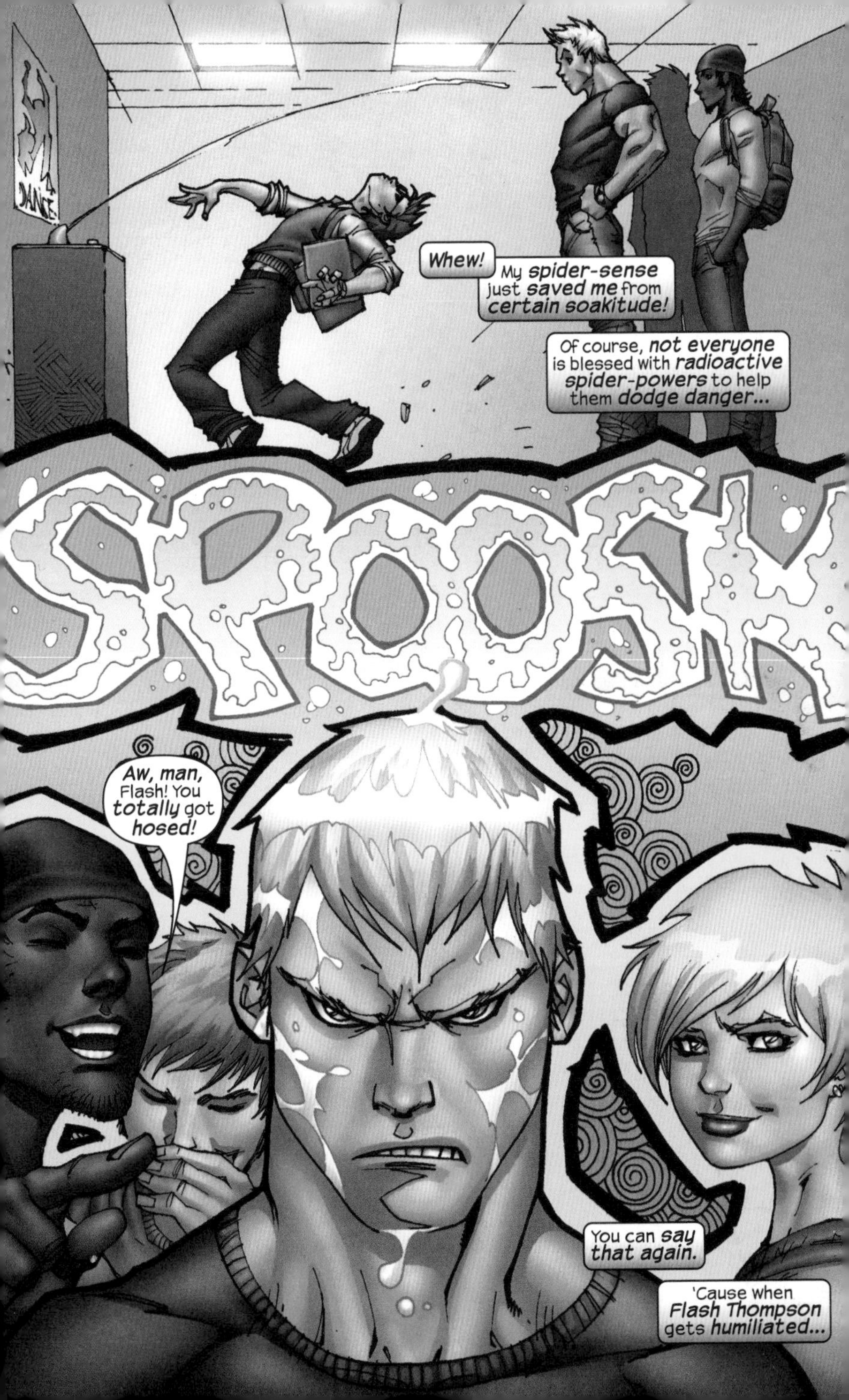
4 DANCE
Whew!
My spider-sense just saved me from certain soakitude!
Of course, not everyone is blessed with radioactive spider-powers to help them dodge danger...
SPOOSH
Aw, man, Flash! You totally got hosed!
You can say that again.
'Cause when Flash Thompson gets humiliated...

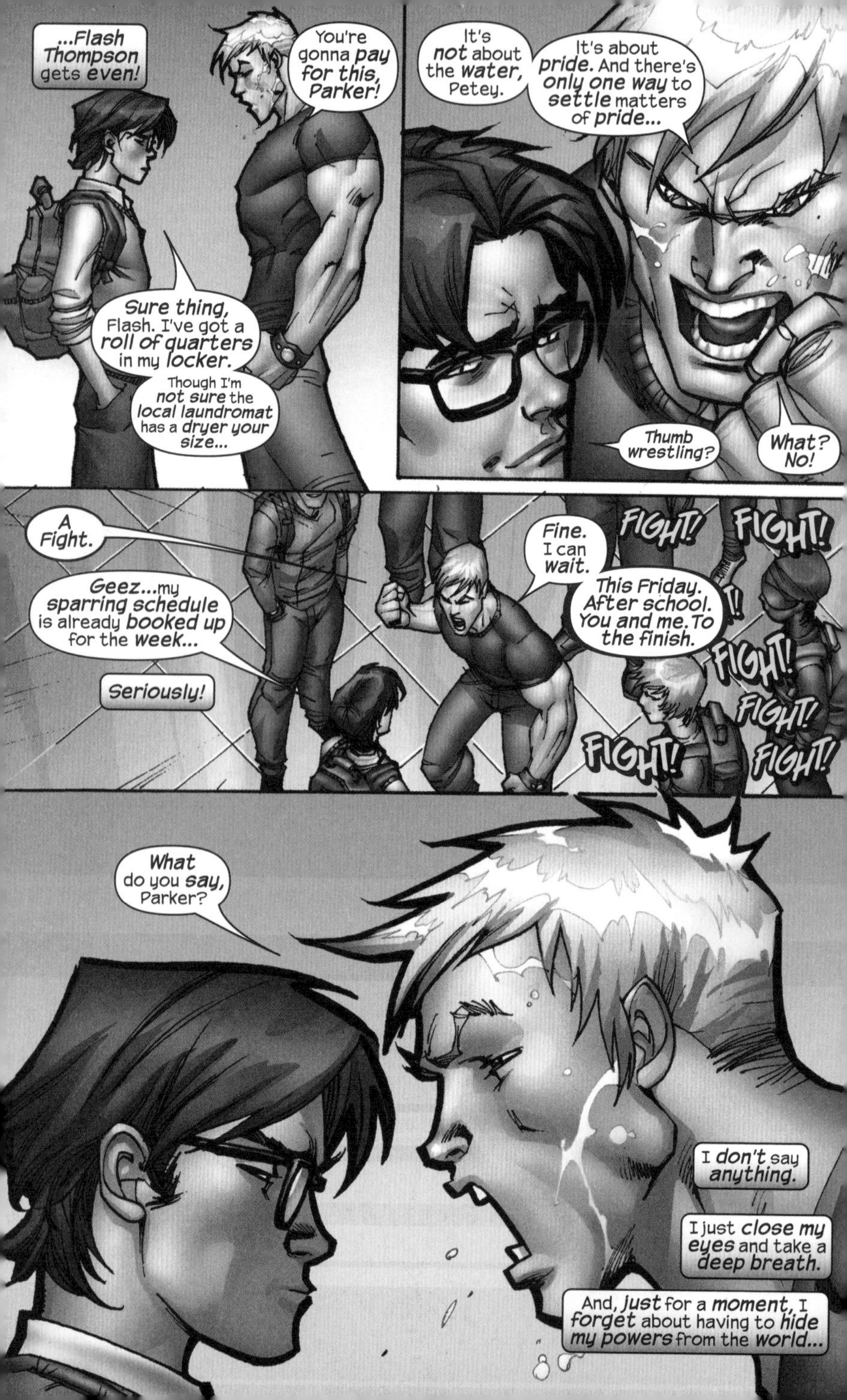
...Flash Thompson gets even!
You're gonna pay for this, Parker!
Sure thing, Flash. I've got a roll of quarters in my locker.
Though I'm not sure the local laundromat has a dryer your size...
It's not about the water, Petey.
It's about pride. And there's only one way to settle matters of pride...
Thumb wrestling?
What? No!
A Fight.
Geez...my sparring schedule is already booked up for the week...
Seriously!
Fine. I can wait.
This Friday. After school. You and me. To the finish.
FIGHT! FIGHT! FIGHT! FIGHT! FIGHT! FIGHT!
What do you say, Parker?
I don't say anything.
I just close my eyes and take a deep breath.
And, just for a moment, I forget about having to hide my powers from the world...

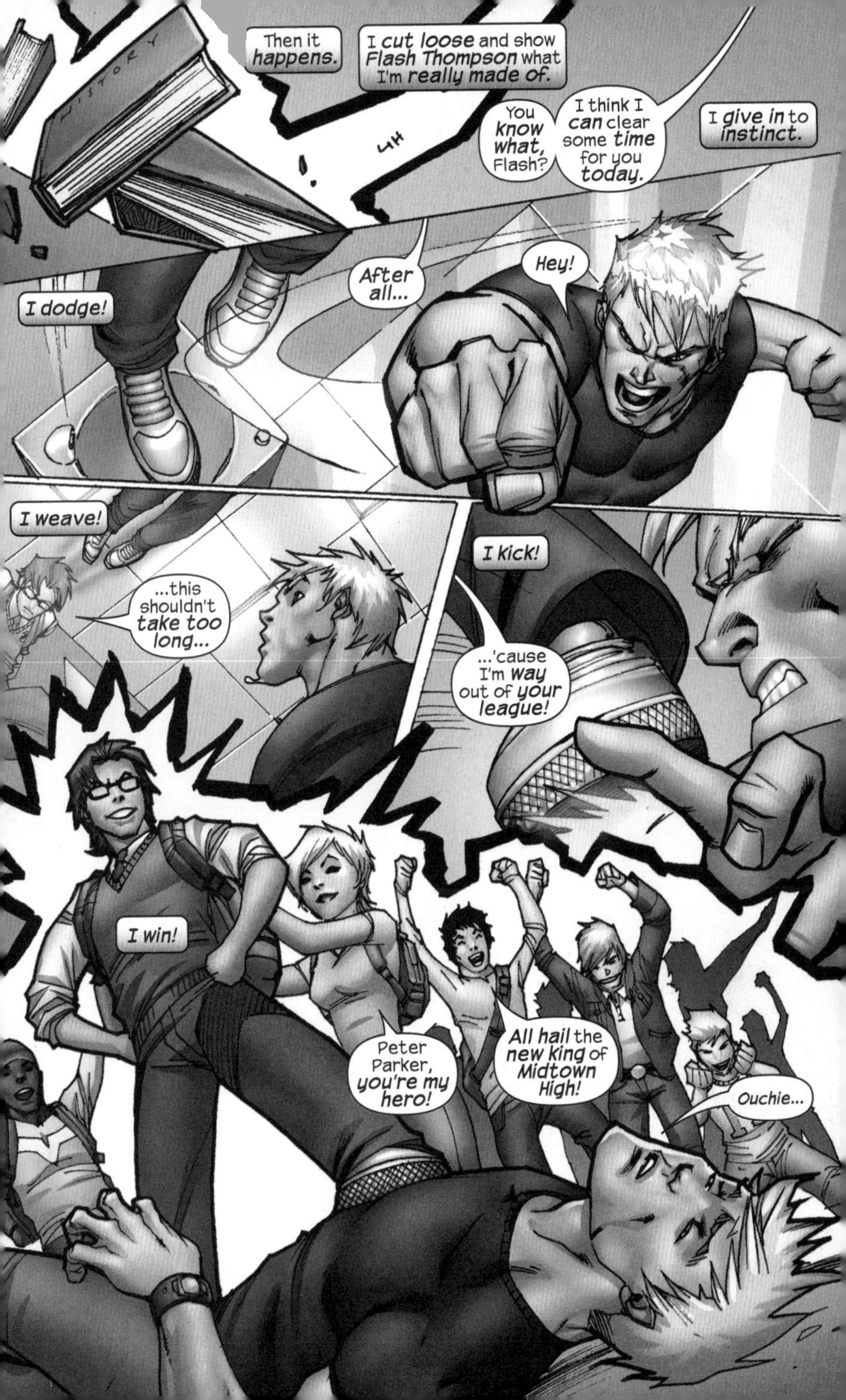
Then it happens.
I cut loose and show Flash Thompson what I'm really made of.
You know what, Flash?
I think I can clear some time for you today.
I give in to instinct.
I dodge!
After all...
Hey!
I weave!
...this shouldn't take too long...
I kick!
...'cause I'm way out of your league!
I win!
Peter Parker, you're my hero!
All hail the new king of Midtown High!
Ouchie...

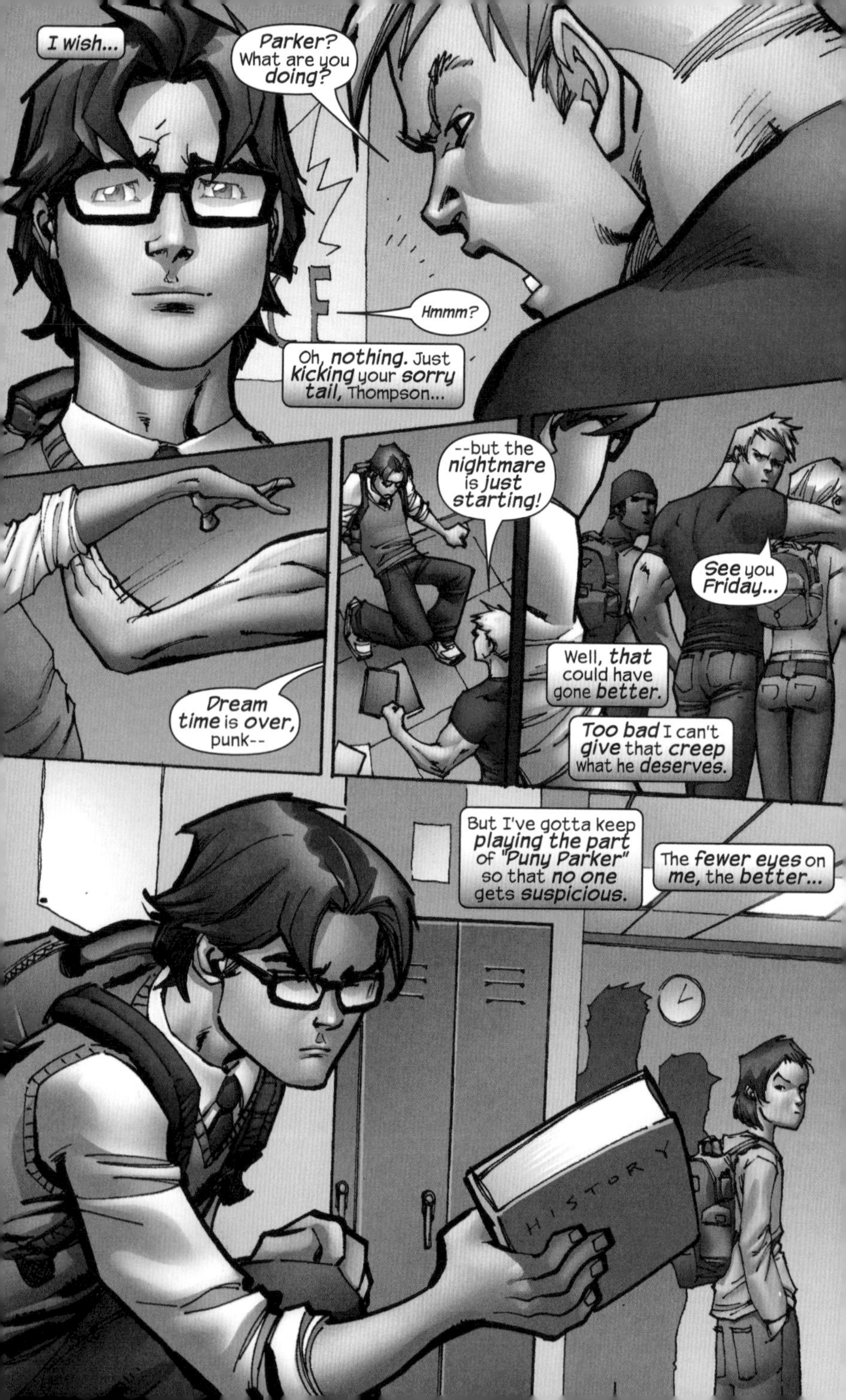
I wish...
Parker? What are you doing?
Hmmm?
Oh, nothing. Just kicking your sorry tail, Thompson...
Dream time is over, punk--
--but the nightmare is just starting!
See you Friday...
Well, that could have gone better.
Too bad I can't give that creep what he deserves.
But I've gotta keep playing the part of "Puny Parker" so that no one gets suspicious.
The fewer eyes on me, the better...
HISTORY

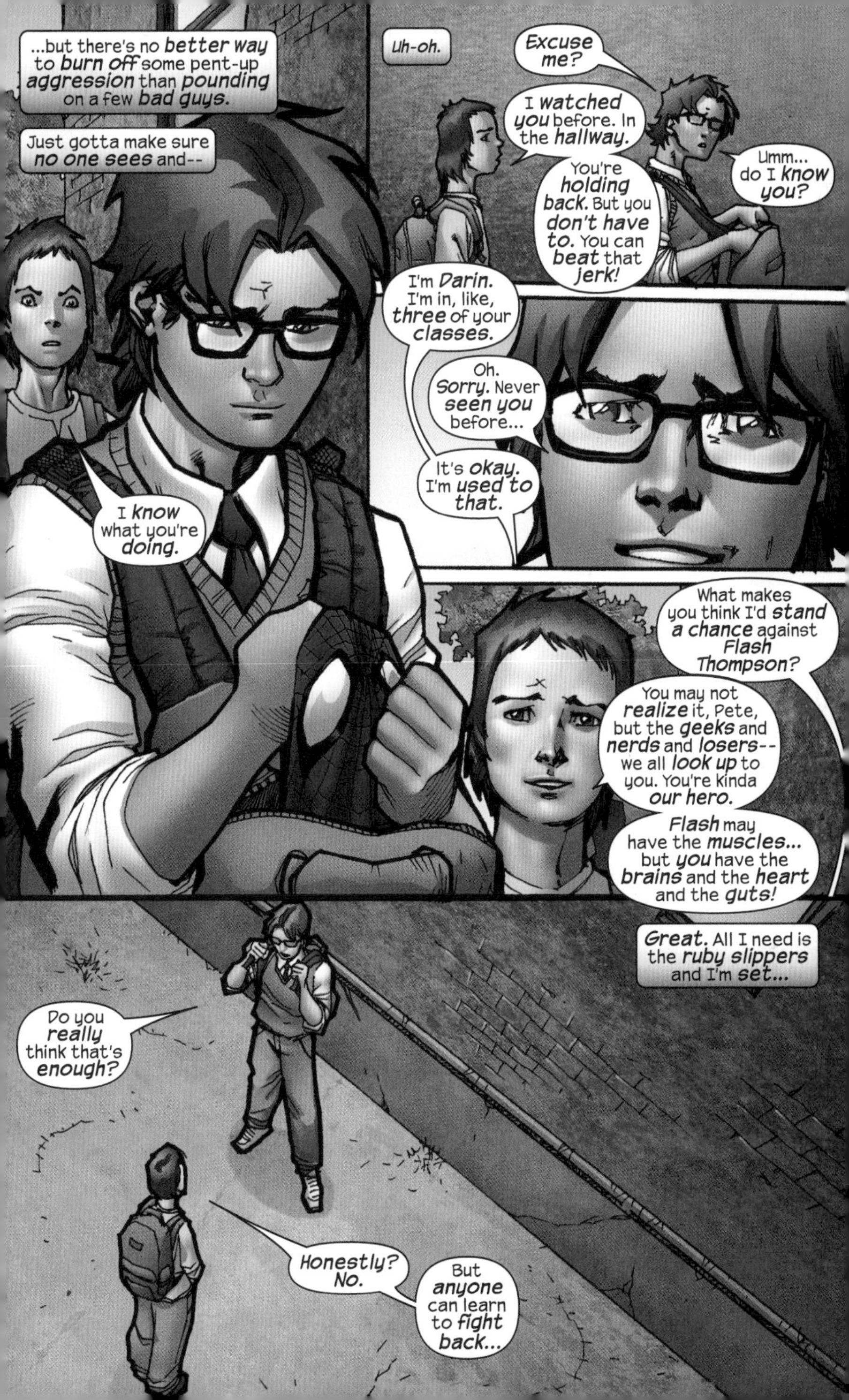
...but there's no better way to burn off some pent-up aggression than pounding on a few bad guys.
Just gotta make sure no one sees and--
I know what you're doing.
Uh-oh.
Excuse me?
I watched you before. In the hallway.
You're holding back. But you don't have to. You can beat that jerk!
Umm... do I know you?
I'm Darin. I'm in, like, three of your classes.
Oh. Sorry. Never seen you before...
It's okay. I'm used to that.
What makes you think I'd stand a chance against Flash Thompson?
You may not realize it, Pete, but the geeks and nerds and losers-- we all look up to you. You're kinda our hero.
Flash may have the muscles... but you have the brains and the heart and the guts!
Great. All I need is the ruby slippers and I'm set...
Do you really think that's enough?
Honestly? No.
But anyone can learn to fight back...

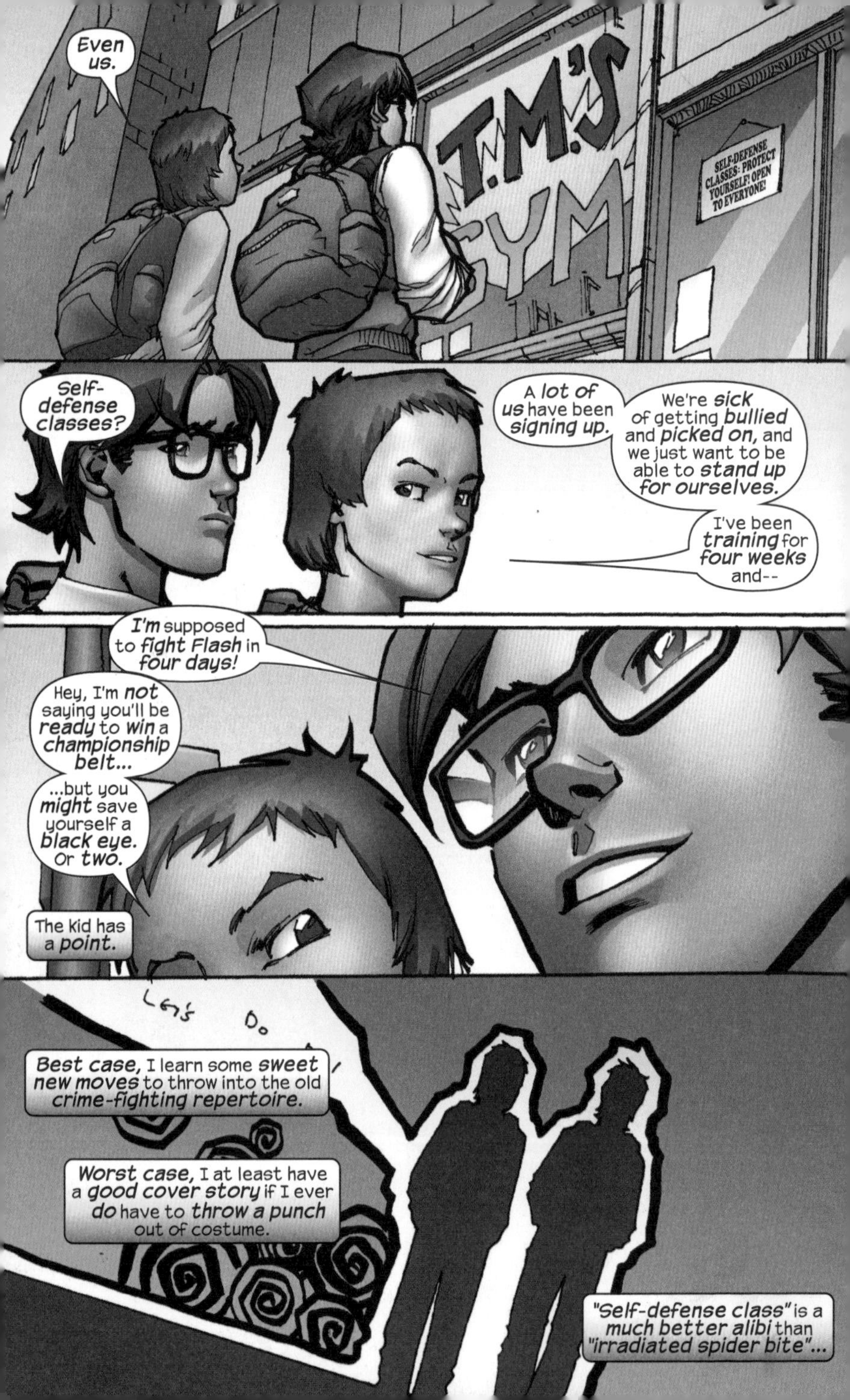
Even us.
SELF-DEFENSE CLASSES: PROTECT YOURSELF! OPEN TO EVERYONE!
T.M.'S GYM
Self-defense classes?
A lot of us have been signing up.
We're sick of getting bullied and picked on, and we just want to be able to stand up for ourselves.
I've been training for four weeks and--
I'm supposed to fight Flash in four days!
Hey, I'm not saying you'll be ready to win a championship belt...
...but you might save yourself a black eye. Or two.
The kid has a point.
Best case, I learn some sweet new moves to throw into the old crime-fighting repertoire.
Worst case, I at least have a good cover story if I ever do have to throw a punch out of costume.
"Self-defense class" is a much better alibi than "irradiated spider bite"...

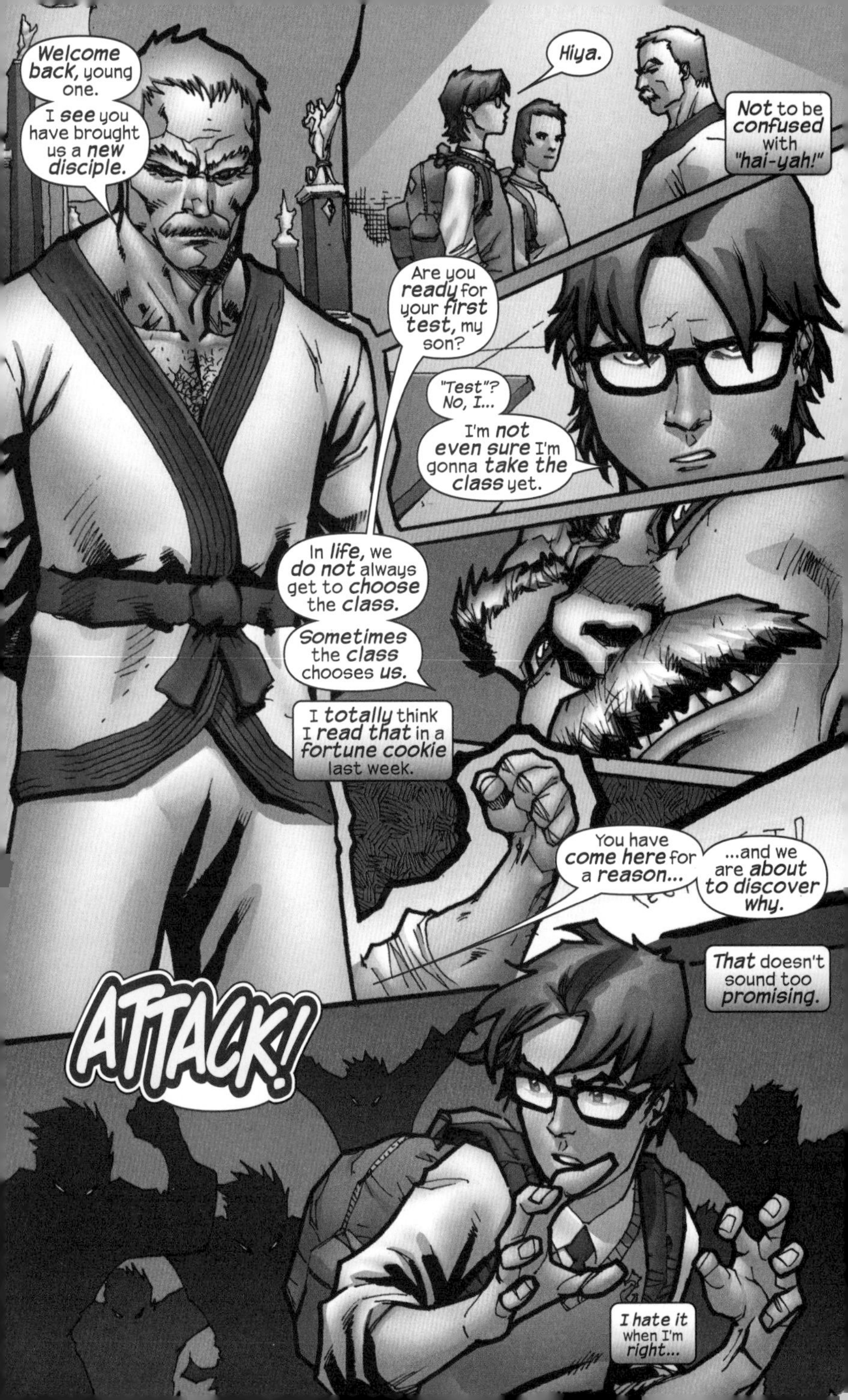
Welcome back, young one.
I see you have brought us a new disciple.
Hiya.
Not to be confused with "hai-yah!"
Are you ready for your first test, my son?
"Test"? No, I...
I'm not even sure I'm gonna take the class yet.
In life, we do not always get to choose the class.
Sometimes the class chooses us.
I totally think I read that in a fortune cookie last week.
You have come here for a reason...
...and we are about to discover why.
That doesn't sound too promising.
ATTACK!
I hate it when I'm right...

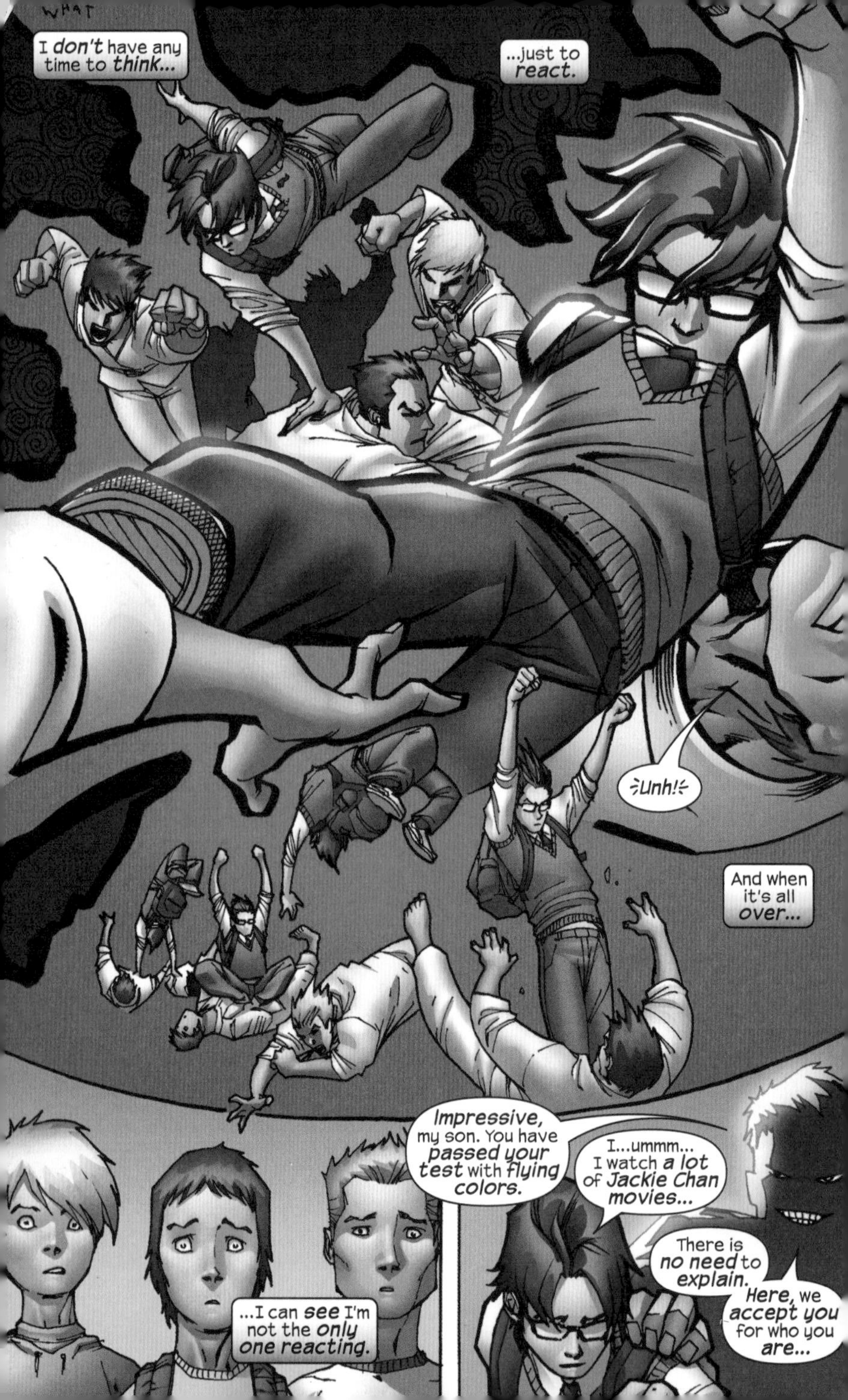
WHAT
I don't have any time to think...
...just to react.
Unh!
And when it's all over...
...I can see I'm not the only one reacting.
Impressive, my son. You have passed your test with flying colors.
I...ummm... I watch a lot of Jackie Chan movies...
There is no need to explain.
Here, we accept you for who you are...

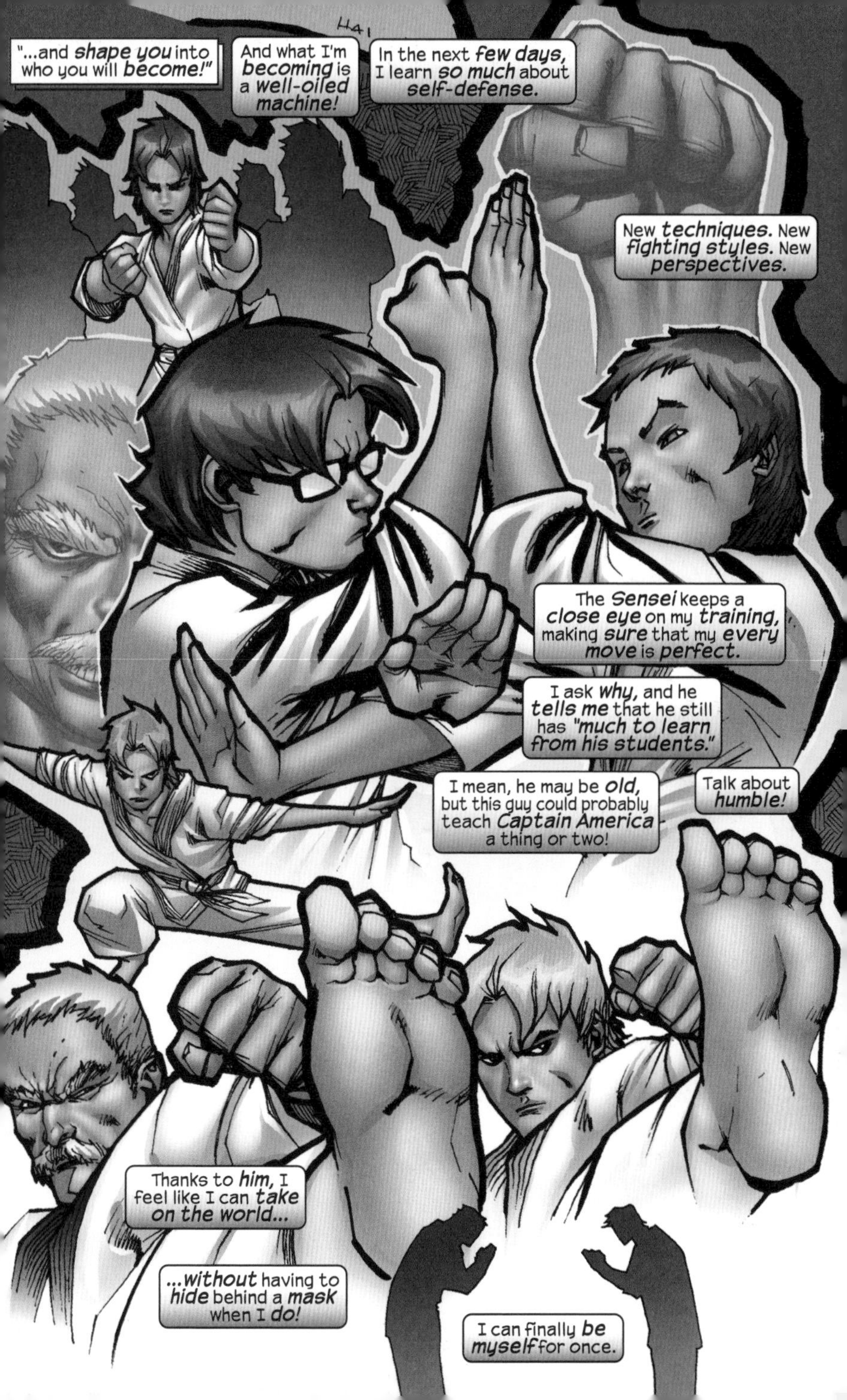

"...and shape you into who you will become!"
And what I'm becoming is a well-oiled machine!
In the next few days, I learn so much about self-defense.
New techniques. New fighting styles. New perspectives.
The Sensei keeps a close eye on my training, making sure that my every move is perfect.
I ask why, and he tells me that he still has "much to learn from his students."
Talk about humble!
I mean, he may be old, but this guy could probably teach Captain America a thing or two!
Thanks to him, I feel like I can take on the world...
...without having to hide behind a mask when I do!
I can finally be myself for once.

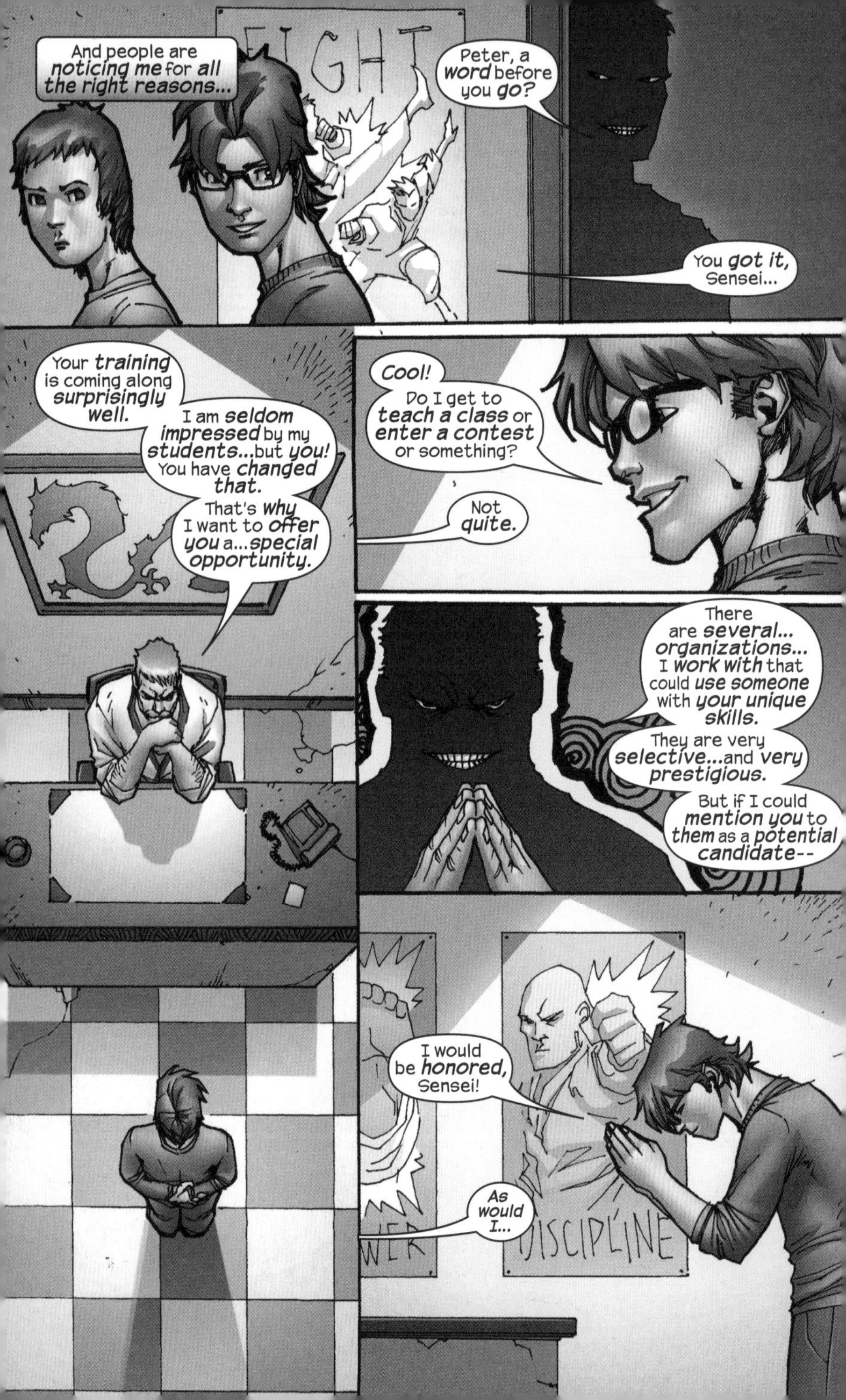
And people are noticing me for all the right reasons...
Peter, a word before you go?
You got it, Sensei...
Your training is coming along surprisingly well.
I am seldom impressed by my students...but you! You have changed that.
That's why I want to offer you a...special opportunity.
Cool!
Do I get to teach a class or enter a contest or something?
Not quite.
There are several... organizations... I work with that could use someone with your unique skills.
They are very selective...and very prestigious.
But if I could mention you to them as a potential candidate--
I would be honored, Sensei!
As would I...
DISCIPLINE

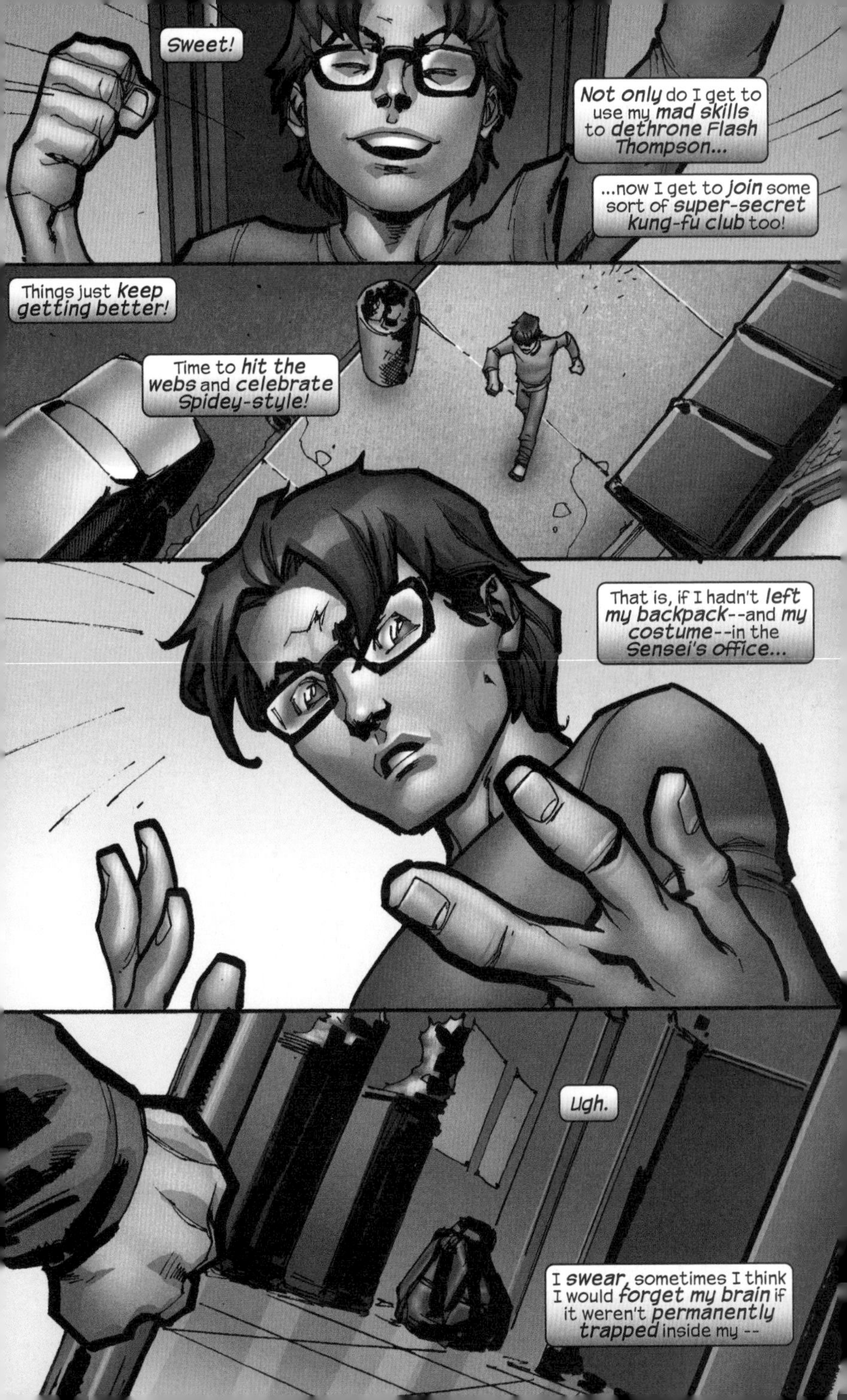
Sweet!
Not only do I get to use my mad skills to dethrone Flash Thompson...
...now I get to join some sort of super-secret kung-fu club too!
Things just keep getting better!
Time to hit the webs and celebrate Spidey-style!
That is, if I hadn't left my backpack--and my costume--in the Sensei's office...
Ugh.
I swear, sometimes I think I would forget my brain if it weren't permanently trapped inside my --

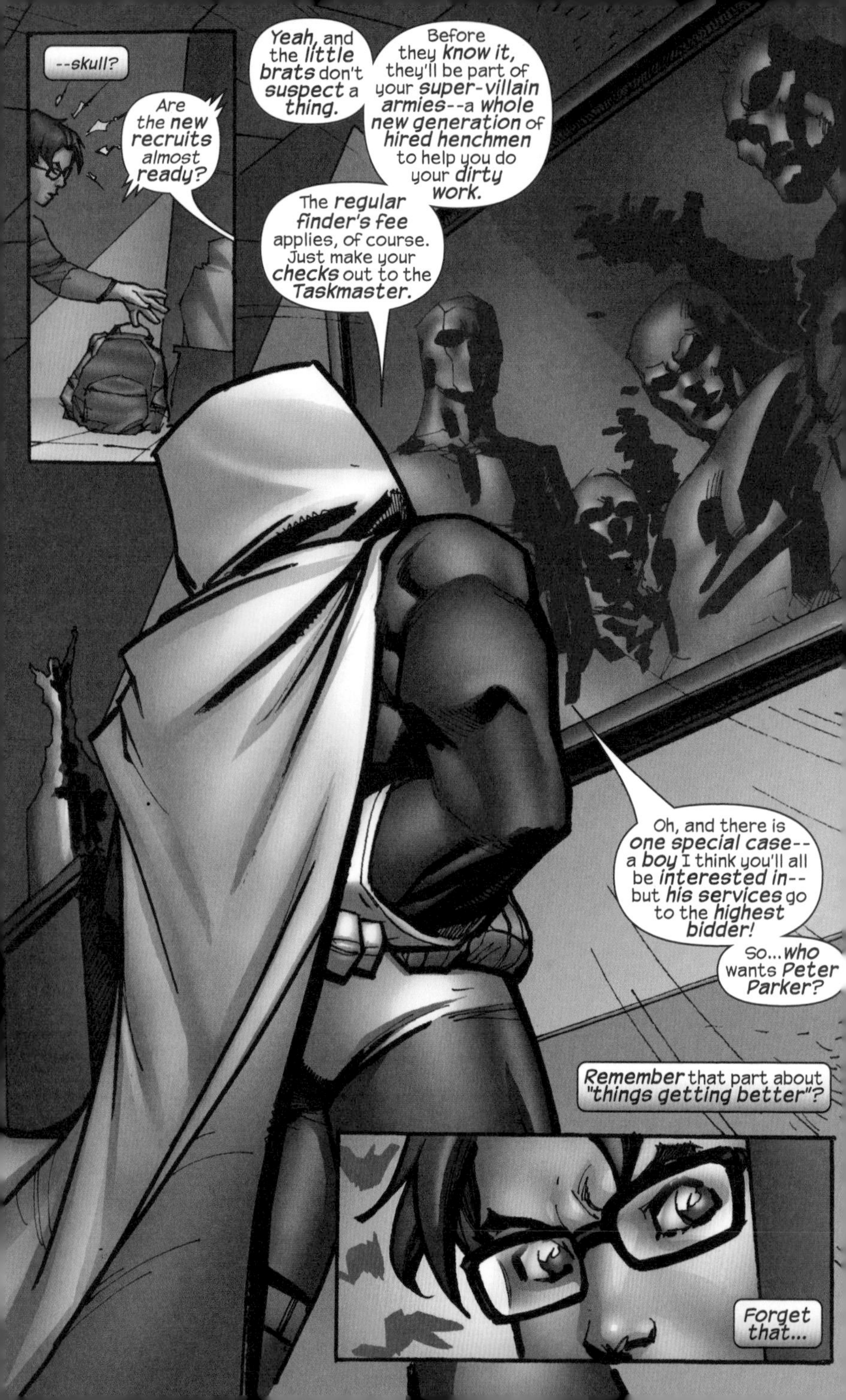
--skull?
Are the new recruits almost ready?
Yeah, and the little brats don't suspect a thing.
Before they know it, they'll be part of your super-villain armies--a whole new generation of hired henchmen to help you do your dirty work.
The regular finder's fee applies, of course. Just make your checks out to the Taskmaster.
Oh, and there is one special case--a boy I think you'll all be interested in--but his services go to the highest bidder!
So...who wants Peter Parker?
Remember that part about "things getting better"?
Forget that...

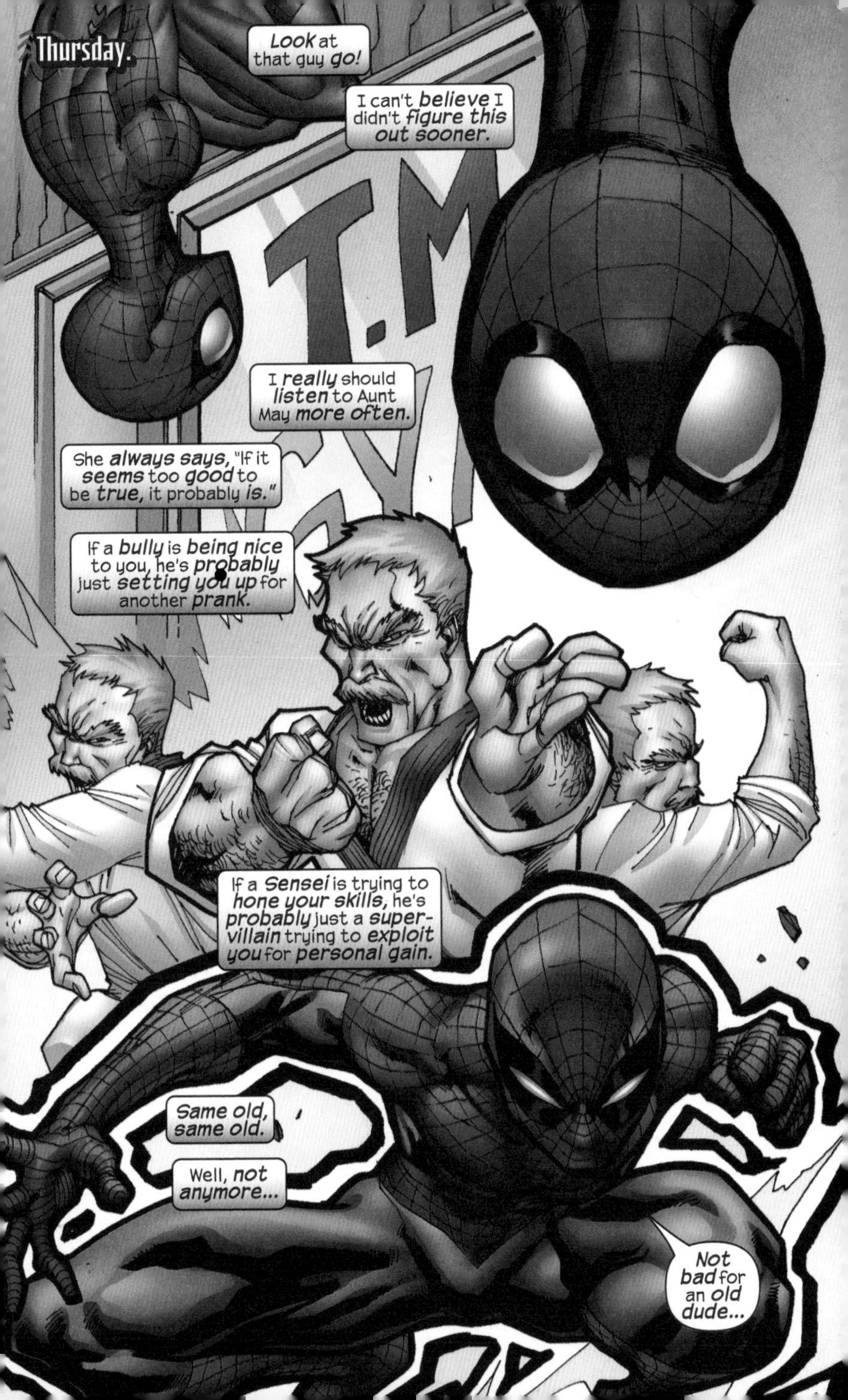
Thursday.
Look at that guy go!
I can't believe I didn't figure this out sooner.
T.M
I really should listen to Aunt May more often.
She always says, "If it seems too good to be true, it probably is."
If a bully is being nice to you, he's probably just setting you up for another prank.
If a Sensei is trying to hone your skills, he's probably just a super-villain trying to exploit you for personal gain.
Same old, same old.
Well, not anymore...
Not bad for an old dude...

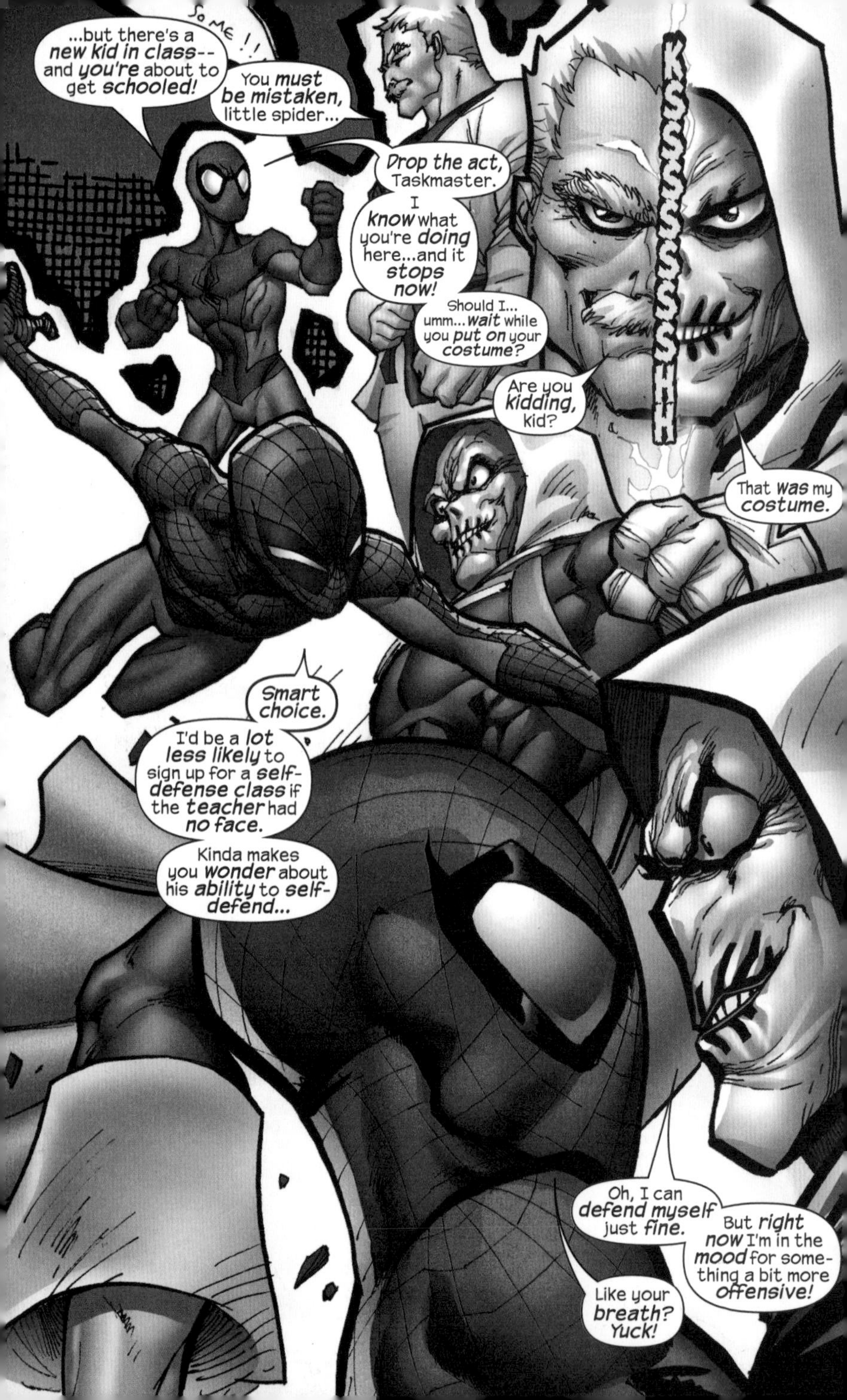

...but there's a new kid in class-- and you're about to get schooled!
You must be mistaken, little spider...
Drop the act, Taskmaster.
I know what you're doing here...and it stops now!
Should I... umm...wait while you put on your costume?
KSSSSSSSSHH
Are you kidding, kid?
That was my costume.
Smart choice.
I'd be a lot less likely to sign up for a self-defense class if the teacher had no face.
Kinda makes you wonder about his ability to self-defend...
Oh, I can defend myself just fine.
But right now I'm in the mood for something a bit more offensive!
Like your breath? Yuck!

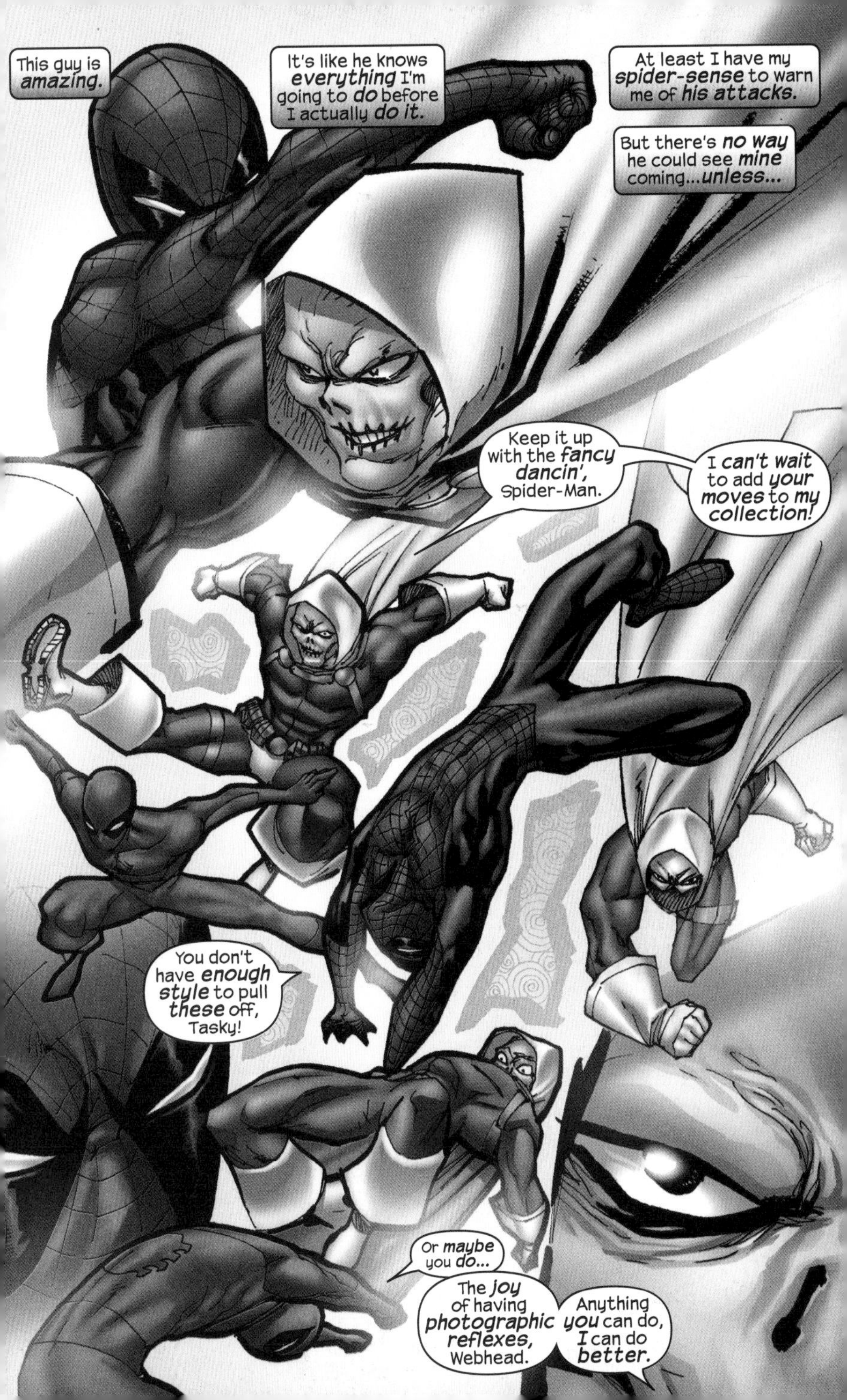
This guy is amazing.
It's like he knows everything I'm going to do before I actually do it.
At least I have my spider-sense to warn me of his attacks.
But there's no way he could see mine coming...unless...
Keep it up with the fancy dancin', Spider-Man.
I can't wait to add your moves to my collection!
You don't have enough style to pull these off, Tasky!
Or maybe you do...
The joy of having photographic reflexes, Webhead.
Anything you can do, I can do better.

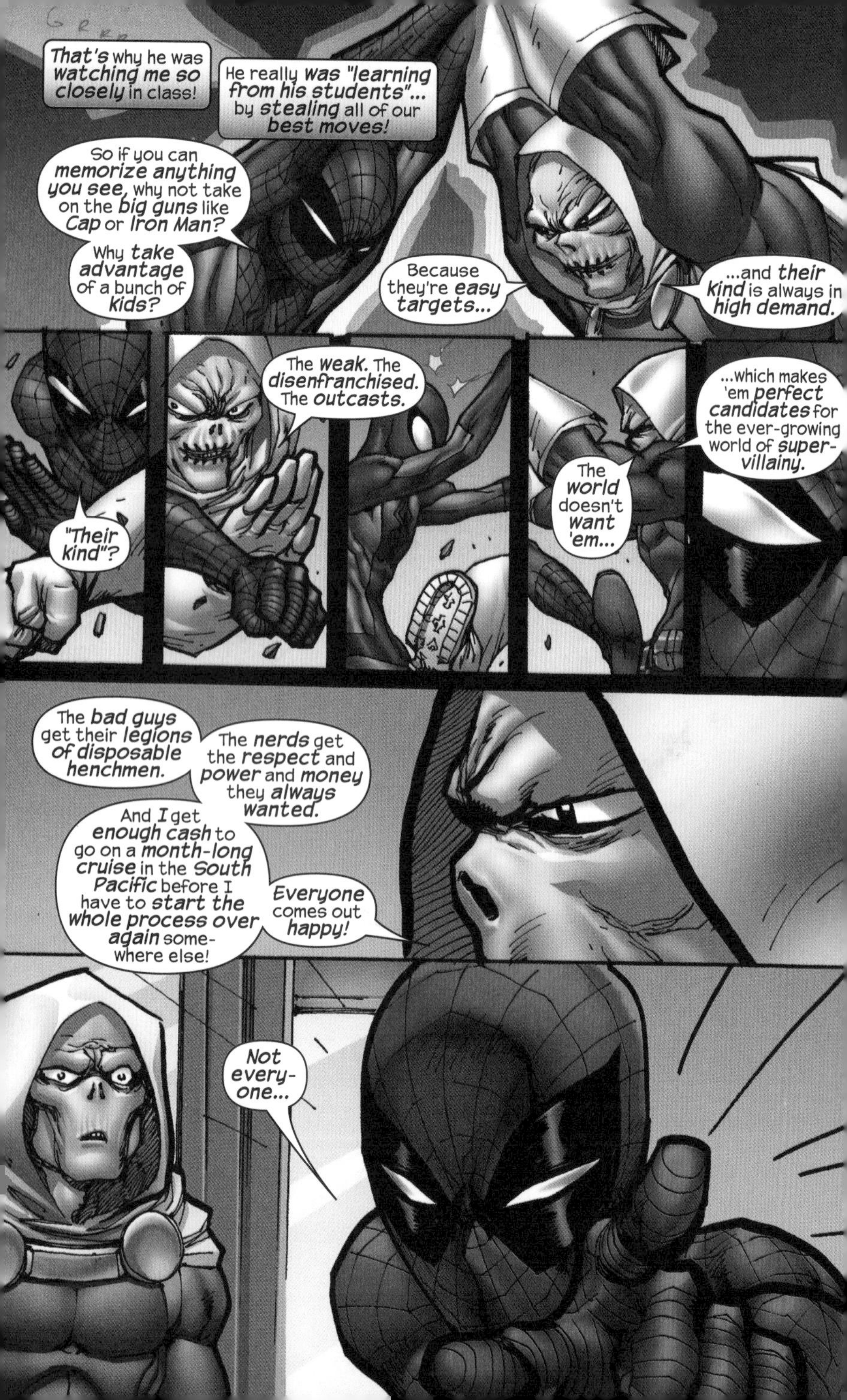

That's why he was watching me so closely in class!
He really was "learning from his students"... by stealing all of our best moves!
So if you can memorize anything you see, why not take on the big guns like Cap or Iron Man?
Why take advantage of a bunch of kids?
Because they're easy targets...
...and their kind is always in high demand.
"Their kind"?
The weak. The disenfranchised. The outcasts.
The world doesn't want 'em...
...which makes 'em perfect candidates for the ever-growing world of super-villainy.
The bad guys get their legions of disposable henchmen.
The nerds get the respect and power and money they always wanted.
And I get enough cash to go on a month-long cruise in the South Pacific before I have to start the whole process over again some-where else!
Everyone comes out happy!
Not every-one...

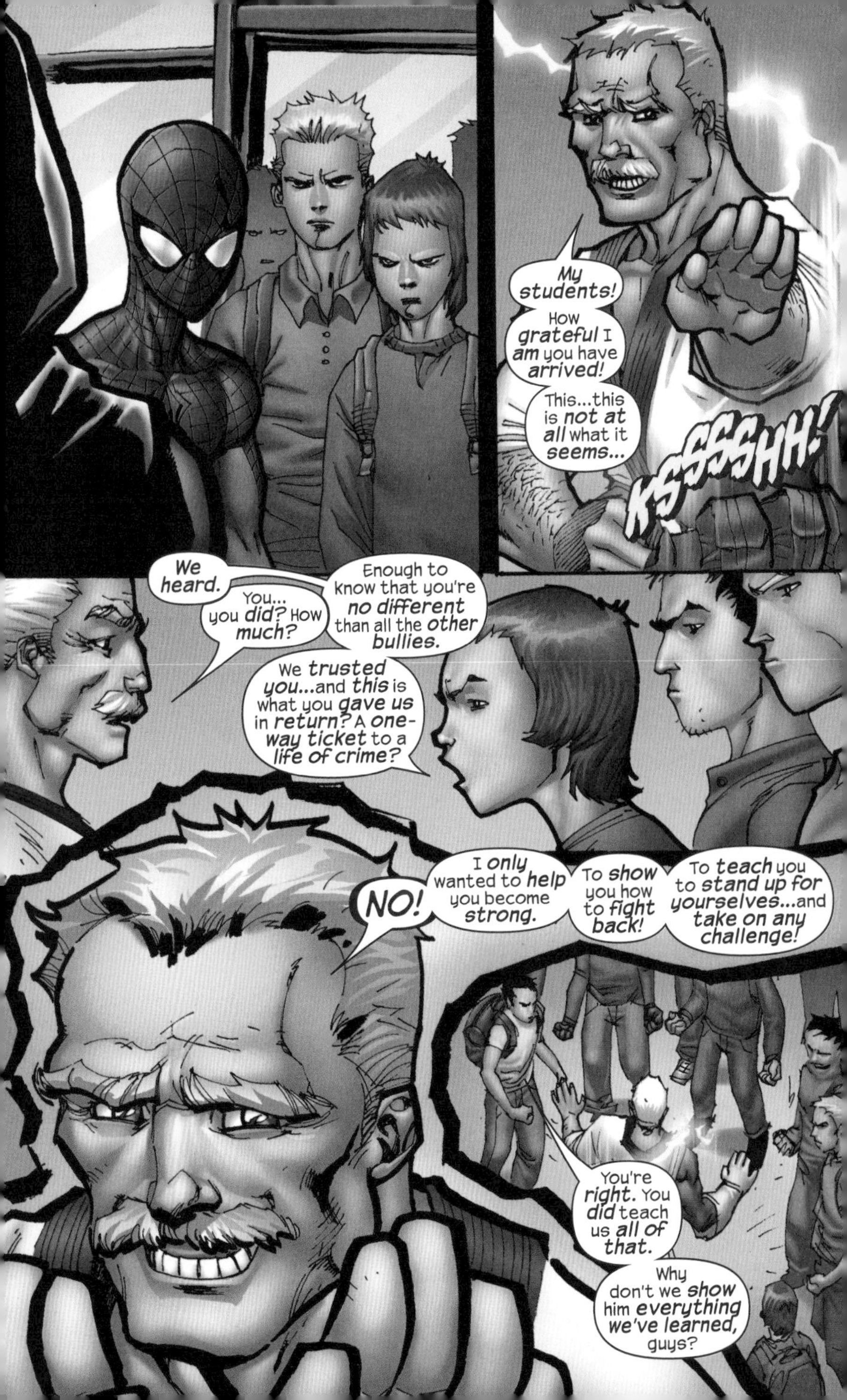
My students!
How grateful I am you have arrived!
This...this is not at all what it seems...
KSSSSHH!
We heard.
You... you did? How much?
Enough to know that you're no different than all the other bullies.
We trusted you...and this is what you gave us in return? A one-way ticket to a life of crime?
NO!
I only wanted to help you become strong.
To show you how to fight back!
To teach you to stand up for yourselves...and take on any challenge!
You're right. You did teach us all of that.
Why don't we show him everything we've learned, guys?

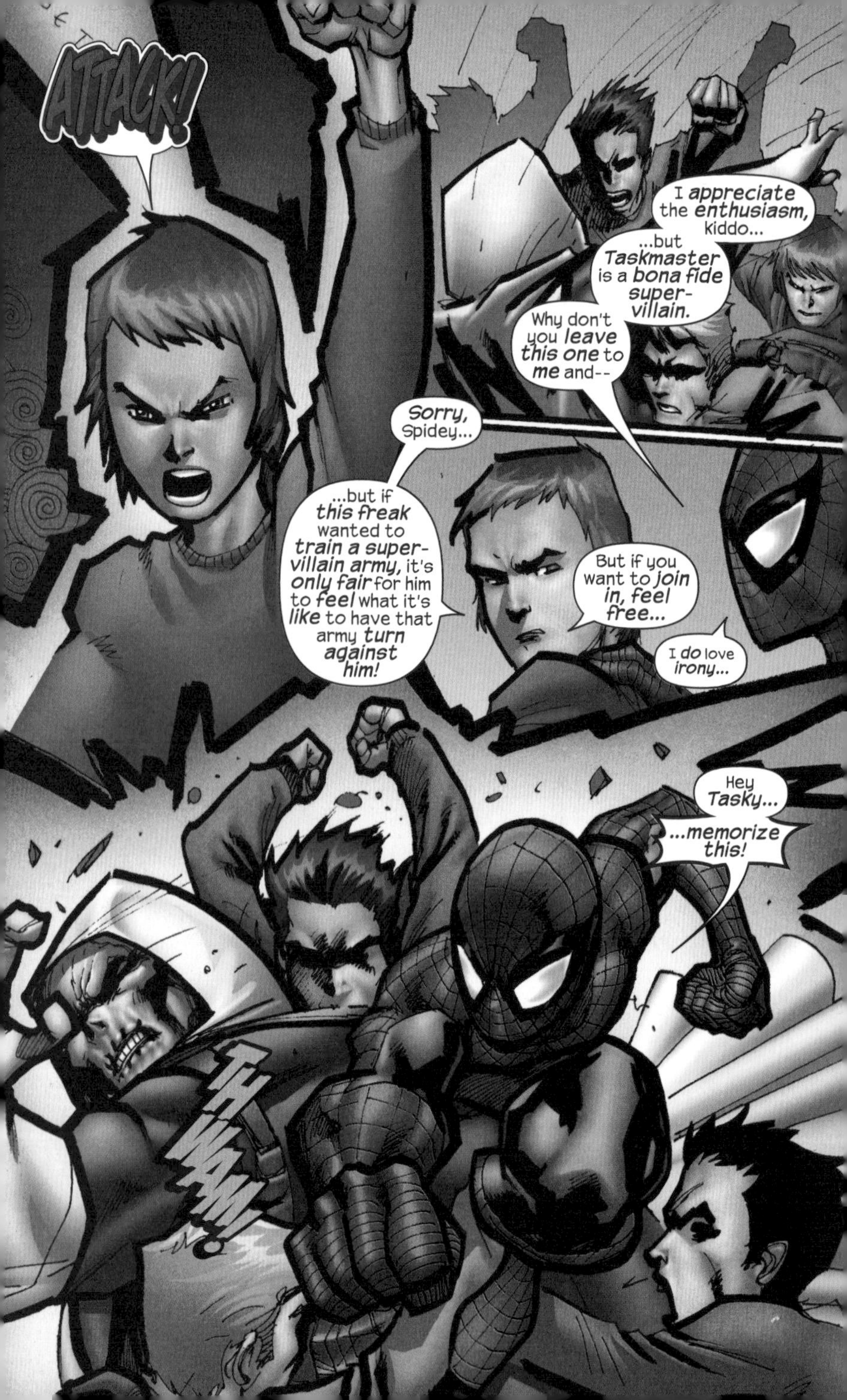
ATTACK!
I appreciate the enthusiasm, kiddo...
...but Taskmaster is a bona fide super-villain.
Why don't you leave this one to me and--
Sorry, Spidey...
...but if this freak wanted to train a super-villain army, it's only fair for him to feel what it's like to have that army turn against him!
But if you want to join in, feel free...
I do love irony...
Hey Tasky...
...memorize this!
THWAM!

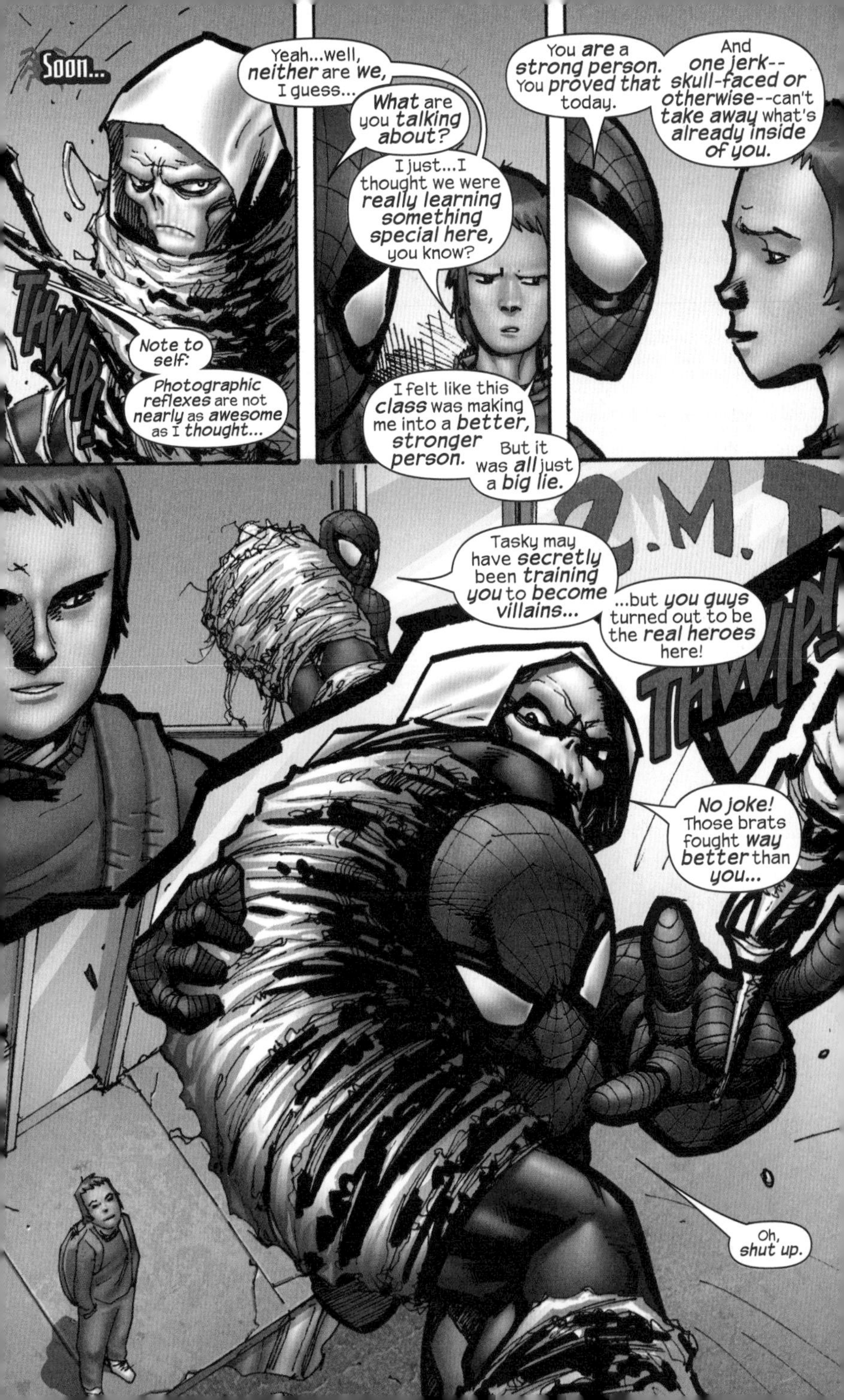
Soon...
THWIP!
Note to self:
Photographic reflexes are not nearly as awesome as I thought...
Yeah...well, neither are we, I guess...
What are you talking about?
I just...I thought we were really learning something special here, you know?
I felt like this class was making me into a better, stronger person.
But it was all just a big lie.
You are a strong person. You proved that today.
And one jerk--skull-faced or otherwise--can't take away what's already inside of you.
Tasky may have secretly been training you to become villains...
...but you guys turned out to be the real heroes here!
THWIP!
No joke! Those brats fought way better than you...
Oh, shut up.

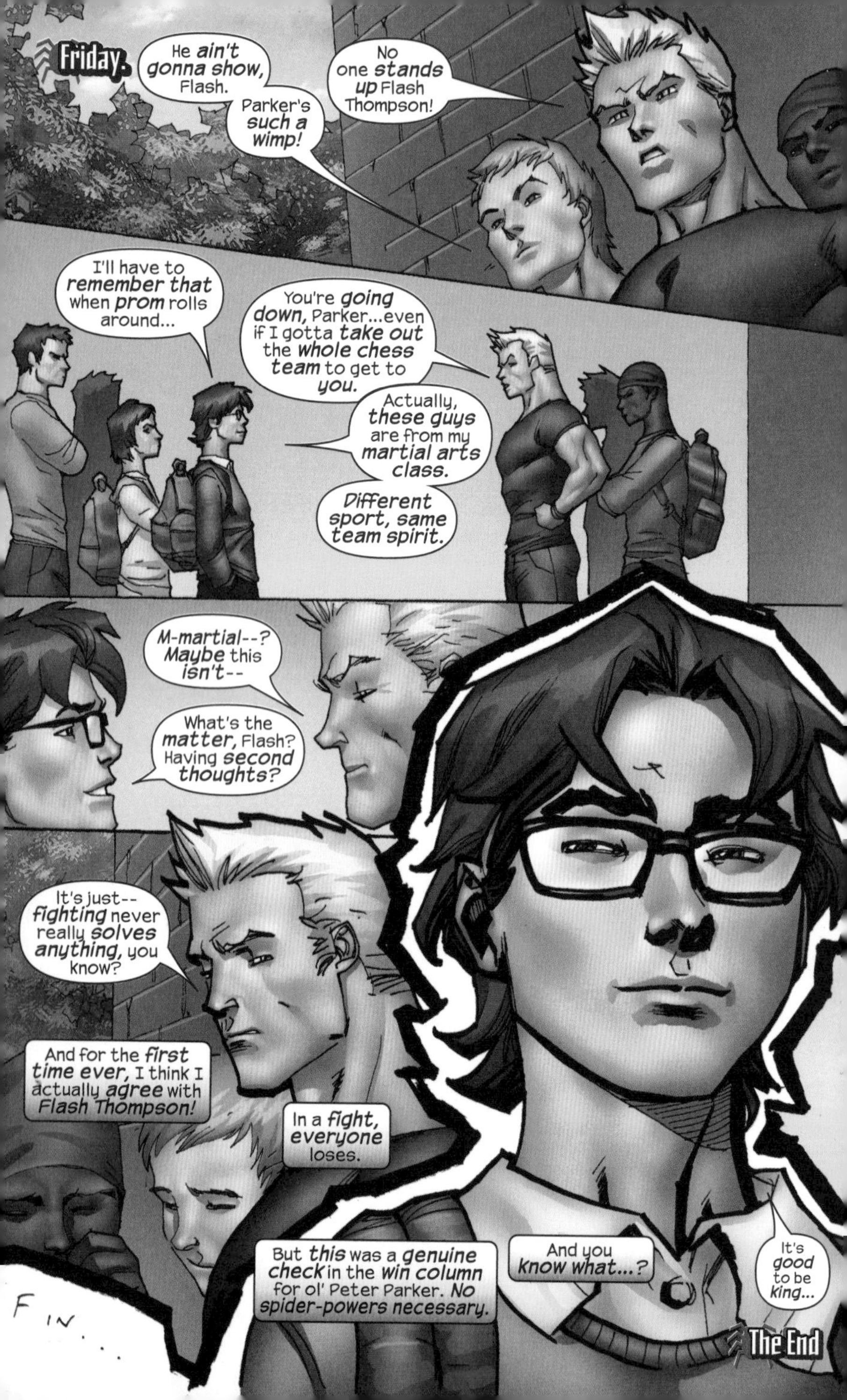

Friday.
He ain't gonna show, Flash.
Parker's such a wimp!
No one stands up Flash Thompson!
I'll have to remember that when prom rolls around...
You're going down, Parker...even if I gotta take out the whole chess team to get to you.
Actually, these guys are from my martial arts class.
Different sport, same team spirit.
M-martial--? Maybe this isn't--
What's the matter, Flash? Having second thoughts?
It's just--fighting never really solves anything, you know?
And for the first time ever, I think I actually agree with Flash Thompson!
In a fight, everyone loses.
But this was a genuine check in the win column for ol' Peter Parker. No spider-powers necessary.
And you know what...?
It's good to be king...
FIN...
The End

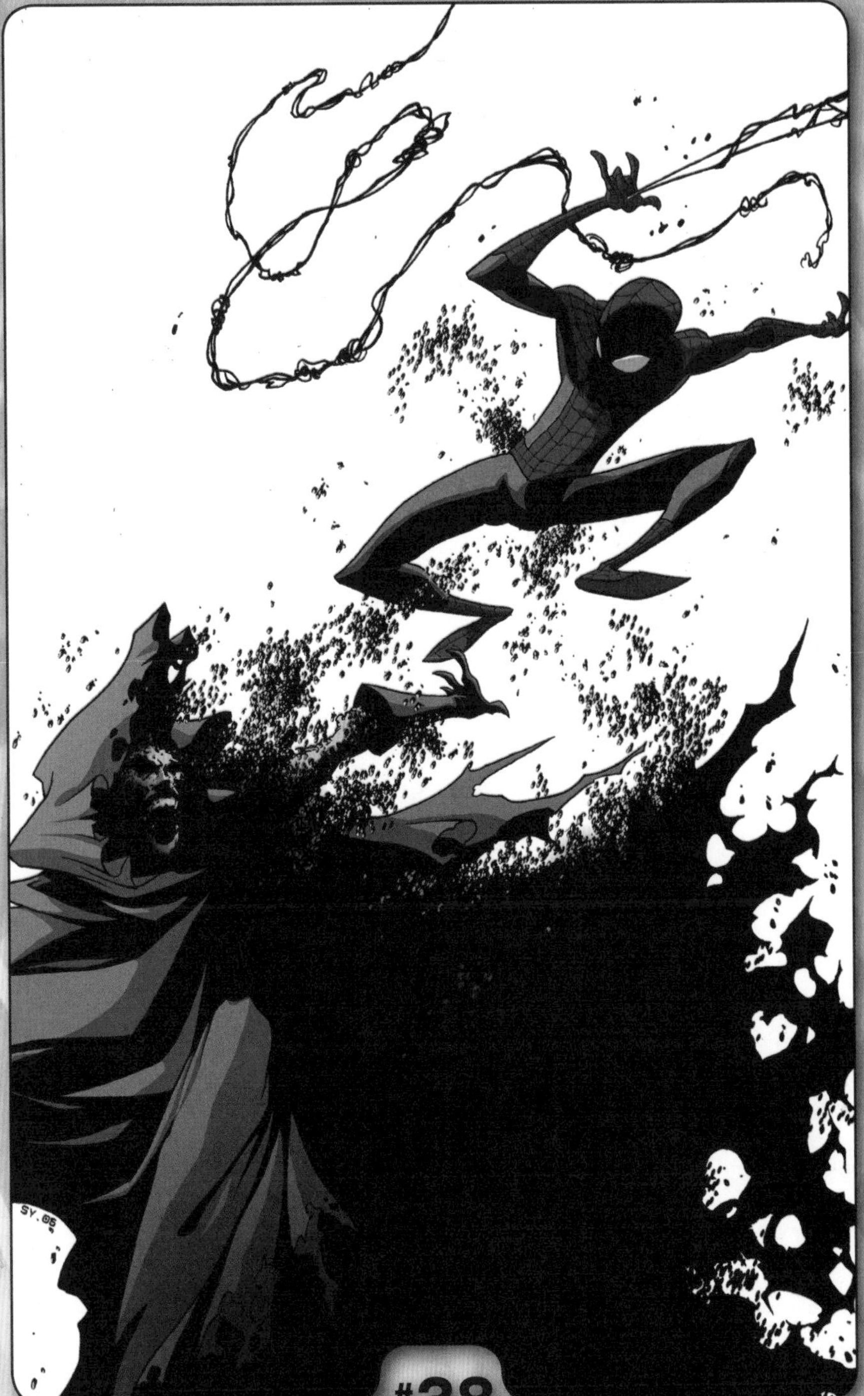
SY.05

#38

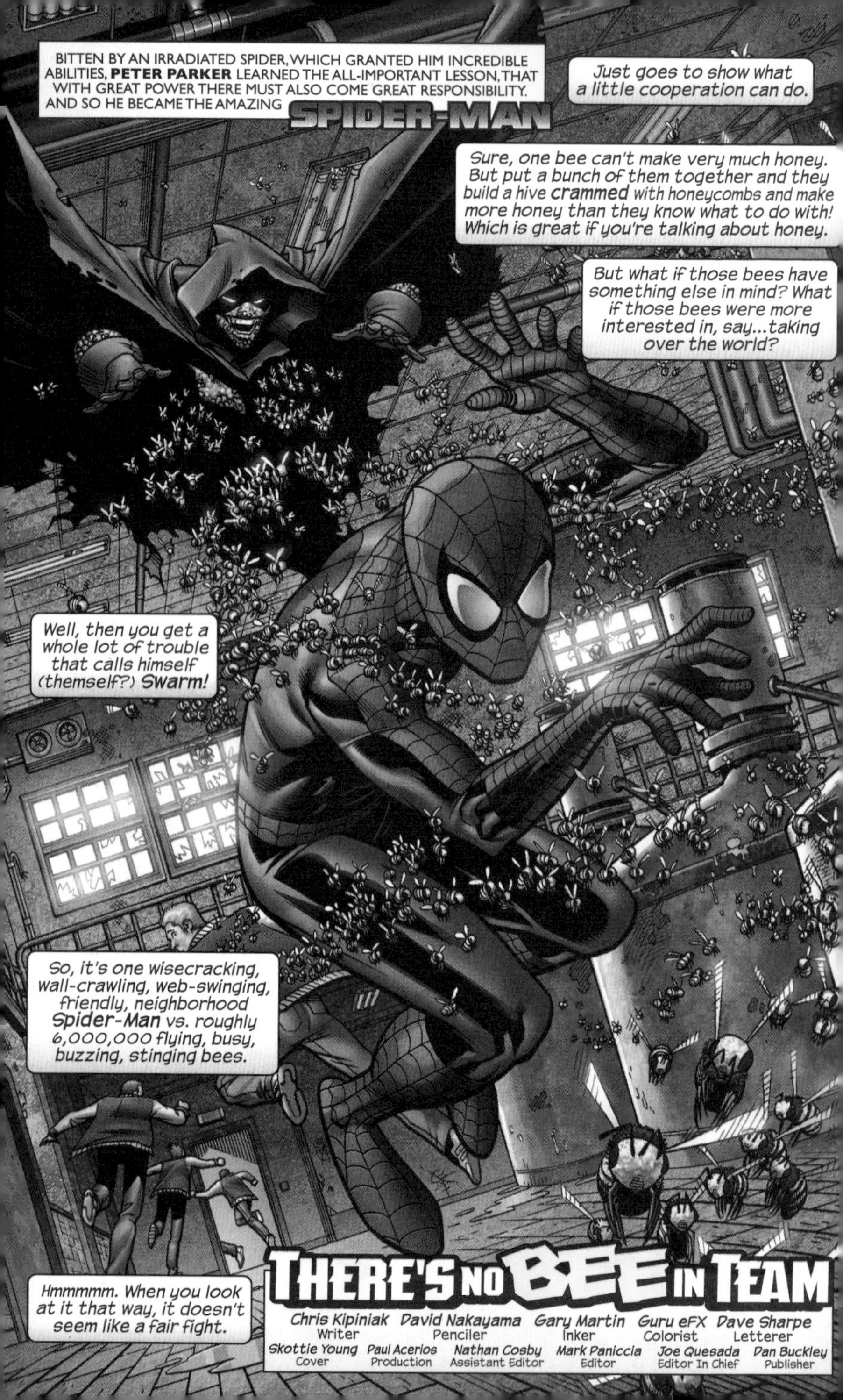

BITTEN BY AN IRRADIATED SPIDER, WHICH GRANTED HIM INCREDIBLE ABILITIES, PETER PARKER LEARNED THE ALL-IMPORTANT LESSON, THAT WITH GREAT POWER THERE MUST ALSO COME GREAT RESPONSIBILITY. AND SO HE BECAME THE AMAZING
SPIDER-MAN
Just goes to show what a little cooperation can do.
Sure, one bee can't make very much honey. But put a bunch of them together and they build a hive crammed with honeycombs and make more honey than they know what to do with! Which is great if you're talking about honey.
But what if those bees have something else in mind? What if those bees were more interested in, say...taking over the world?
Well, then you get a whole lot of trouble that calls himself (themself?) Swarm!
So, it's one wisecracking, wall-crawling, web-swinging, friendly, neighborhood Spider-Man vs. roughly 6,000,000 flying, busy, buzzing, stinging bees.
Hmmmmm. When you look at it that way, it doesn't seem like a fair fight.
THERE'S NO BEE IN TEAM
Chris Kipiniak Writer
David Nakayama Penciler
Gary Martin Inker
Guru eFX Colorist
Dave Sharpe Letterer
Skottie Young Cover
Paul Acerios Production
Nathan Cosby Assistant Editor
Mark Paniccia Editor
Joe Quesada Editor In Chief
Dan Buckley Publisher

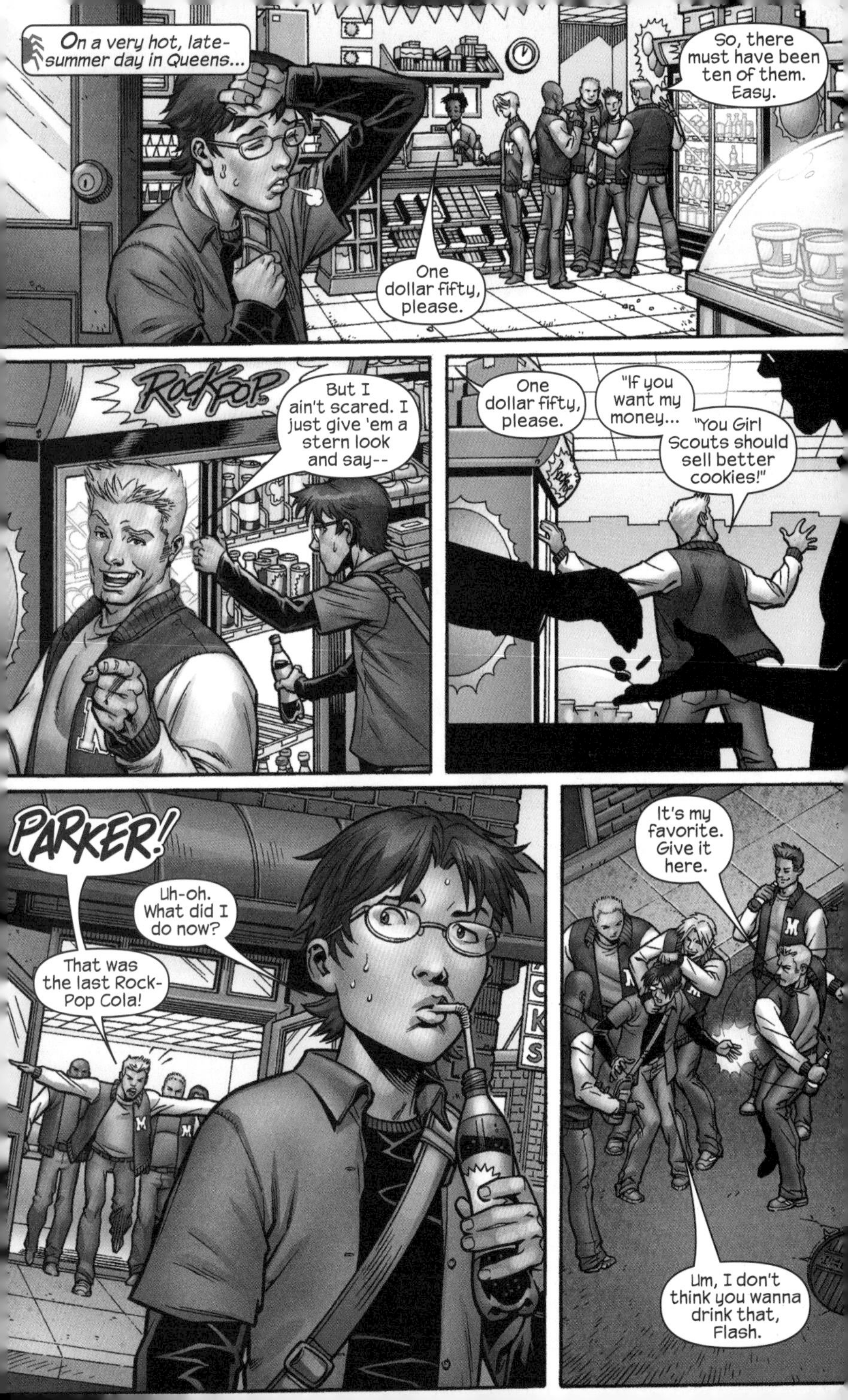
On a very hot, late-summer day in Queens...
So, there must have been ten of them. Easy.
One dollar fifty, please.
ROCKPOP
But I ain't scared. I just give 'em a stern look and say--
One dollar fifty, please.
"If you want my money...
"You Girl Scouts should sell better cookies!"
PARKER!
Uh-oh. What did I do now?
That was the last Rock-Pop Cola!
It's my favorite. Give it here.
Um, I don't think you wanna drink that, Flash.

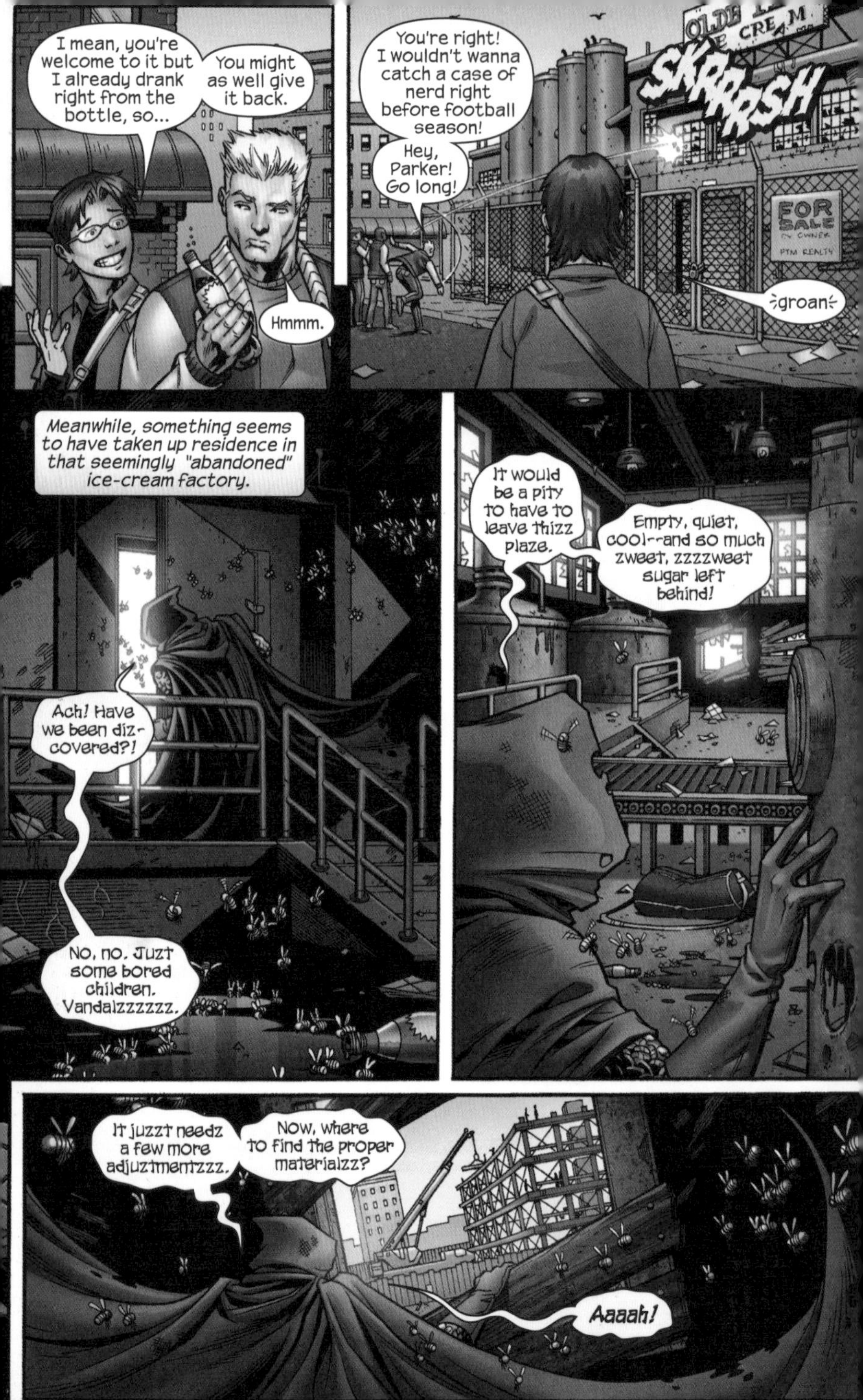
I mean, you're welcome to it but I already drank right from the bottle, so...
You might as well give it back.
Hmmm.
You're right! I wouldn't wanna catch a case of nerd right before football season!
Hey, Parker! Go long!
OLDE
CREAM
SKRRRSH
FOR SALE
groan
Meanwhile, something seems to have taken up residence in that seemingly "abandoned" ice-cream factory.
Ach! Have we been diz-covered?!
No, no. Juzt some bored children. Vandalzzzzzz.
It would be a pity to have to leave thizz plaze.
Empty, quiet, cool--and so much zweet, zzzzweet sugar left behind!
It juzzt needz a few more adjuztmentzzz.
Now, where to find the proper materialzz?
Aaaah!

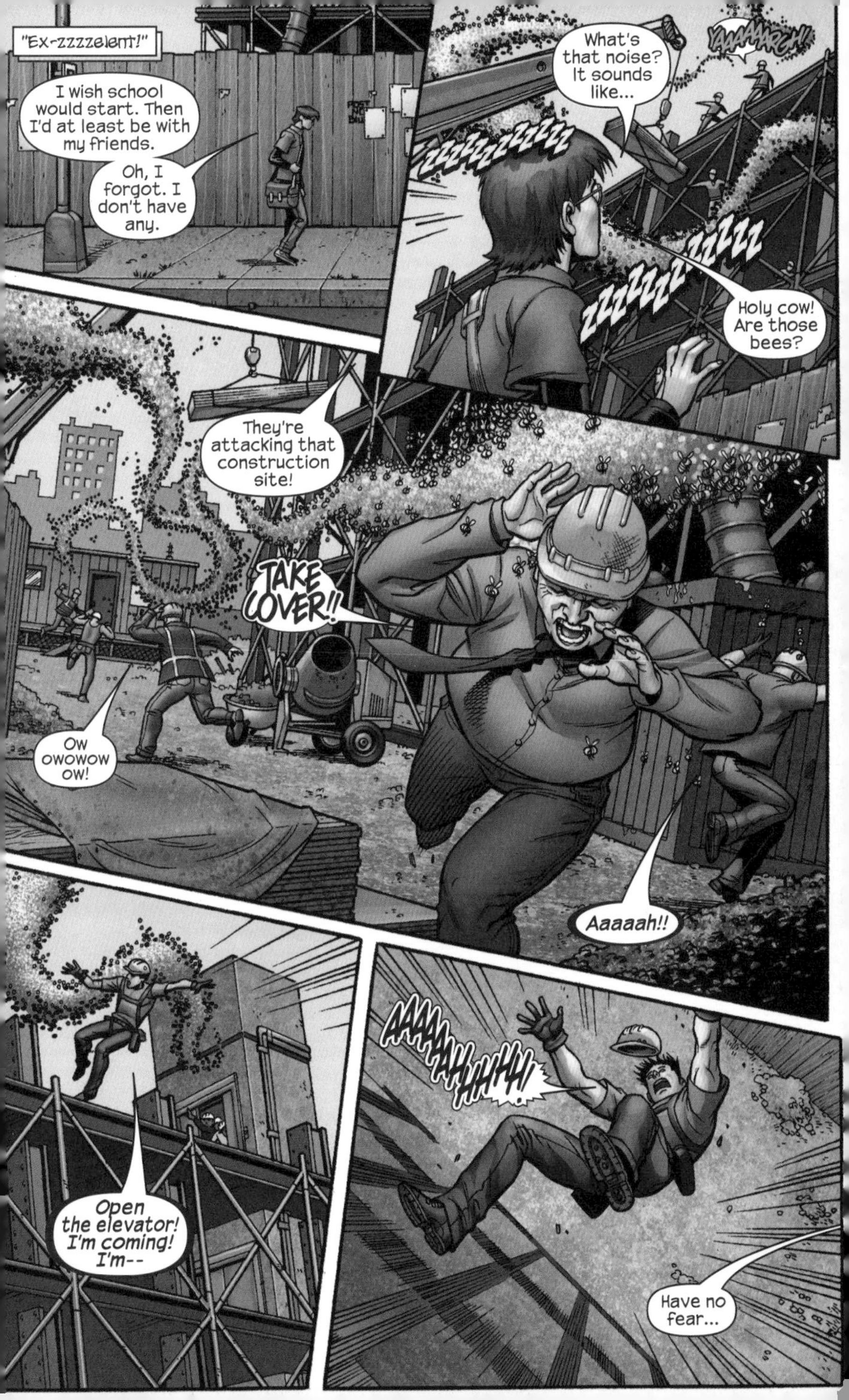
"Ex-zzzzelent!"
I wish school would start. Then I'd at least be with my friends.
Oh, I forgot. I don't have any.
What's that noise? It sounds like...
YAAAAARGH!!
ZZZZZZZZZZZZZ
ZZZZZZZZZZZZZZ
Holy cow! Are those bees?
They're attacking that construction site!
TAKE COVER!!
Ow owowow ow!
Aaaaah!!
Open the elevator! I'm coming! I'm--
AAAAAAHHHHHH!
Have no fear...

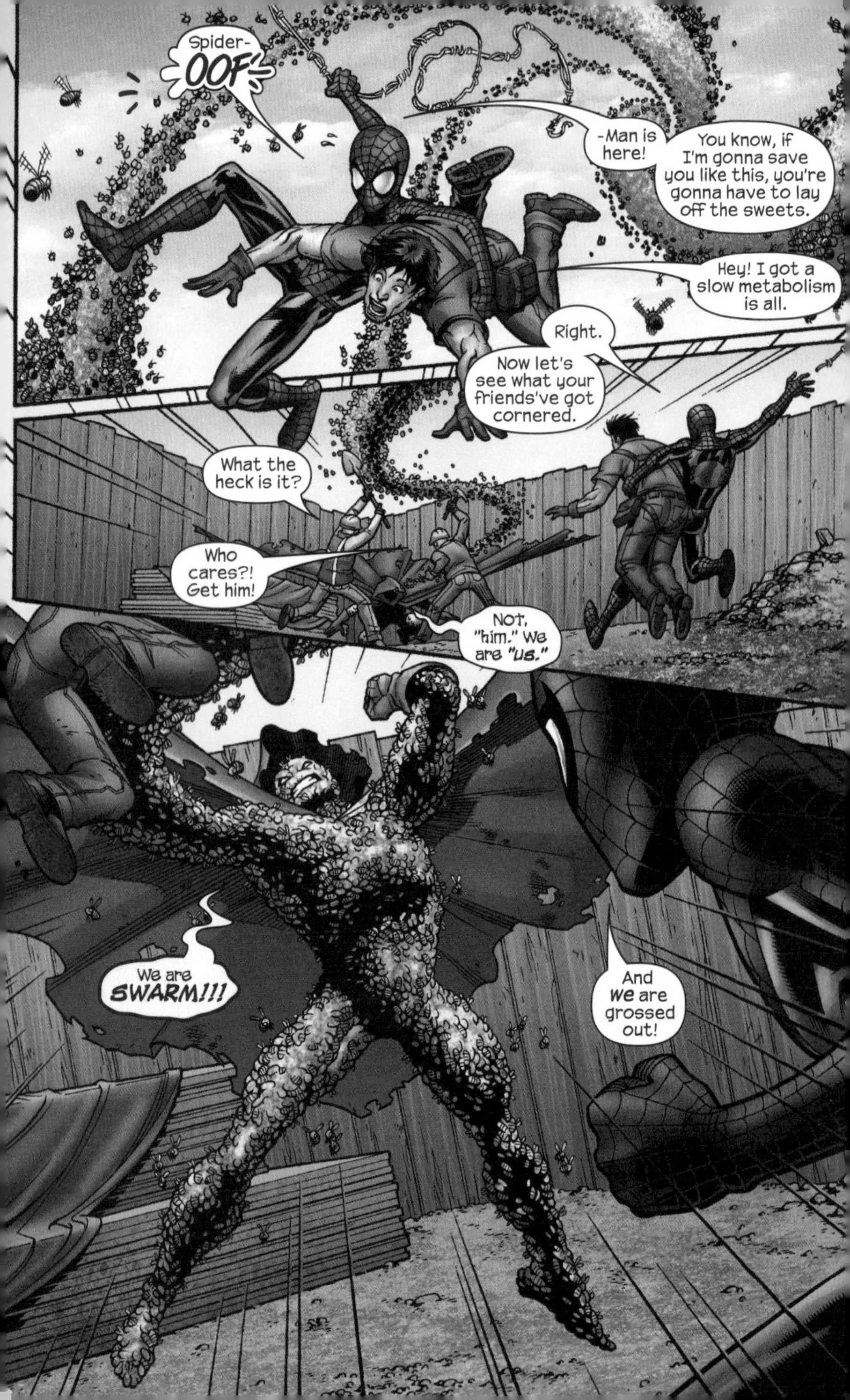
Spider-
OOF!
-Man is here!
You know, if I'm gonna save you like this, you're gonna have to lay off the sweets.
Hey! I got a slow metabolism is all.
Right.
Now let's see what your friends've got cornered.
What the heck is it?
Who cares?! Get him!
NOT, "him." We are "us."
We are SWARM!!!
And we are grossed out!

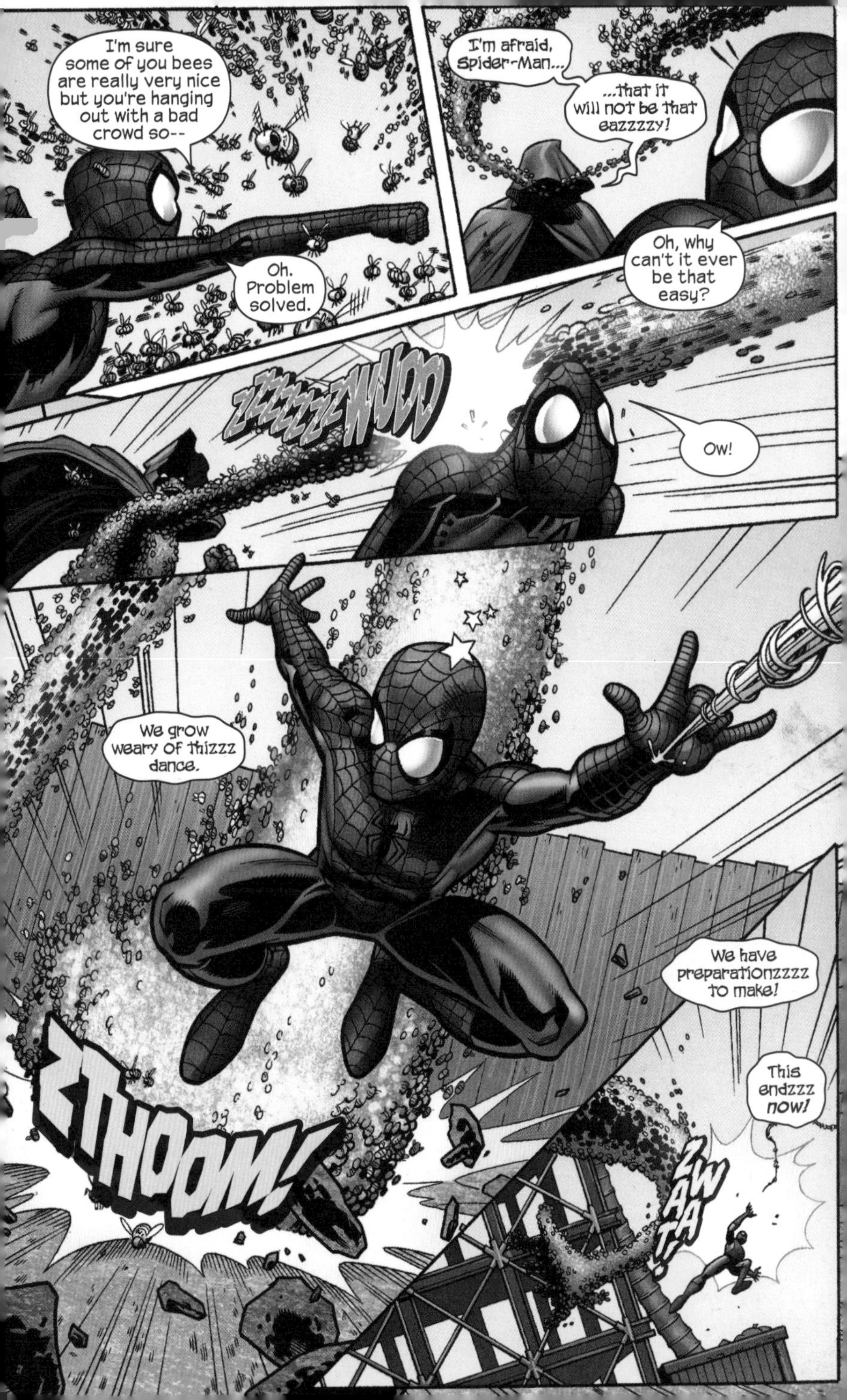
I'm sure some of you bees are really very nice but you're hanging out with a bad crowd so--
Oh. Problem solved.
I'm afraid, Spider-Man...
...that it will not be that eazzzzy!
Oh, why can't it ever be that easy?
ZZZZZZZZWUDD
Ow!
We grow weary of thizzz dance.
We have preparationzzzz to make!
This endzzz now!
ZTHOOM!
ZWAAT!

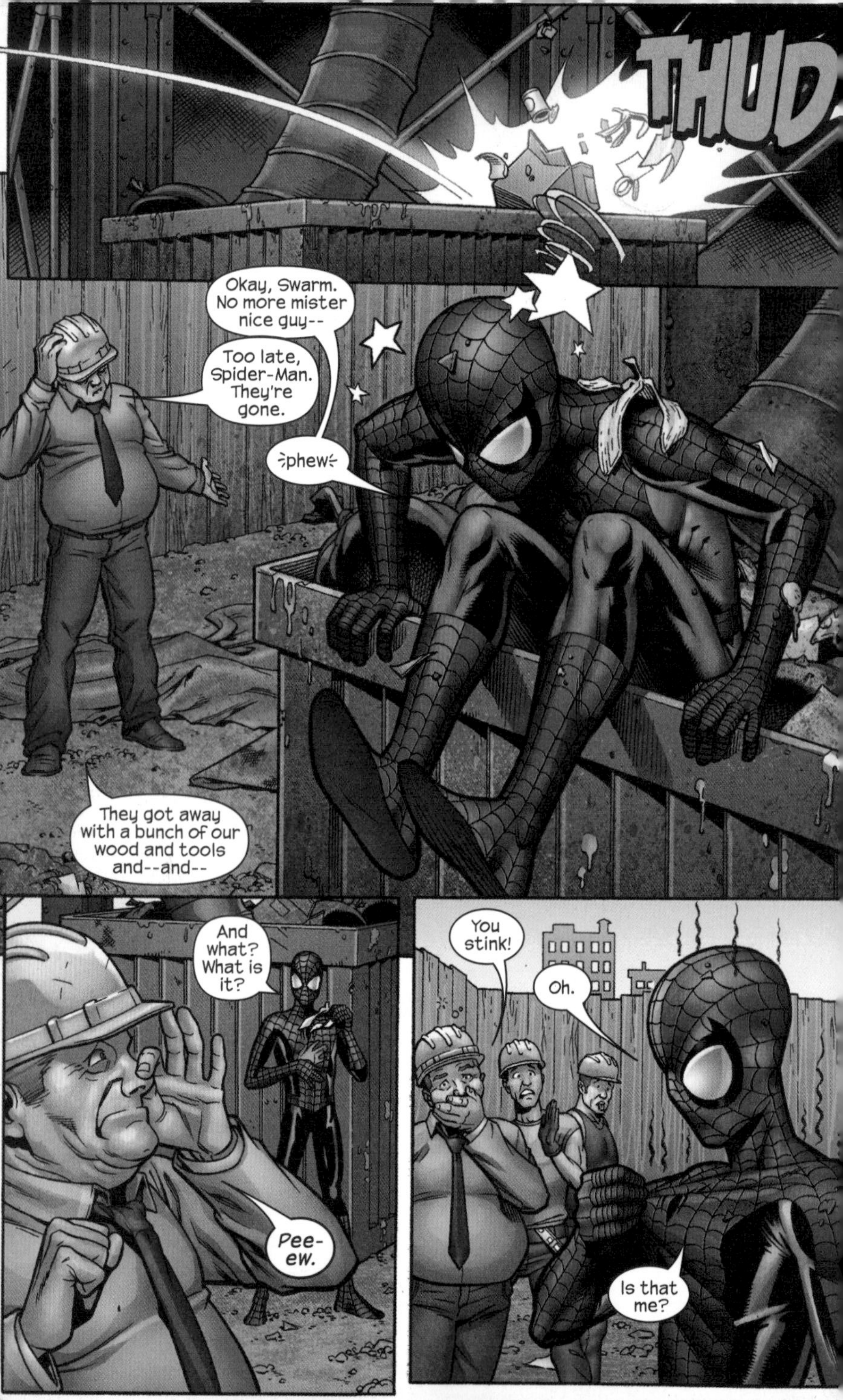
THUD
Okay, Swarm. No more mister nice guy--
Too late, Spider-Man. They're gone.
phew
They got away with a bunch of our wood and tools and--and--
And what? What is it?
Pee-ew.
You stink!
Oh.
Is that me?

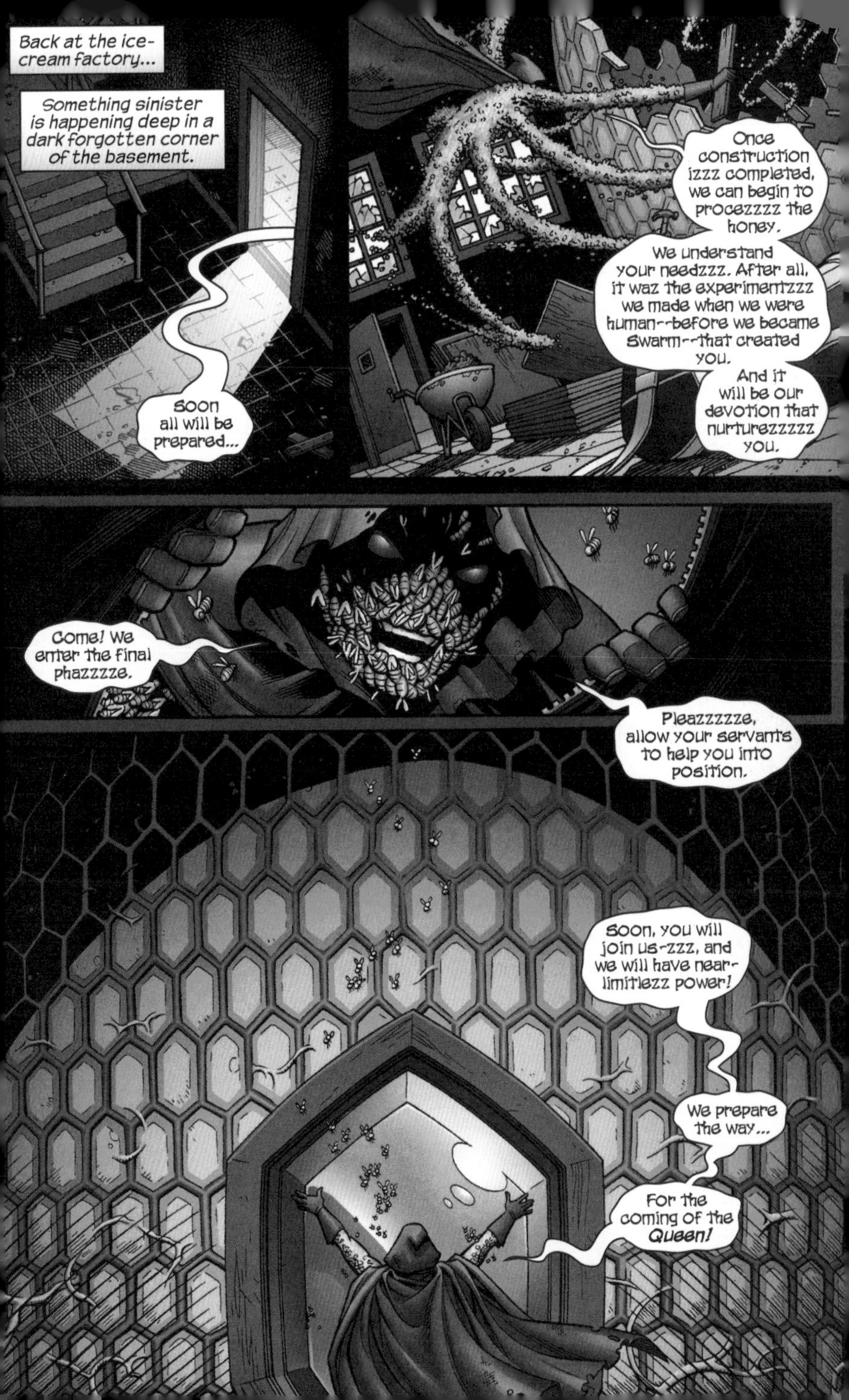
Back at the ice-cream factory...
Something sinister is happening deep in a dark forgotten corner of the basement.
Soon all will be prepared...
Once construction izzz completed, we can begin to procezzzz the honey.
We understand your needzzz. After all, it waz the experimentzzz we made when we were human--before we became Swarm--that created you.
And it will be our devotion that nurturezzzzz you.
Come! We enter the final phazzzze.
Pleazzzzze, allow your servants to help you into position.
Soon, you will join us-zzz, and we will have near-limitlezz power!
We prepare the way...
For the coming of the Queen!

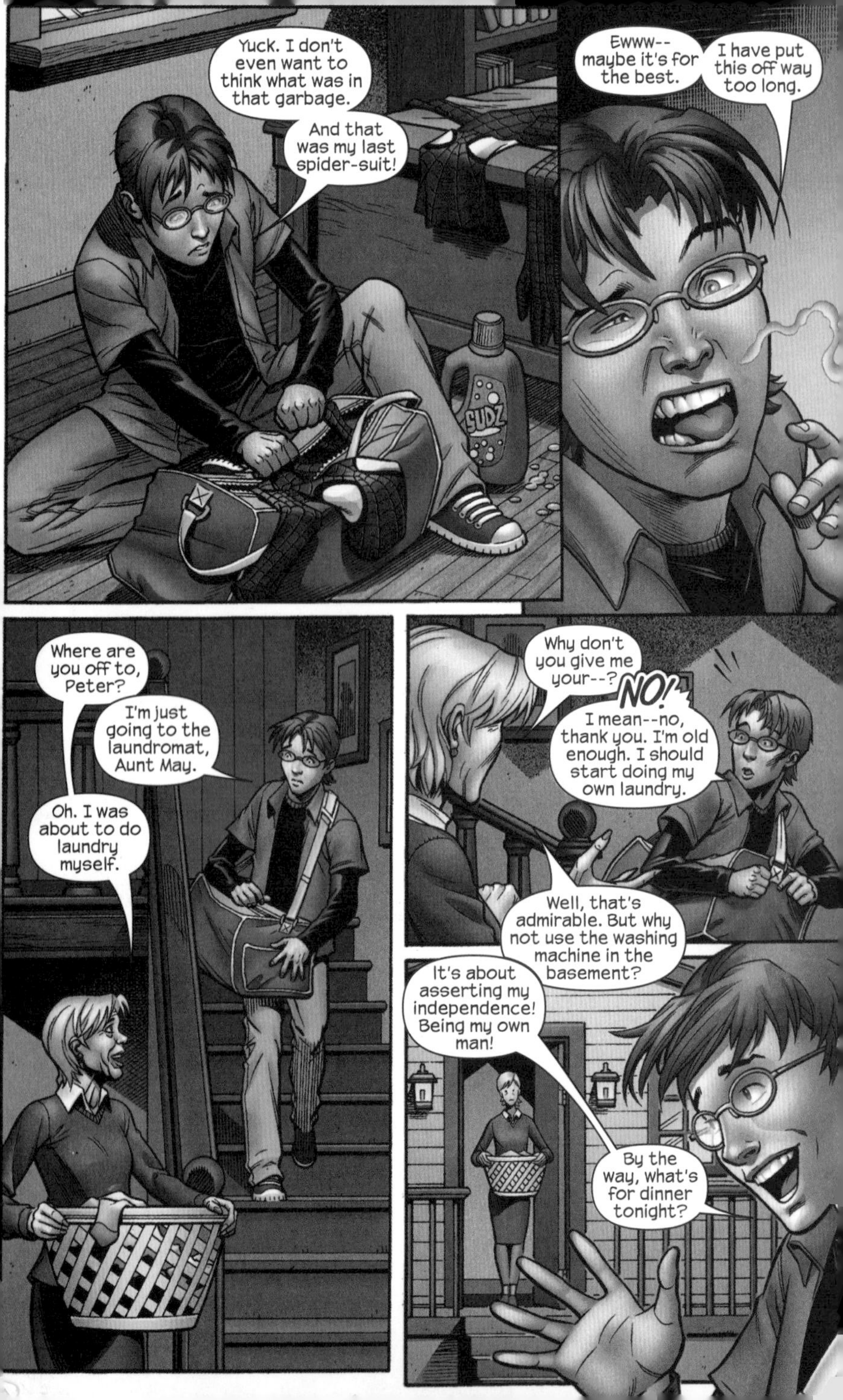
Yuck. I don't even want to think what was in that garbage.
And that was my last spider-suit!
Ewww-- maybe it's for the best.
I have put this off way too long.
SUDZ
Where are you off to, Peter?
I'm just going to the laundromat, Aunt May.
Oh. I was about to do laundry myself.
Why don't you give me your--?
NO!
I mean--no, thank you. I'm old enough. I should start doing my own laundry.
Well, that's admirable. But why not use the washing machine in the basement?
It's about asserting my independence! Being my own man!
By the way, what's for dinner tonight?

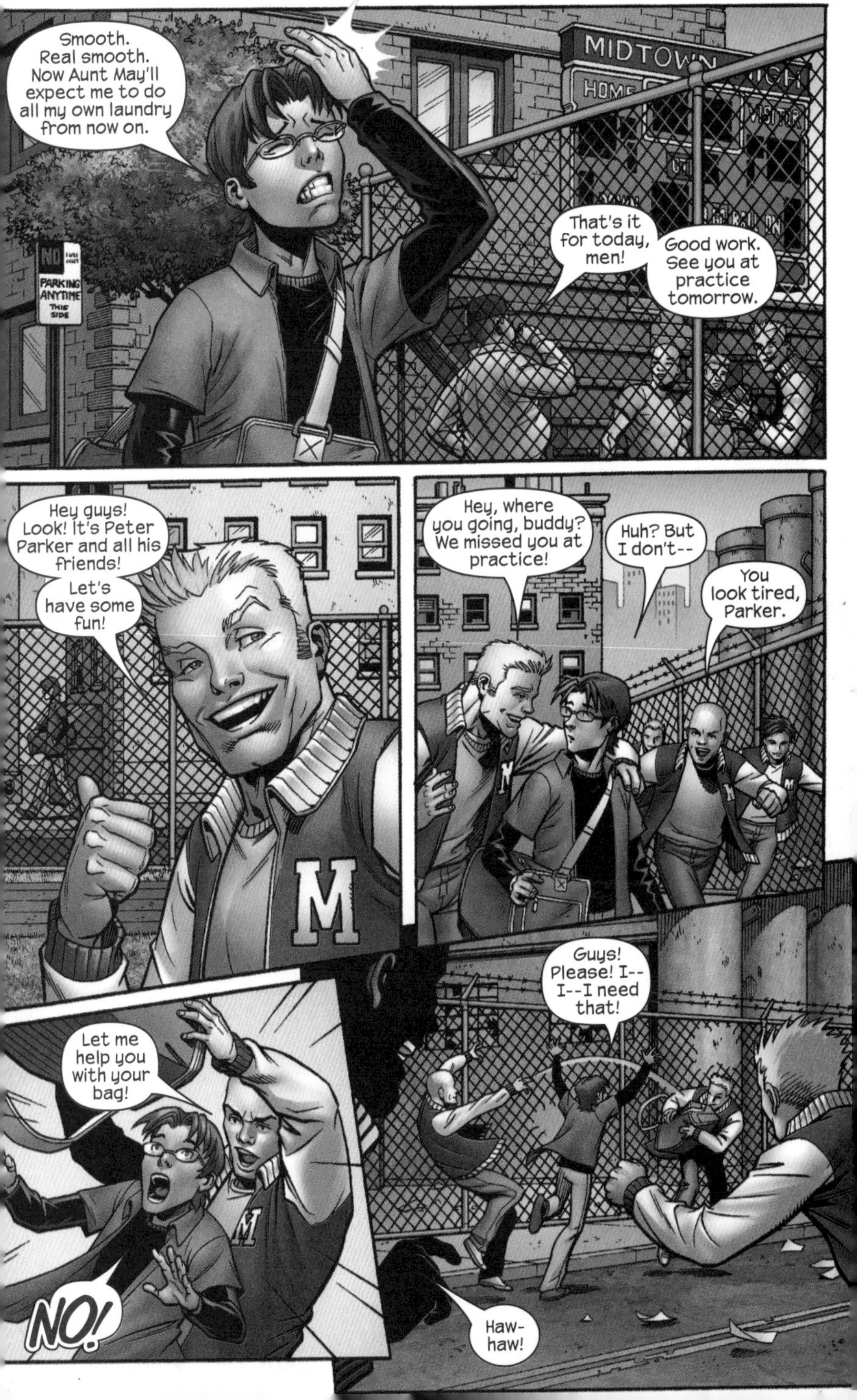

Smooth. Real smooth. Now Aunt May'll expect me to do all my own laundry from now on.
MIDTOWN
HOME
NO
PARKING ANYTIME THIS SIDE
That's it for today, men!
Good work. See you at practice tomorrow.
Hey guys! Look! It's Peter Parker and all his friends!
Let's have some fun!
Hey, where you going, buddy? We missed you at practice!
Huh? But I don't--
You look tired, Parker.
Let me help you with your bag!
NO!
Guys! Please! I-- I--I need that!
Haw-haw!

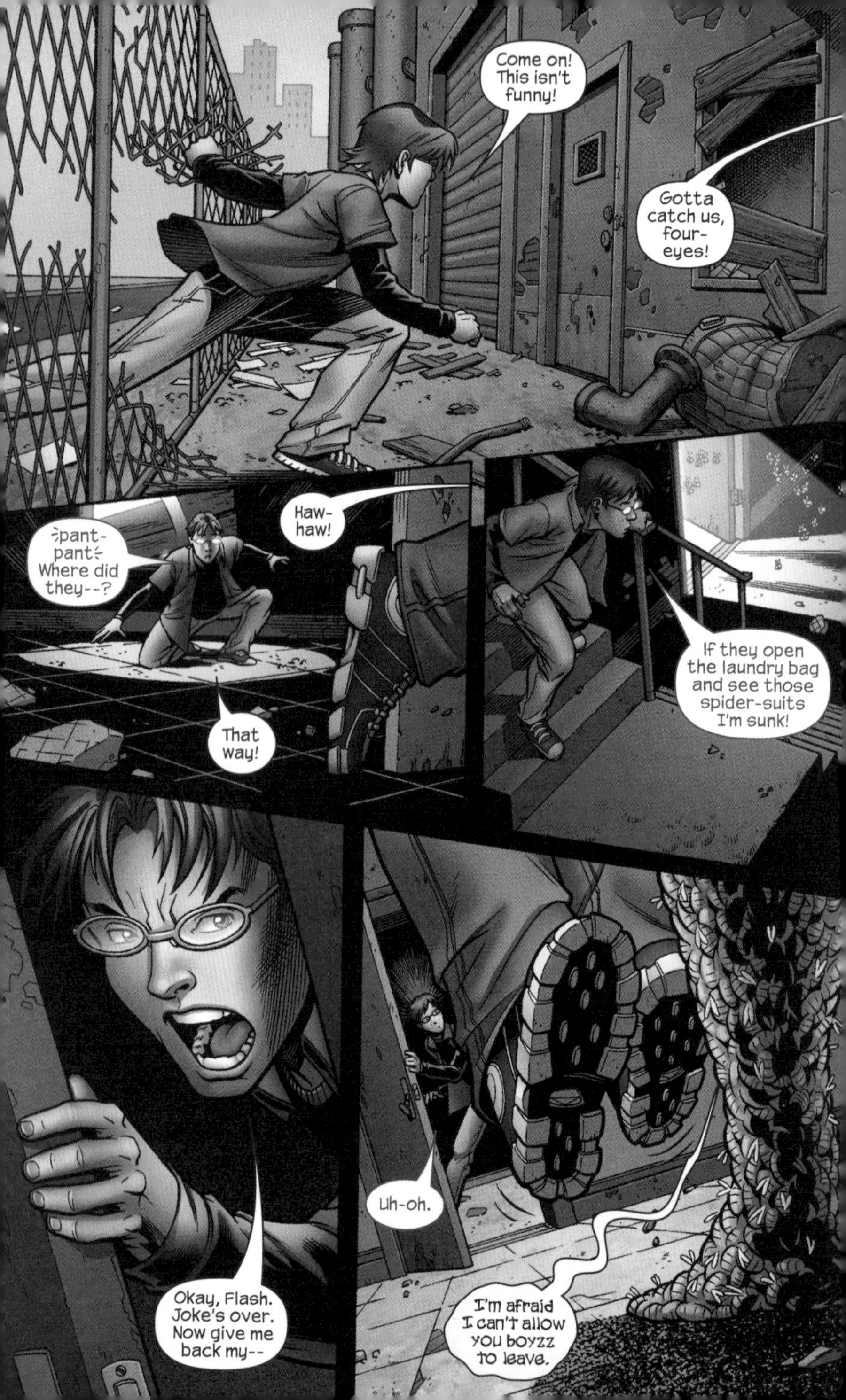
Come on! This isn't funny!
Gotta catch us, four-eyes!
⩫pant-pant⩪ Where did they--?
Haw-haw!
That way!
If they open the laundry bag and see those spider-suits I'm sunk!
Okay, Flash. Joke's over. Now give me back my--
Uh-oh.
I'm afraid I can't allow you boyzz to leave.

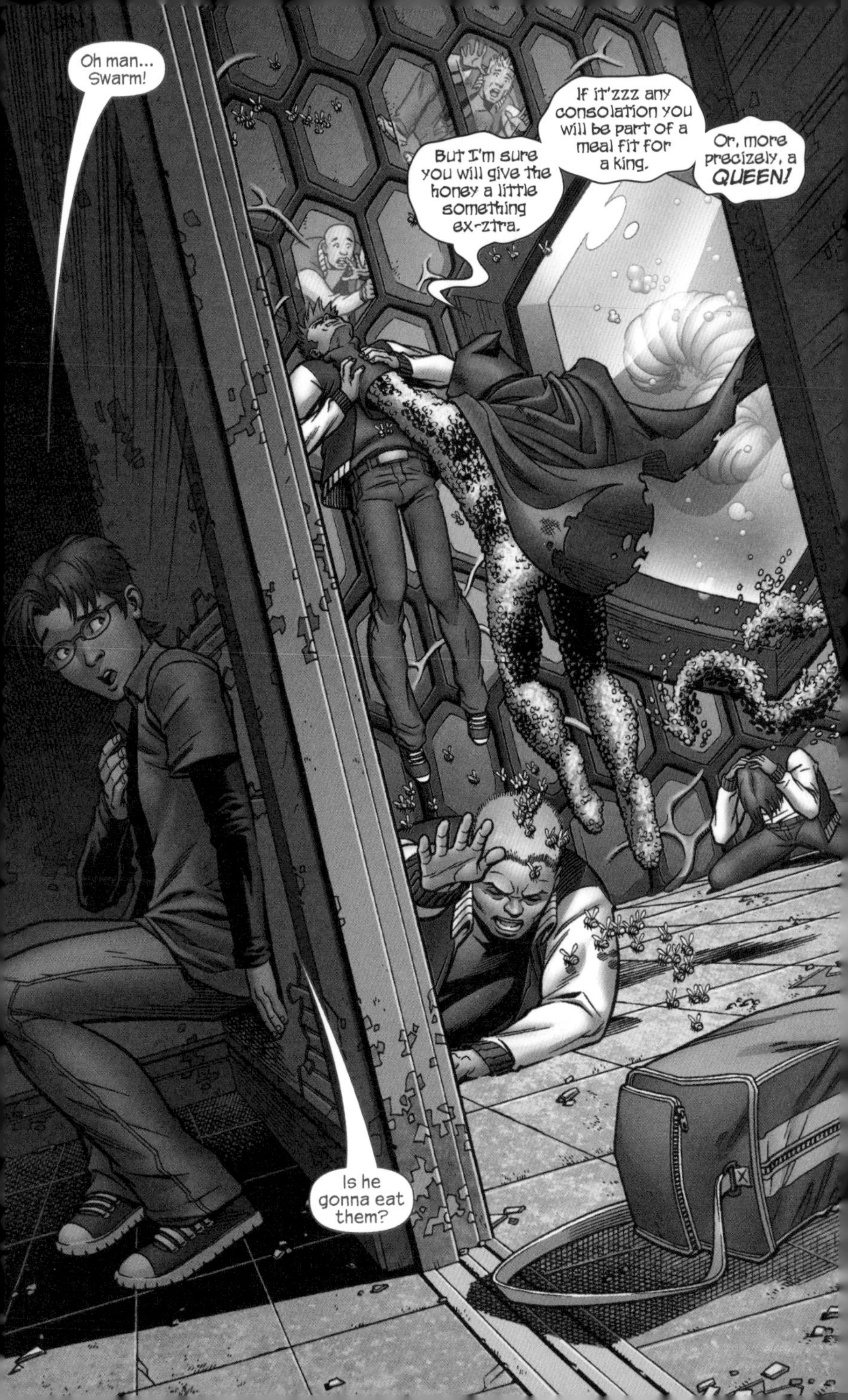
Oh man... Swarm!
But I'm sure you will give the honey a little something ex-ztra.
If it'zzz any consolation you will be part of a meal fit for a king.
Or, more precizely, a QUEEN!
Is he gonna eat them?

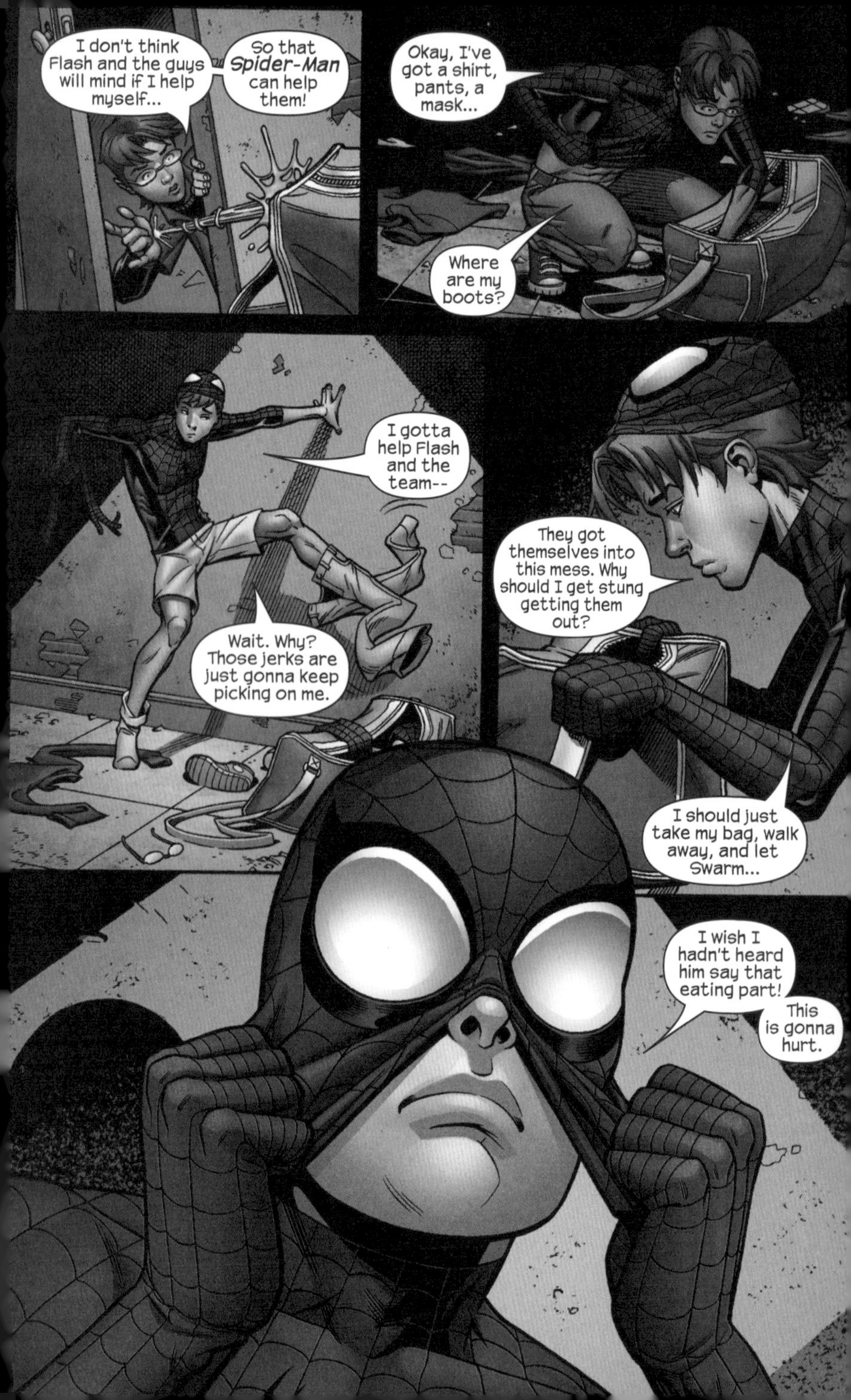
I don't think Flash and the guys will mind if I help myself...
So that *Spider-Man* can help them!
Okay, I've got a shirt, pants, a mask...
Where are my boots?
I gotta help Flash and the team--
Wait. Why? Those jerks are just gonna keep picking on me.
They got themselves into this mess. Why should I get stung getting them out?
I should just take my bag, walk away, and let Swarm...
I wish I hadn't heard him say that eating part!
This is gonna hurt.

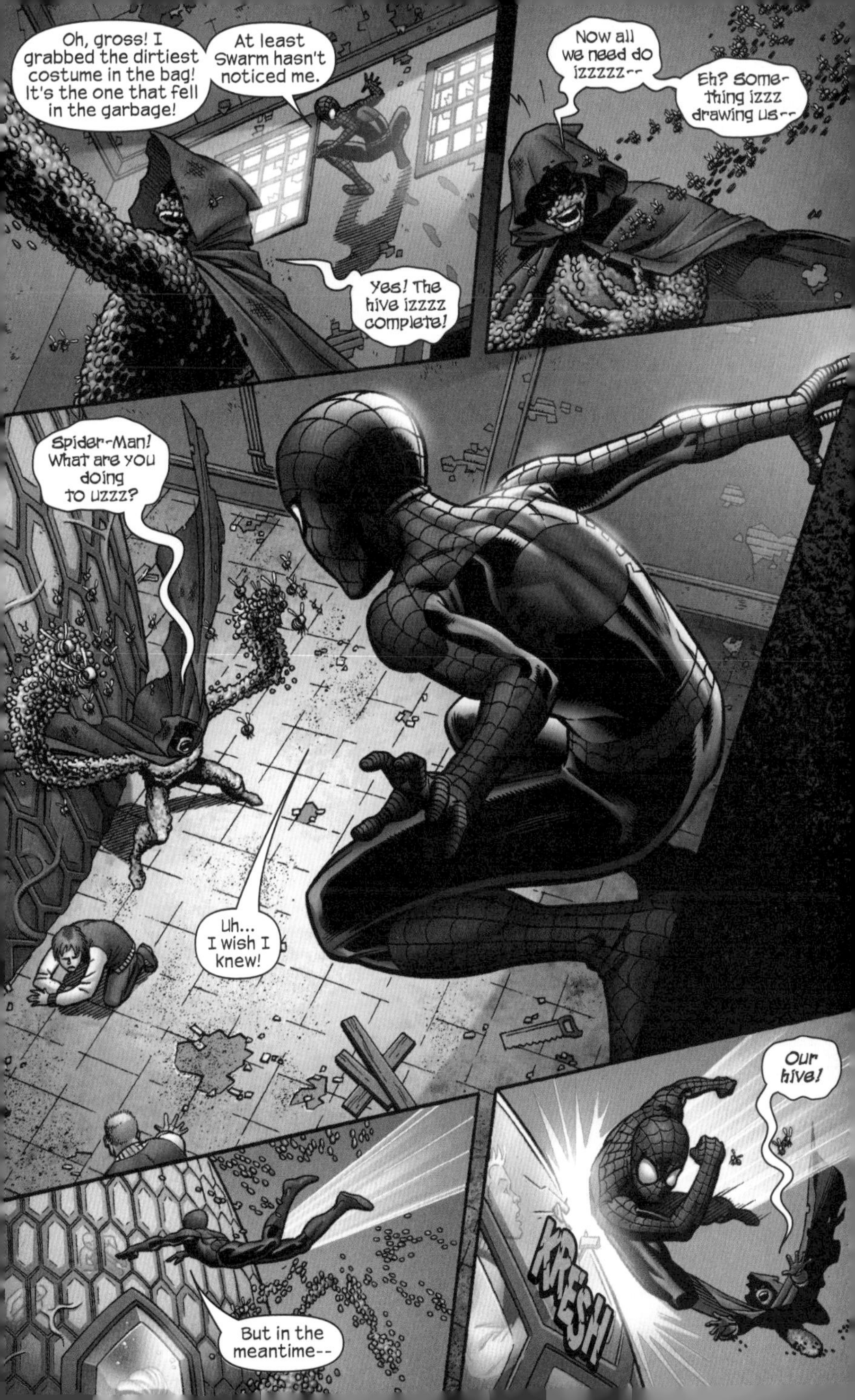
Oh, gross! I grabbed the dirtiest costume in the bag! It's the one that fell in the garbage!
At least Swarm hasn't noticed me.
Yes! The hive izzzz complete!
Now all we need do izzzzz--
Eh? Some-thing izzz drawing us--
Spider-Man! What are you doing to uzzz?
Uh... I wish I knew!
But in the meantime--
KRESH!
Our hive!

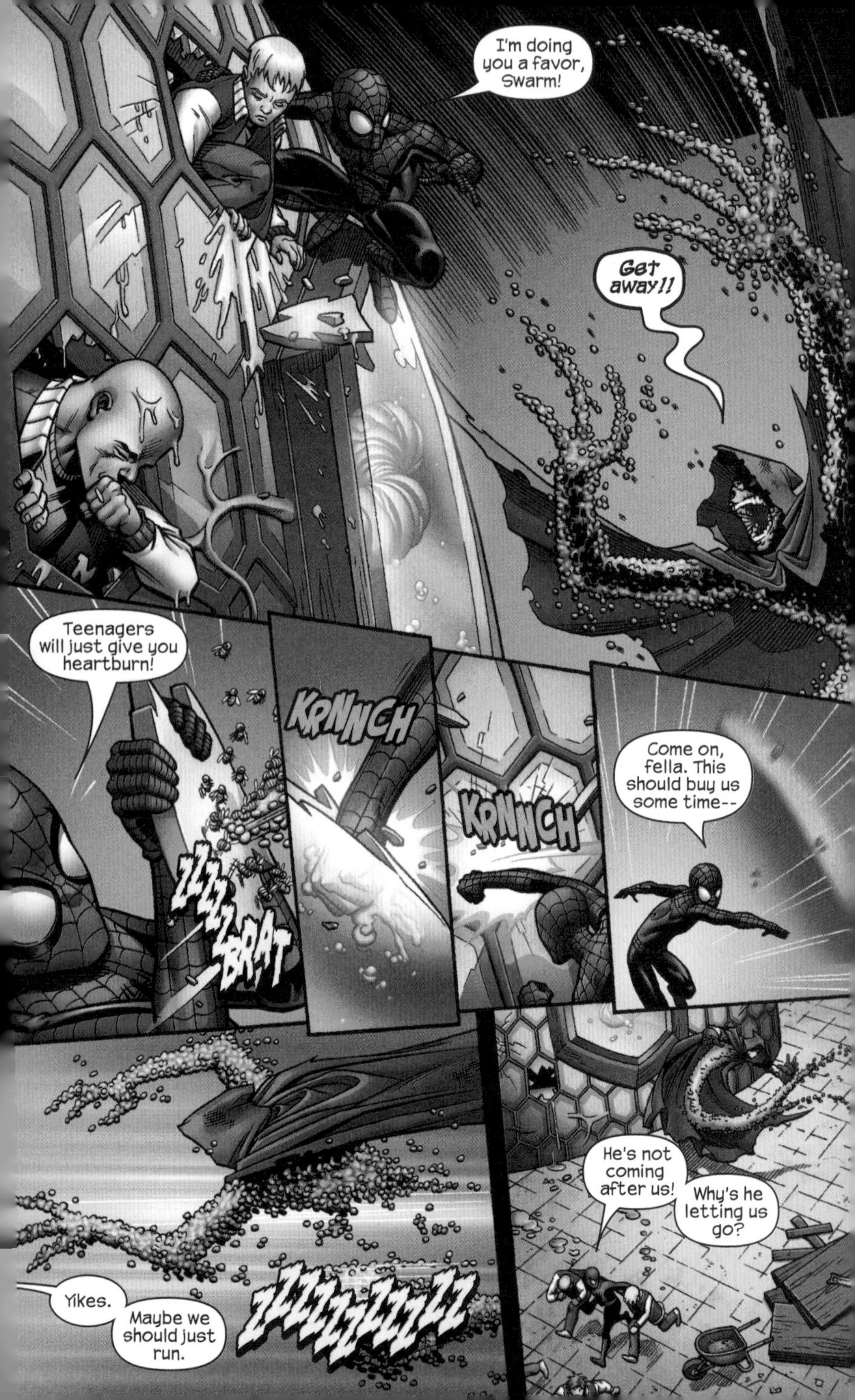
I'm doing you a favor, Swarm!
Get away!!
Teenagers will just give you heartburn!
ZZZZZBRAT
KRNNCH
KRNNCH
Come on, fella. This should buy us some time--
Yikes.
Maybe we should just run.
ZZZZZZZZZZZZ
He's not coming after us!
Why's he letting us go?

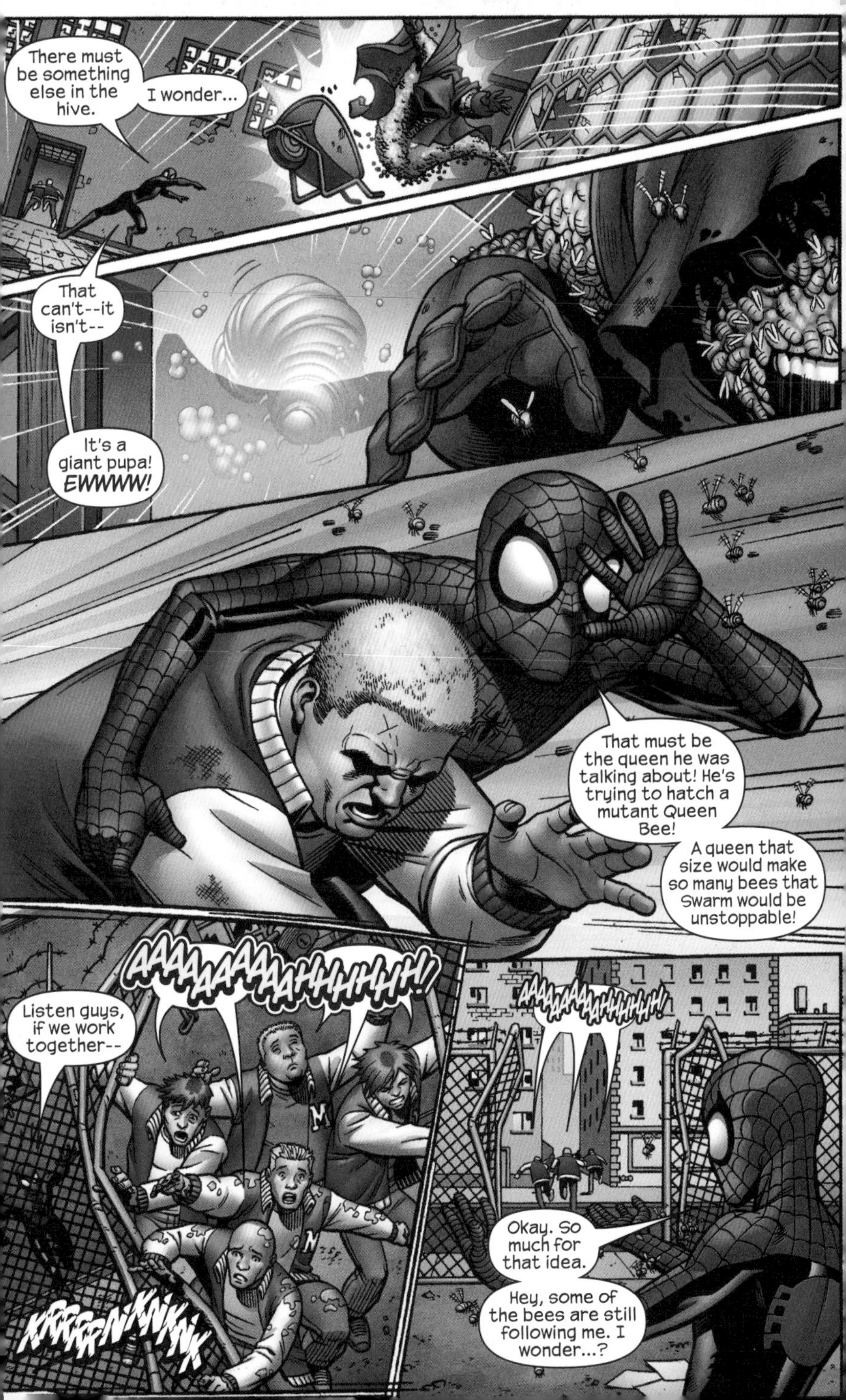
There must be something else in the hive.
I wonder...
That can't--it isn't--
It's a giant pupa! EWWWW!
That must be the queen he was talking about! He's trying to hatch a mutant Queen Bee!
A queen that size would make so many bees that Swarm would be unstoppable!
Listen guys, if we work together--
AAAAAAAAAAHHHHHH!
AAAAAAAAAAHHHHHH!
KRRRRRNKNKNK
Okay. So much for that idea.
Hey, some of the bees are still following me. I wonder...?

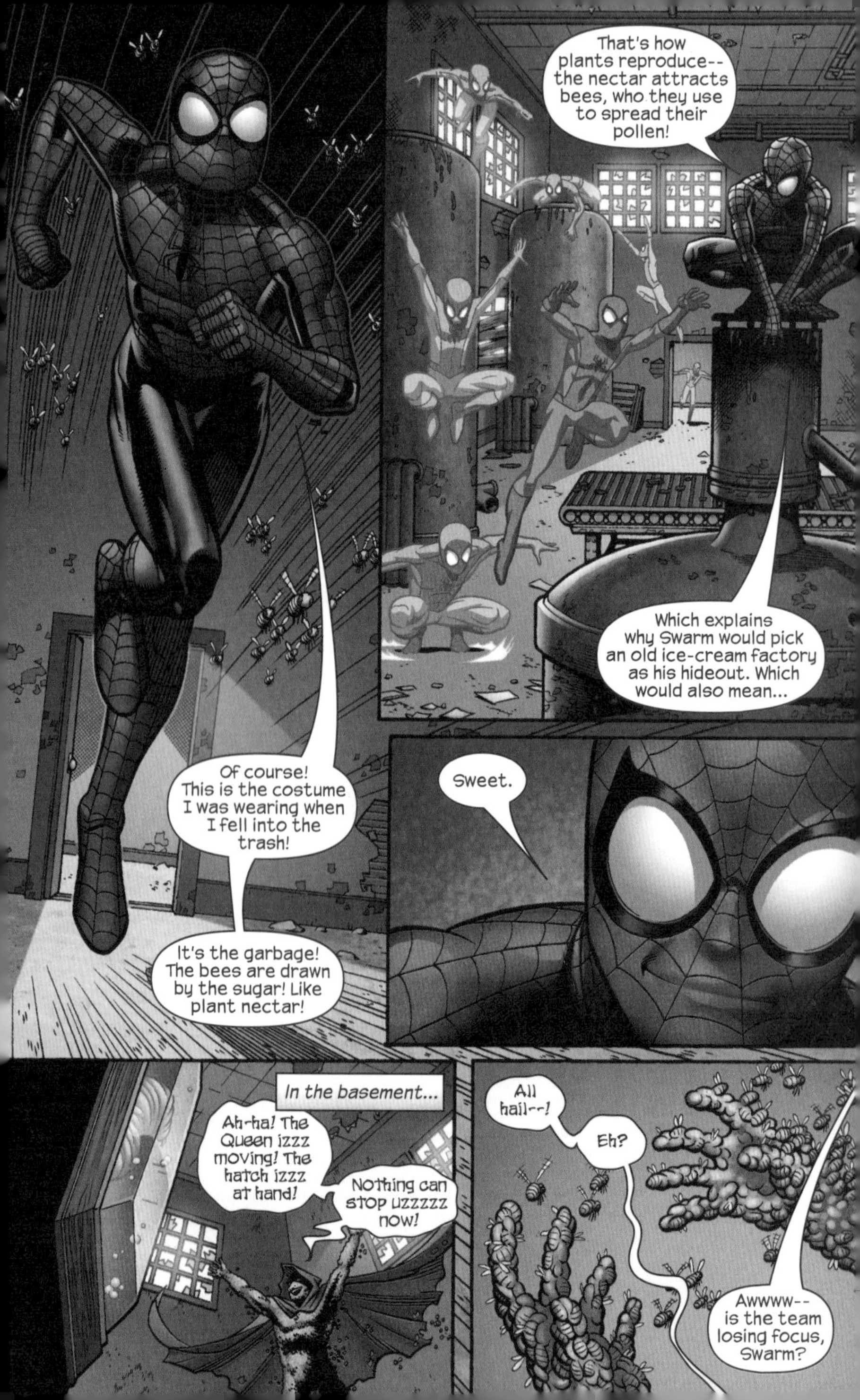
Of course! This is the costume I was wearing when I fell into the trash!
It's the garbage! The bees are drawn by the sugar! Like plant nectar!
That's how plants reproduce-- the nectar attracts bees, who they use to spread their pollen!
Which explains why Swarm would pick an old ice-cream factory as his hideout. Which would also mean...
Sweet.
In the basement...
Ah-ha! The Queen izzz moving! The hatch izzz at hand!
Nothing can stop uzzzzz now!
All hail--!
Eh?
Awwww-- is the team losing focus, Swarm?

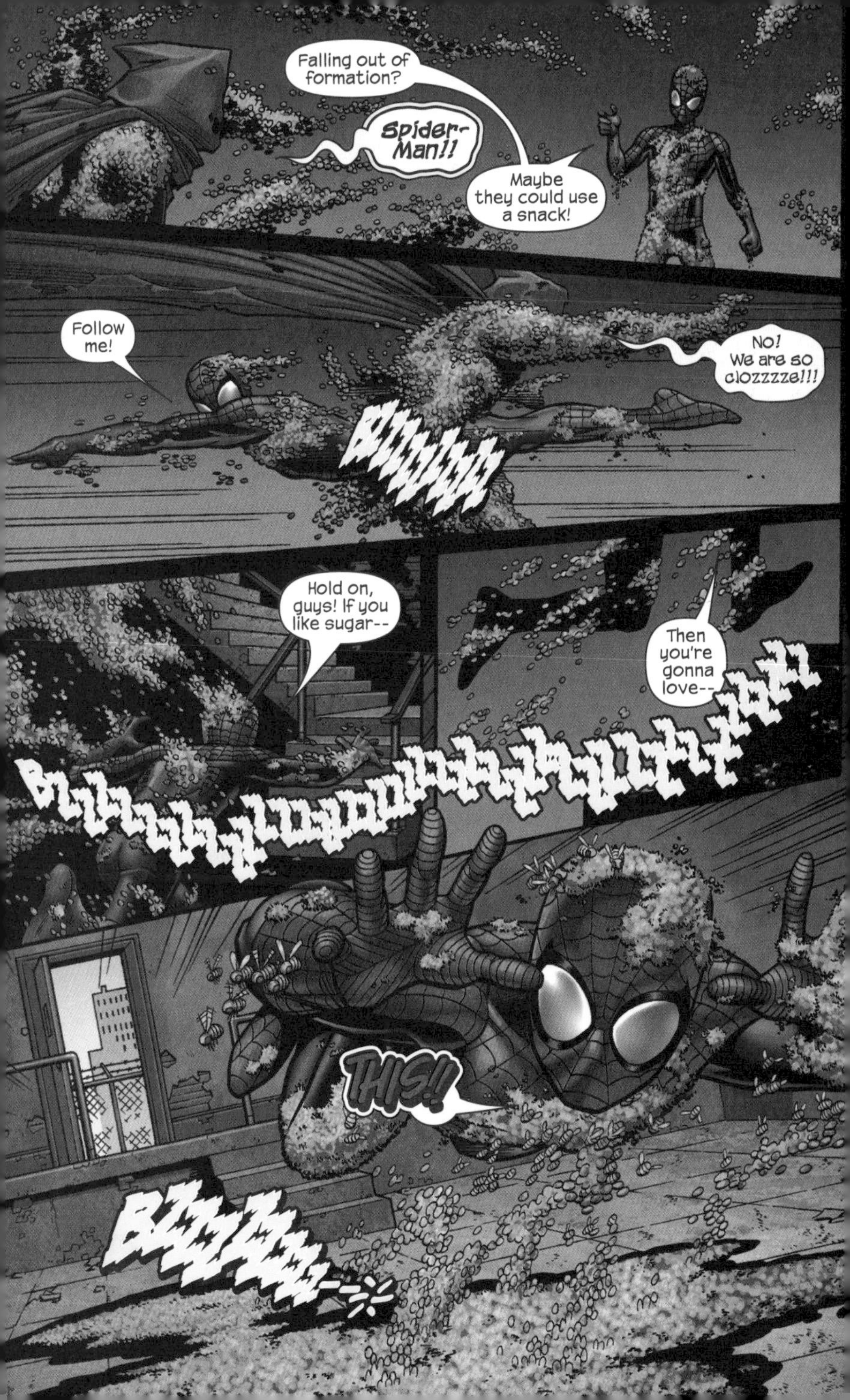
Falling out of formation?
Spider-Man!!
Maybe they could use a snack!
Follow me!
No! We are so clozzzze!!!
Hold on, guys! If you like sugar--
Then you're gonna love--
THIS!!

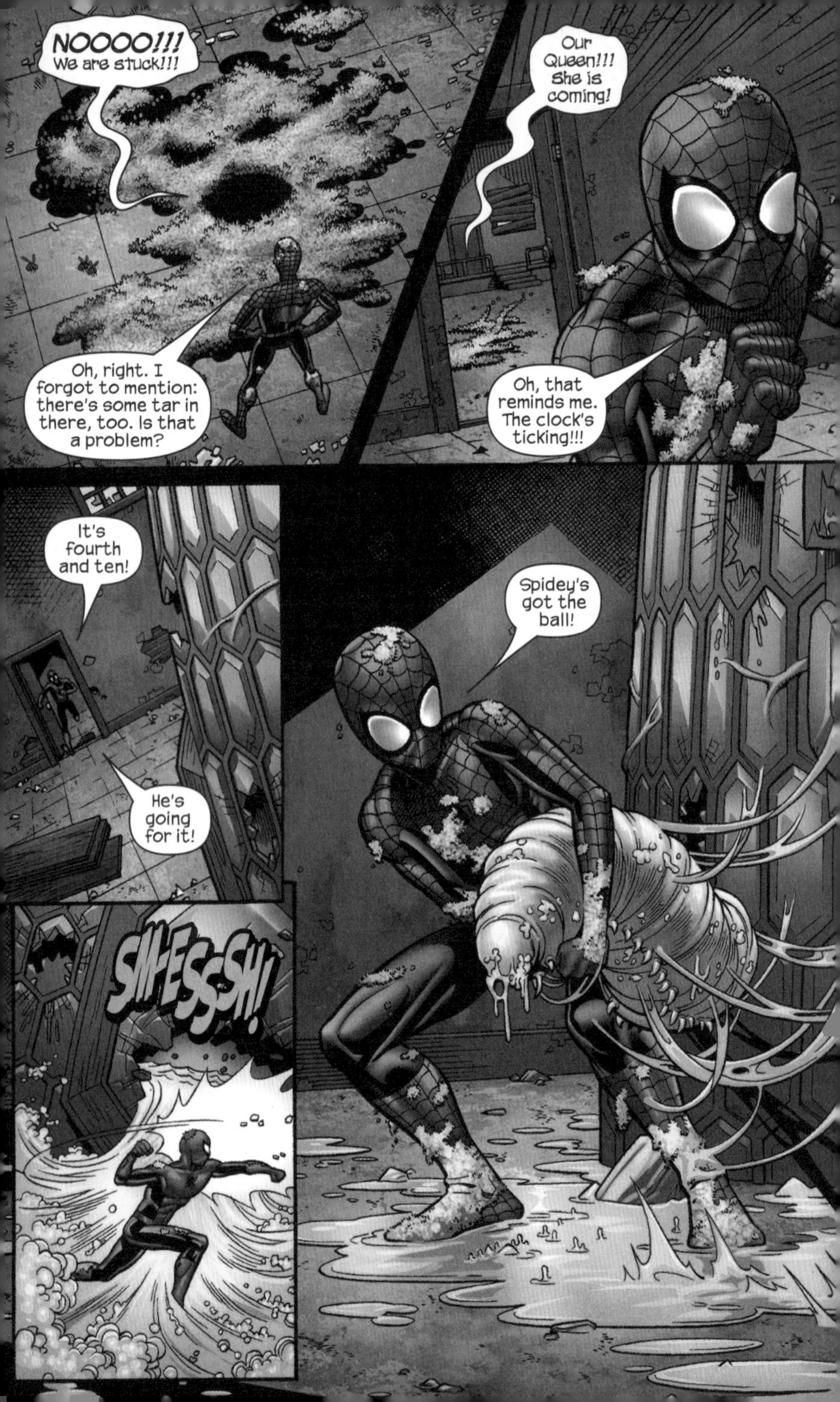

NOOOO!!! We are stuck!!!
Oh, right. I forgot to mention: there's some tar in there, too. Is that a problem?
Our Queen!!! She is coming!
Oh, that reminds me. The clock's ticking!!!
It's fourth and ten!
He's going for it!
Spidey's got the ball!
SMESSSH!

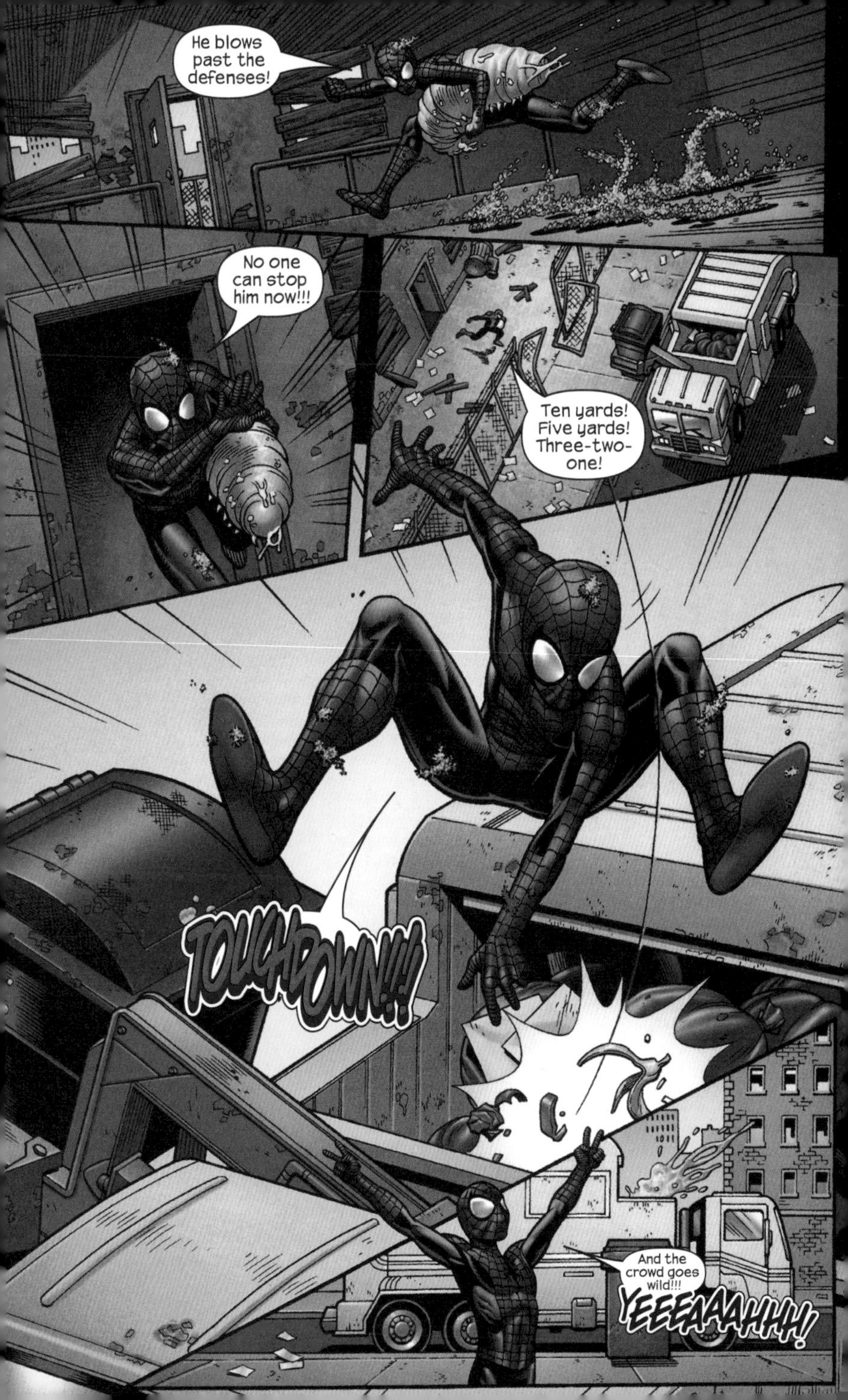
He blows past the defenses!
No one can stop him now!!!
Ten yards! Five yards! Three-two-one!
TOUCHDOWN!!!
And the crowd goes wild!!!
YEEEAAAHHH!

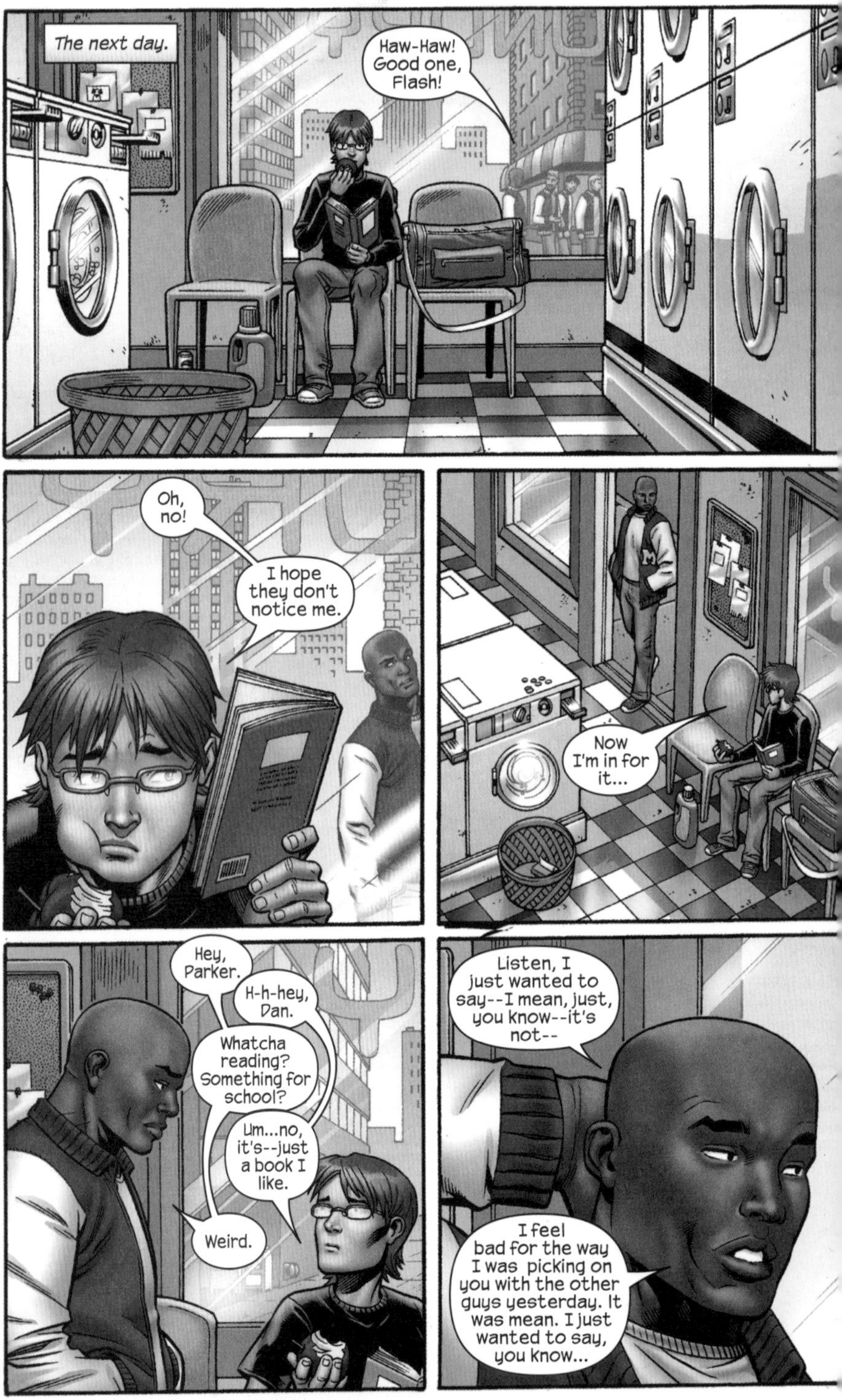
The next day.
Haw-Haw! Good one, Flash!
Oh, no!
I hope they don't notice me.
Now I'm in for it...
Hey, Parker.
H-h-hey, Dan.
Whatcha reading? Something for school?
Um...no, it's--just a book I like.
Weird.
Listen, I just wanted to say--I mean, just, you know--it's not--
I feel bad for the way I was picking on you with the other guys yesterday. It was mean. I just wanted to say, you know...

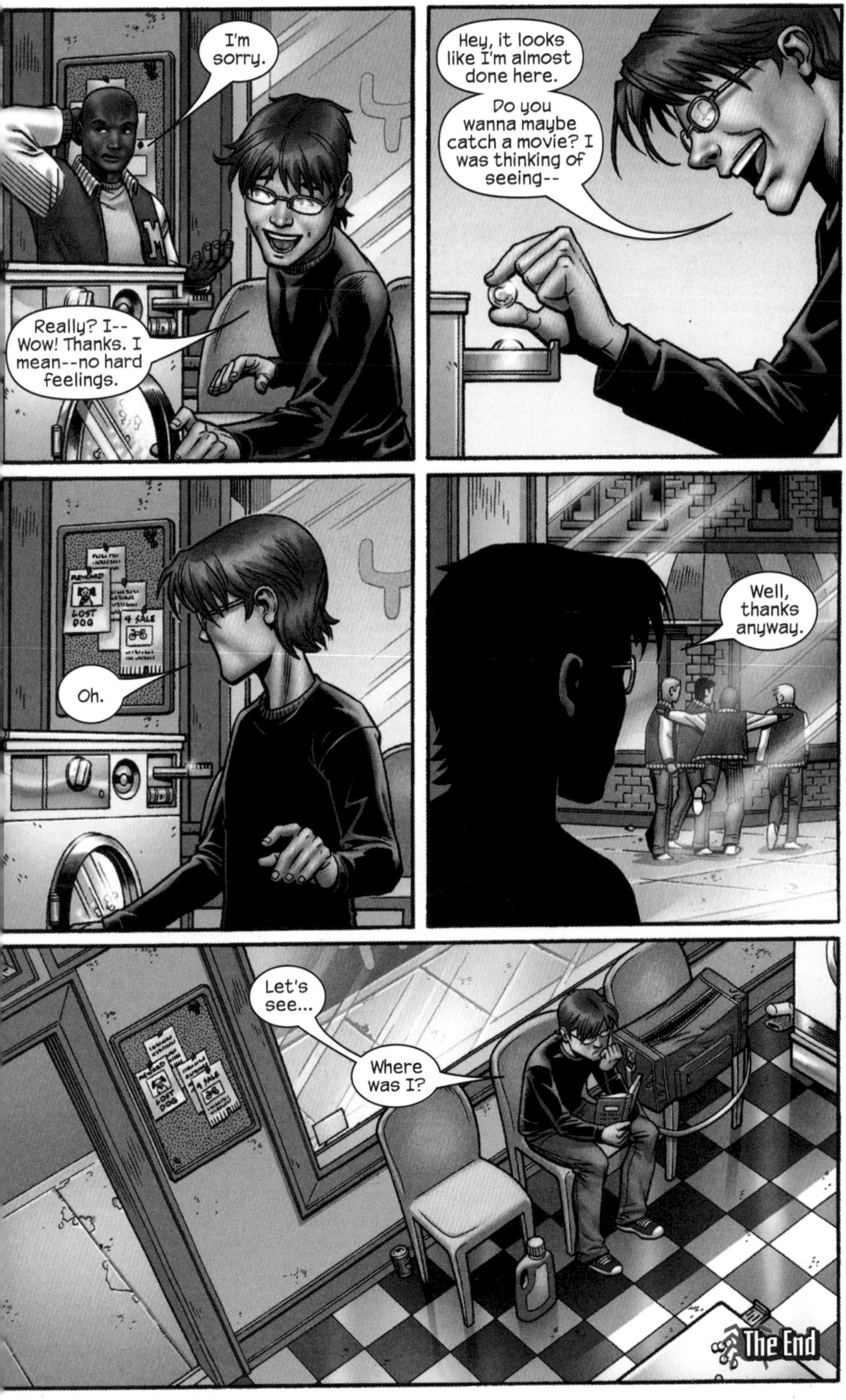
I'm sorry.
Really? I-- Wow! Thanks. I mean--no hard feelings.
Hey, it looks like I'm almost done here.
Do you wanna maybe catch a movie? I was thinking of seeing--
REWARD
LOST DOG
4 SALE
Oh.
Well, thanks anyway.
Let's see...
Where was I?
The End

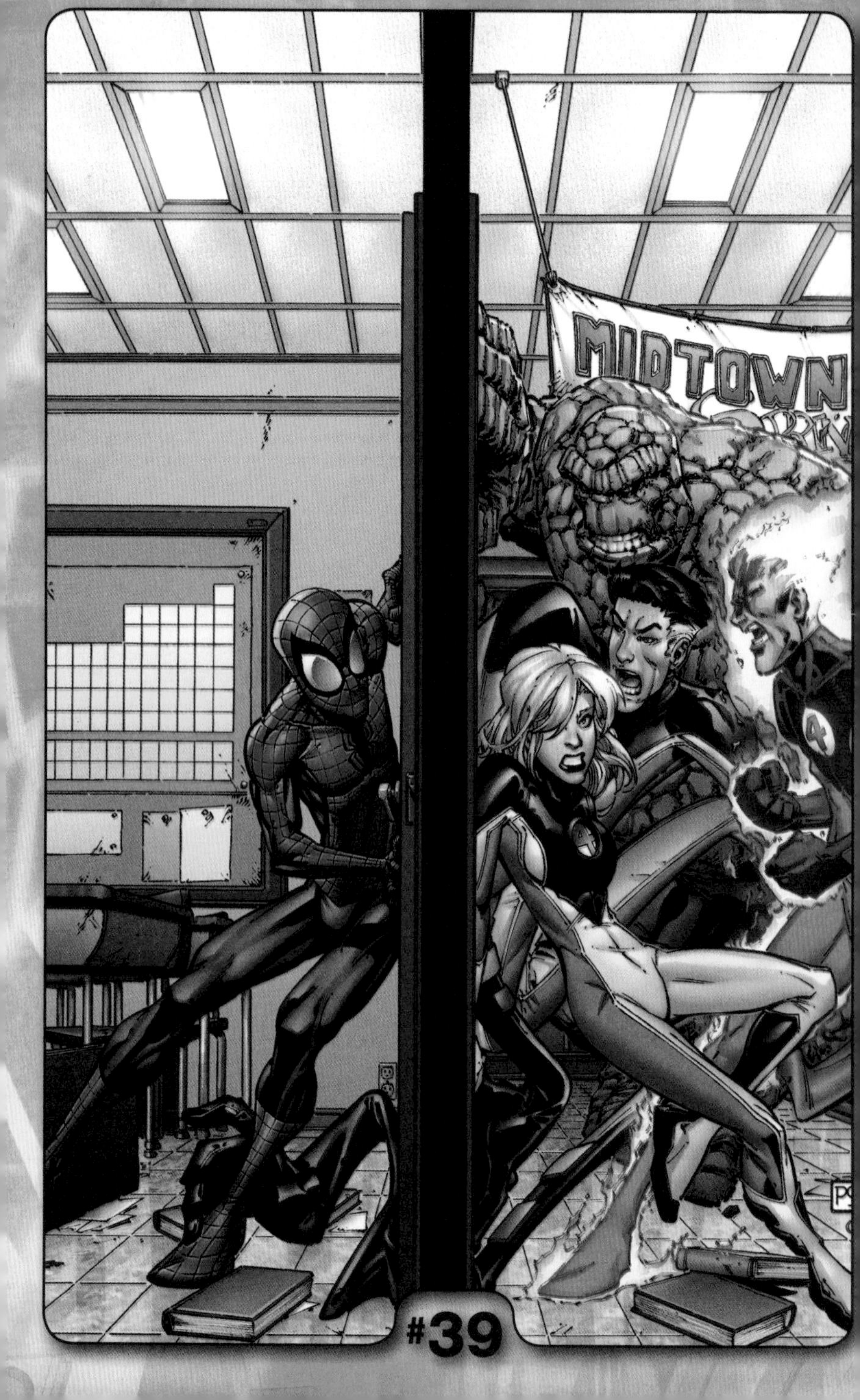
MIDTOWN
#39

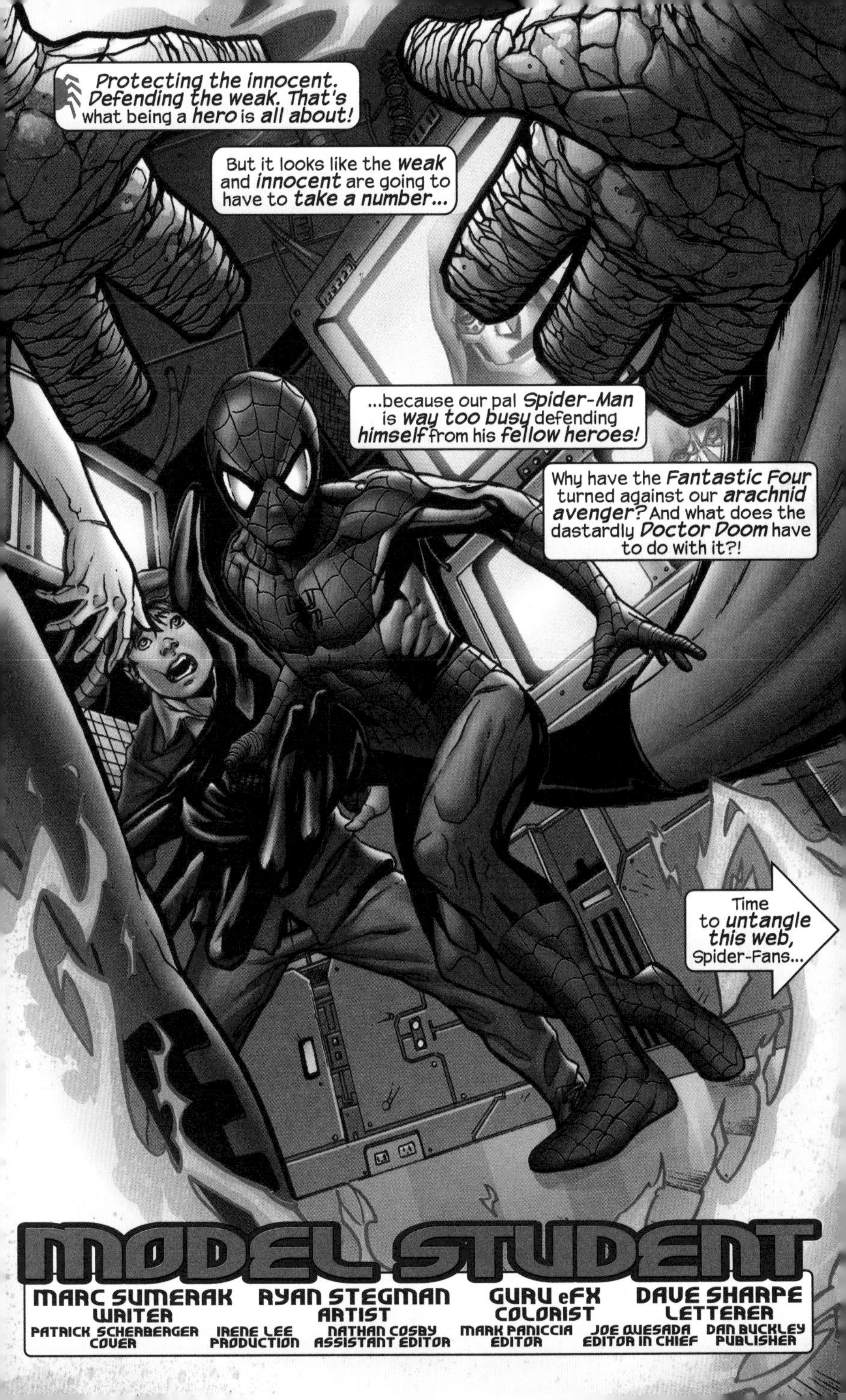

Protecting the innocent. Defending the weak. That's what being a hero is all about!
But it looks like the weak and innocent are going to have to take a number...
...because our pal Spider-Man is way too busy defending himself from his fellow heroes!
Why have the Fantastic Four turned against our arachnid avenger? And what does the dastardly Doctor Doom have to do with it?!
Time to untangle this web, Spider-Fans...
MODEL STUDENT
MARC SUMERAK WRITER
RYAN STEGMAN ARTIST
GURU eFX COLORIST
DAVE SHARPE LETTERER
PATRICK SCHERBERGER COVER
IRENE LEE PRODUCTION
NATHAN COSBY ASSISTANT EDITOR
MARK PANICCIA EDITOR
JOE QUESADA EDITOR IN CHIEF
DAN BUCKLEY PUBLISHER

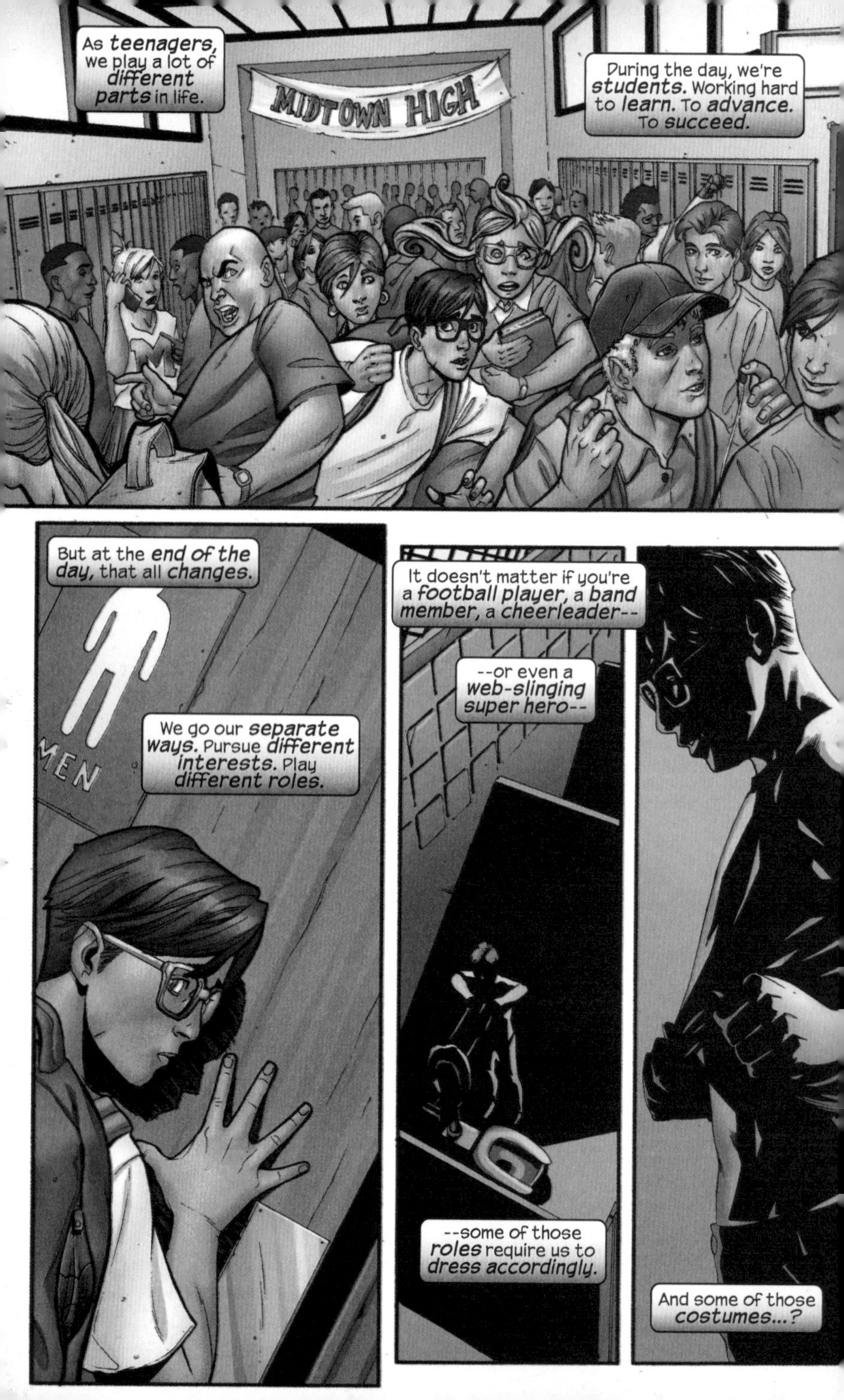

As teenagers, we play a lot of different parts in life.
MIDTOWN HIGH
During the day, we're students. Working hard to learn. To advance. To succeed.
But at the end of the day, that all changes.
MEN
We go our separate ways. Pursue different interests. Play different roles.
It doesn't matter if you're a football player, a band member, a cheerleader--
--or even a web-slinging super hero--
--some of those roles require us to dress accordingly.
And some of those costumes...?

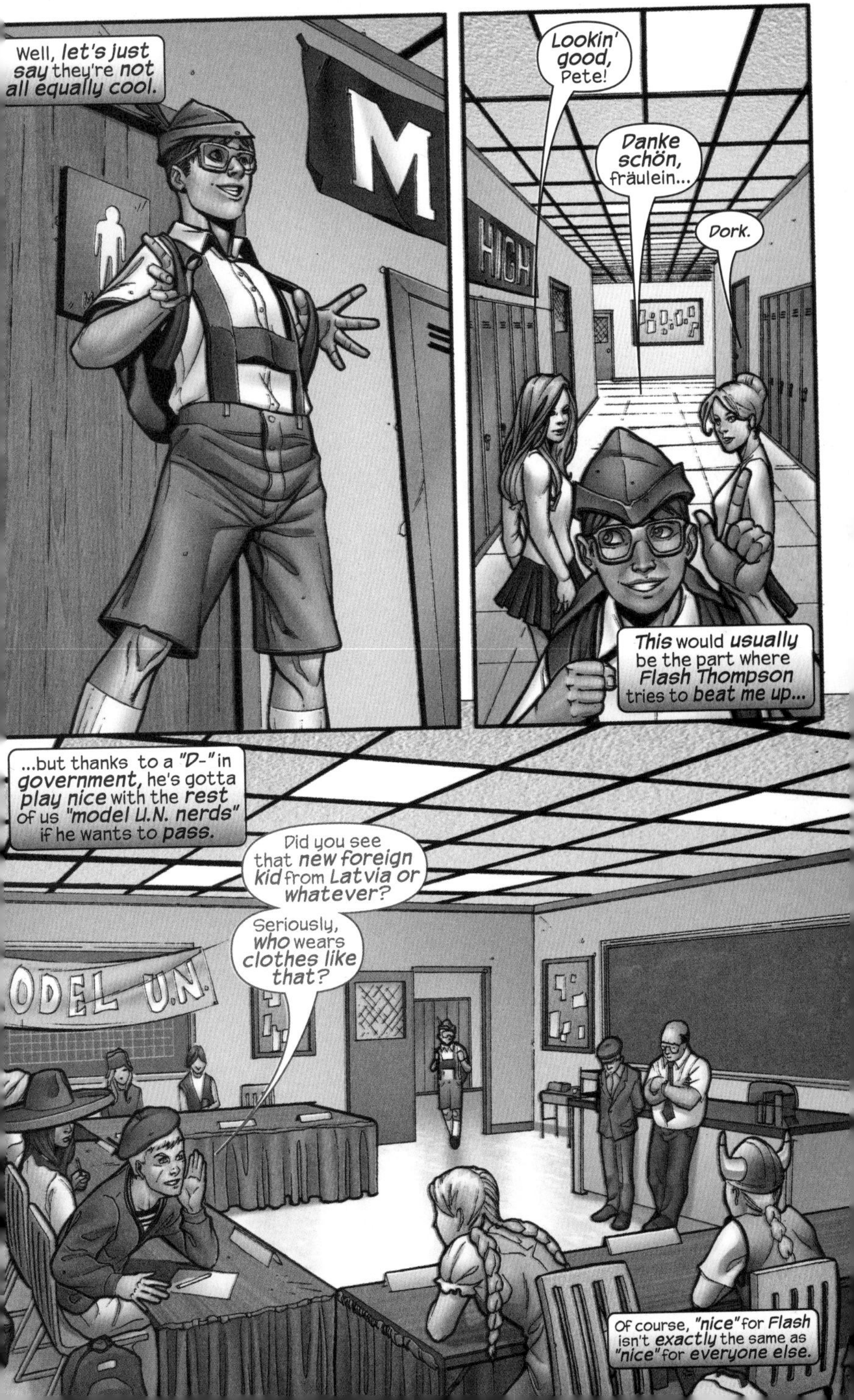
Well, let's just say they're not all equally cool.
Lookin' good, Pete!
Danke schön, fräulein...
Dork.
HIGH
This would usually be the part where Flash Thompson tries to beat me up...
...but thanks to a "D-" in government, he's gotta play nice with the rest of us "model U.N. nerds" if he wants to pass.
Did you see that new foreign kid from Latvia or whatever?
Seriously, who wears clothes like that?
ODEL U.N.
Of course, "nice" for Flash isn't exactly the same as "nice" for everyone else.

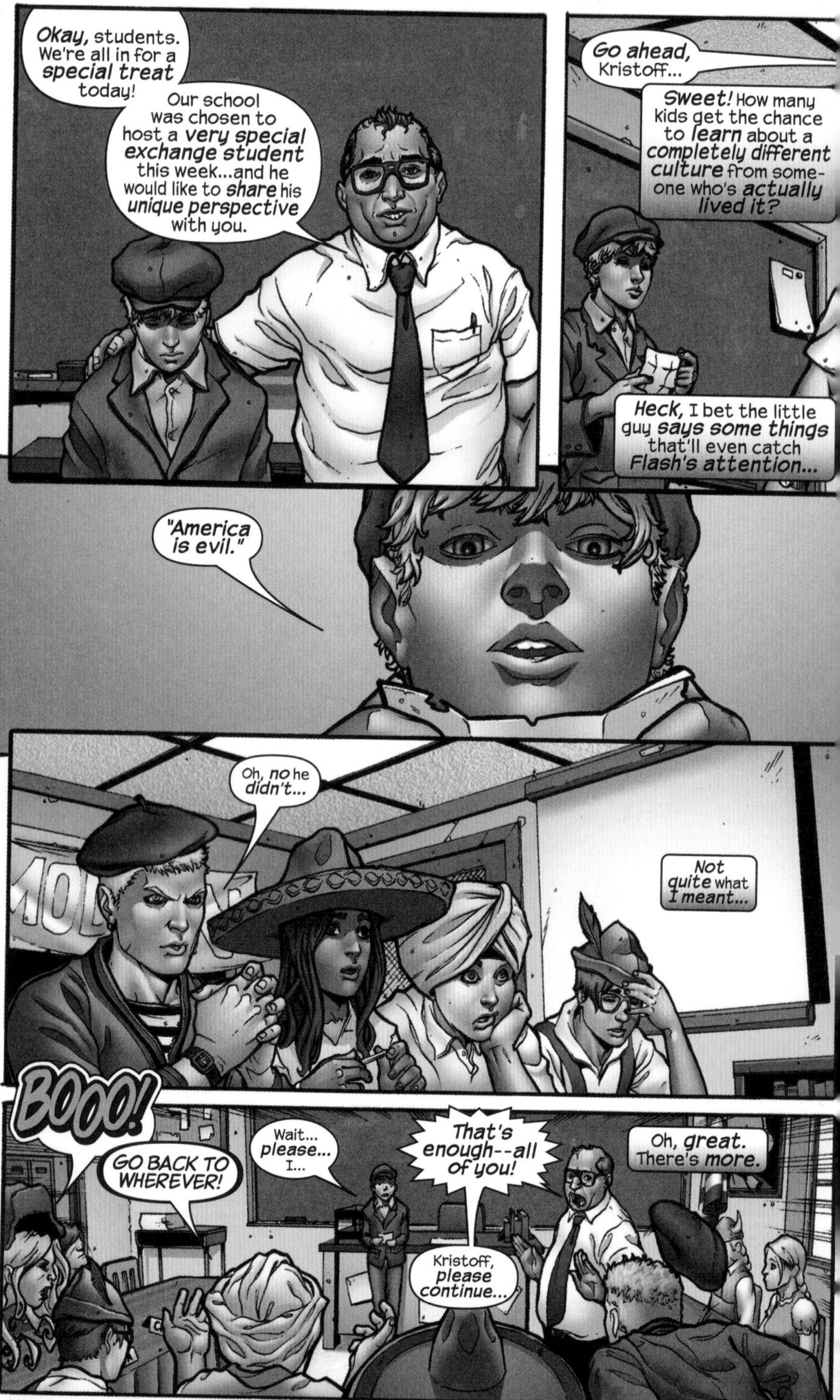
Okay, students. We're all in for a special treat today!
Our school was chosen to host a very special exchange student this week...and he would like to share his unique perspective with you.
Go ahead, Kristoff...
Sweet! How many kids get the chance to learn about a completely different culture from some-one who's actually lived it?
Heck, I bet the little guy says some things that'll even catch Flash's attention...
"America is evil."
Oh, no he didn't...
Not quite what I meant...
BOOO!
GO BACK TO WHEREVER!
Wait... please... I...
That's enough--all of you!
Kristoff, please continue...
Oh, great. There's more.

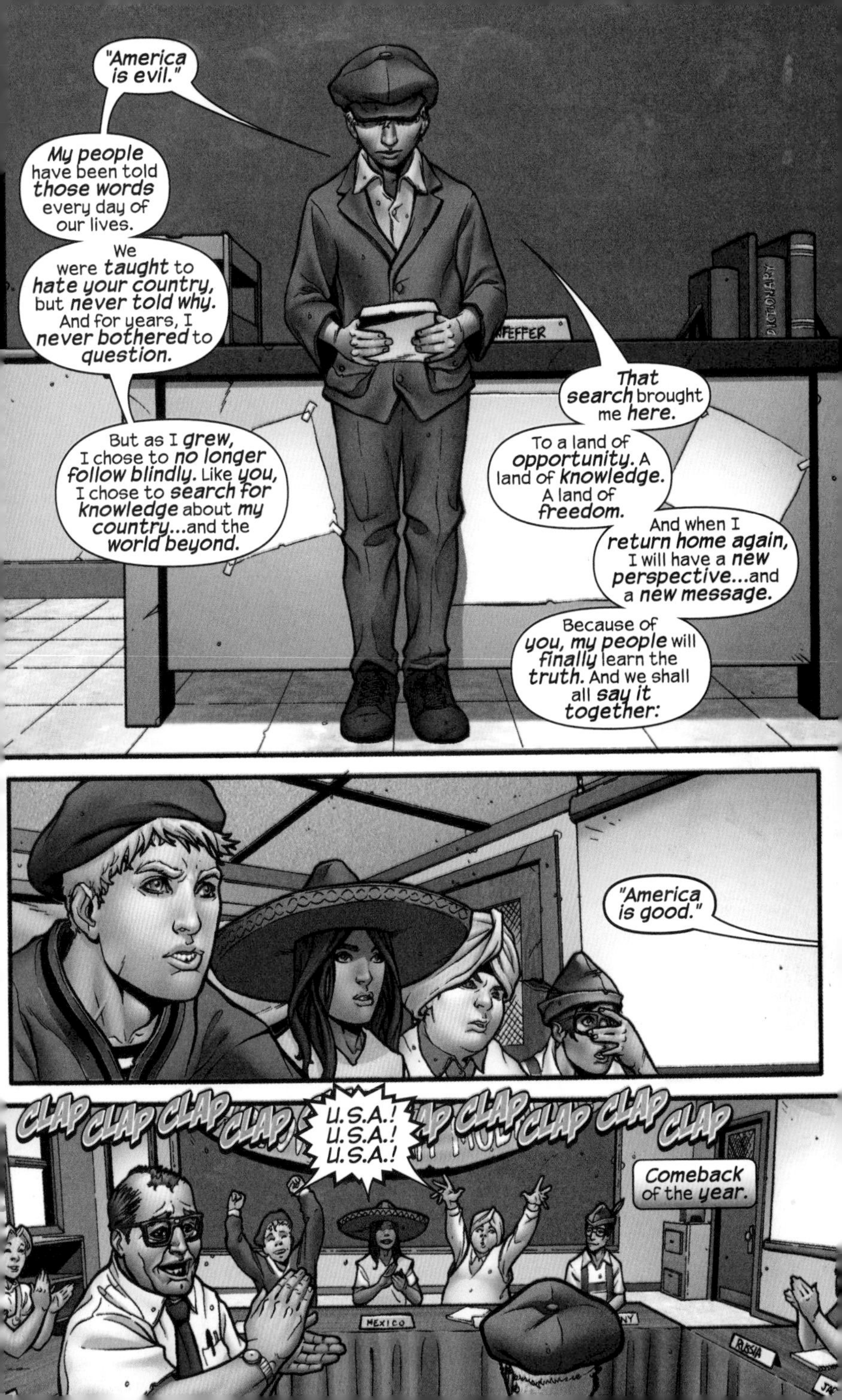

"America is evil."
My people have been told those words every day of our lives.
We were taught to hate your country, but never told why. And for years, I never bothered to question.
But as I grew, I chose to no longer follow blindly. Like you, I chose to search for knowledge about my country...and the world beyond.
That search brought me here.
To a land of opportunity. A land of knowledge. A land of freedom.
And when I return home again, I will have a new perspective...and a new message.
Because of you, my people will finally learn the truth. And we shall all say it together:
DICTIONARY
"America is good."
CLAP CLAP CLAP CLAP
U.S.A.! U.S.A.! U.S.A.!
CLAP CLAP CLAP CLAP CLAP
Comeback of the year.
MEXICO
RUSSIA

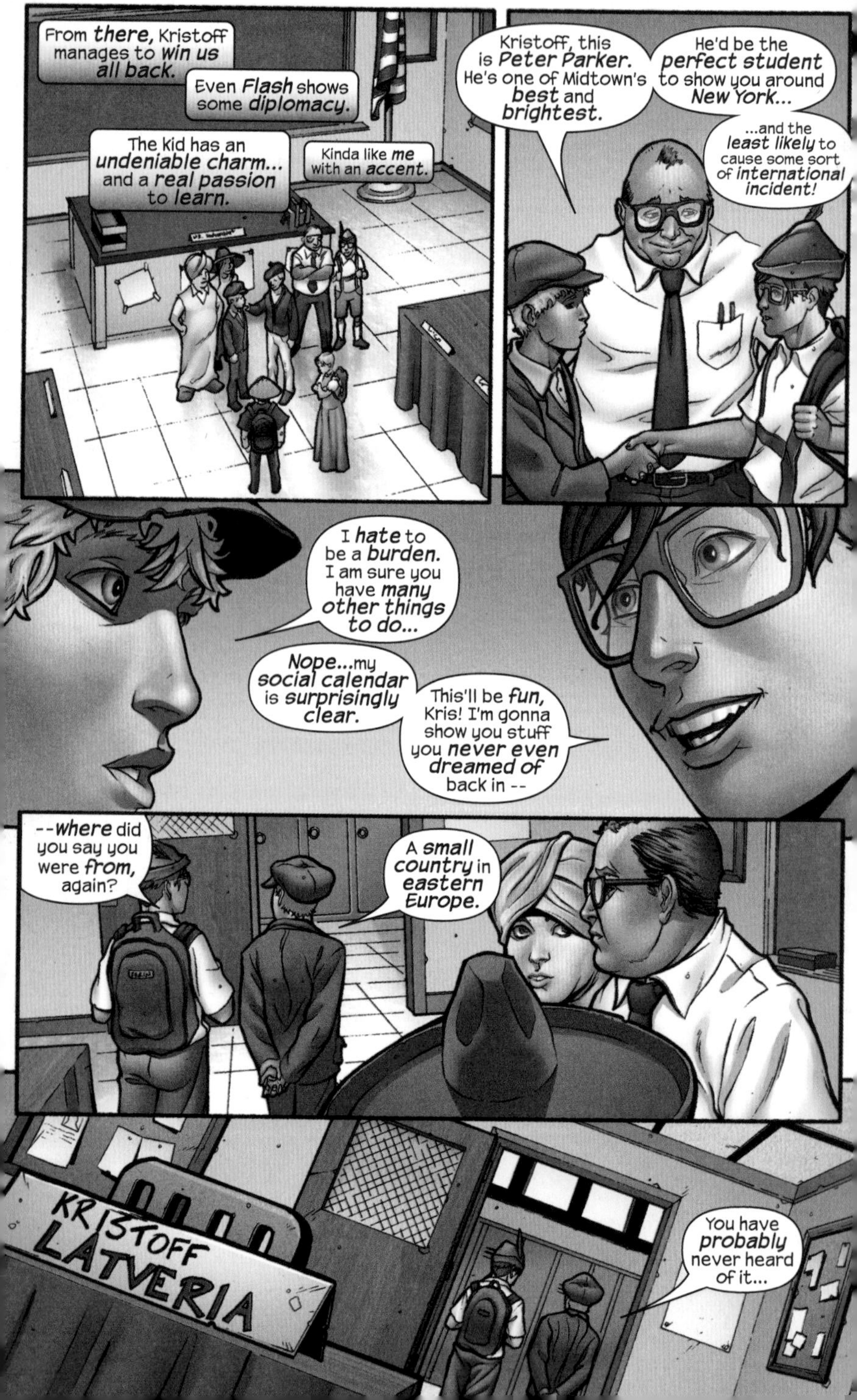
From there, Kristoff manages to win us all back.
Even Flash shows some diplomacy.
The kid has an undeniable charm... and a real passion to learn.
Kinda like me with an accent.
Kristoff, this is Peter Parker. He's one of Midtown's best and brightest.
He'd be the perfect student to show you around New York...
...and the least likely to cause some sort of international incident!
I hate to be a burden. I am sure you have many other things to do...
Nope...my social calendar is surprisingly clear.
This'll be fun, Kris! I'm gonna show you stuff you never even dreamed of back in --
--where did you say you were from, again?
A small country in eastern Europe.
KRISTOFF
LATVERIA
You have probably never heard of it...

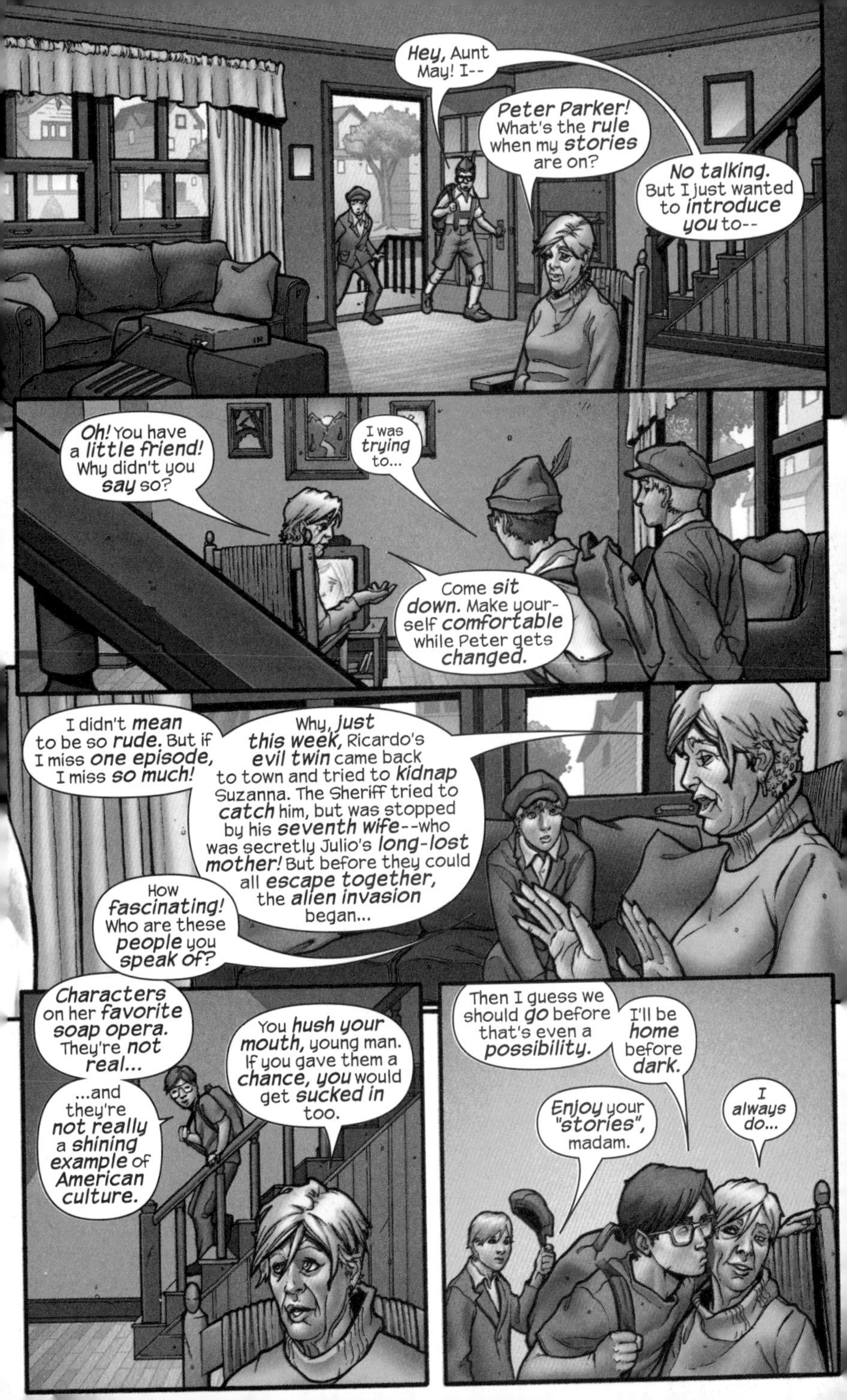
Hey, Aunt May! I--
Peter Parker! What's the rule when my stories are on?
No talking. But I just wanted to introduce you to--
Oh! You have a little friend! Why didn't you say so?
I was trying to...
Come sit down. Make your-self comfortable while Peter gets changed.
I didn't mean to be so rude. But if I miss one episode, I miss so much!
Why, just this week, Ricardo's evil twin came back to town and tried to kidnap Suzanna. The Sheriff tried to catch him, but was stopped by his seventh wife--who was secretly Julio's long-lost mother! But before they could all escape together, the alien invasion began...
How fascinating! Who are these people you speak of?
Characters on her favorite soap opera. They're not real...
...and they're not really a shining example of American culture.
You hush your mouth, young man. If you gave them a chance, you would get sucked in too.
Then I guess we should go before that's even a possibility.
I'll be home before dark.
Enjoy your "stories", madam.
I always do...

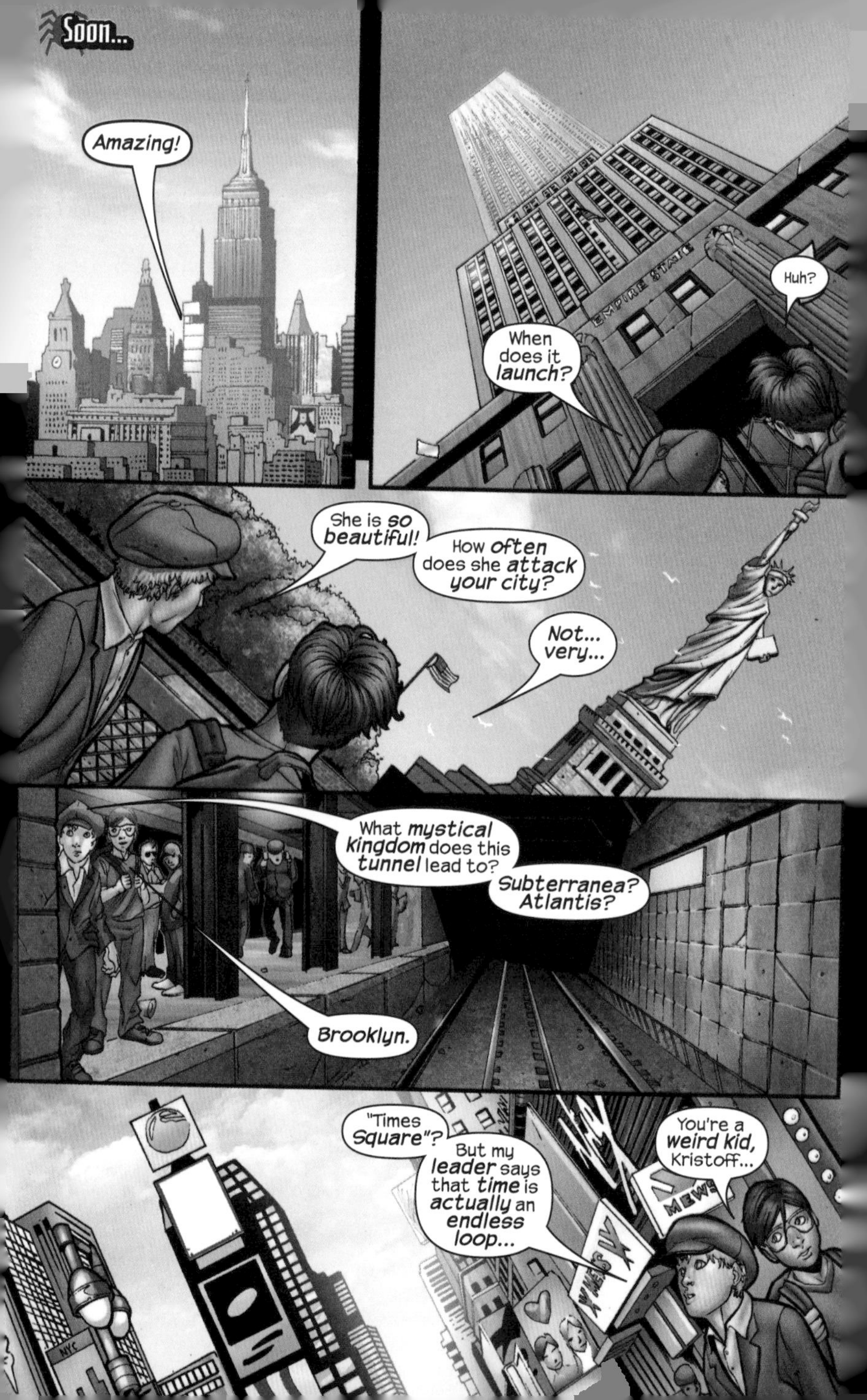
Soon...
Amazing!
When does it launch?
Huh?
She is so beautiful!
How often does she attack your city?
Not... very...
What mystical kingdom does this tunnel lead to?
Subterranea? Atlantis?
Brooklyn.
"Times Square"?
But my leader says that time is actually an endless loop...
You're a weird kid, Kristoff...

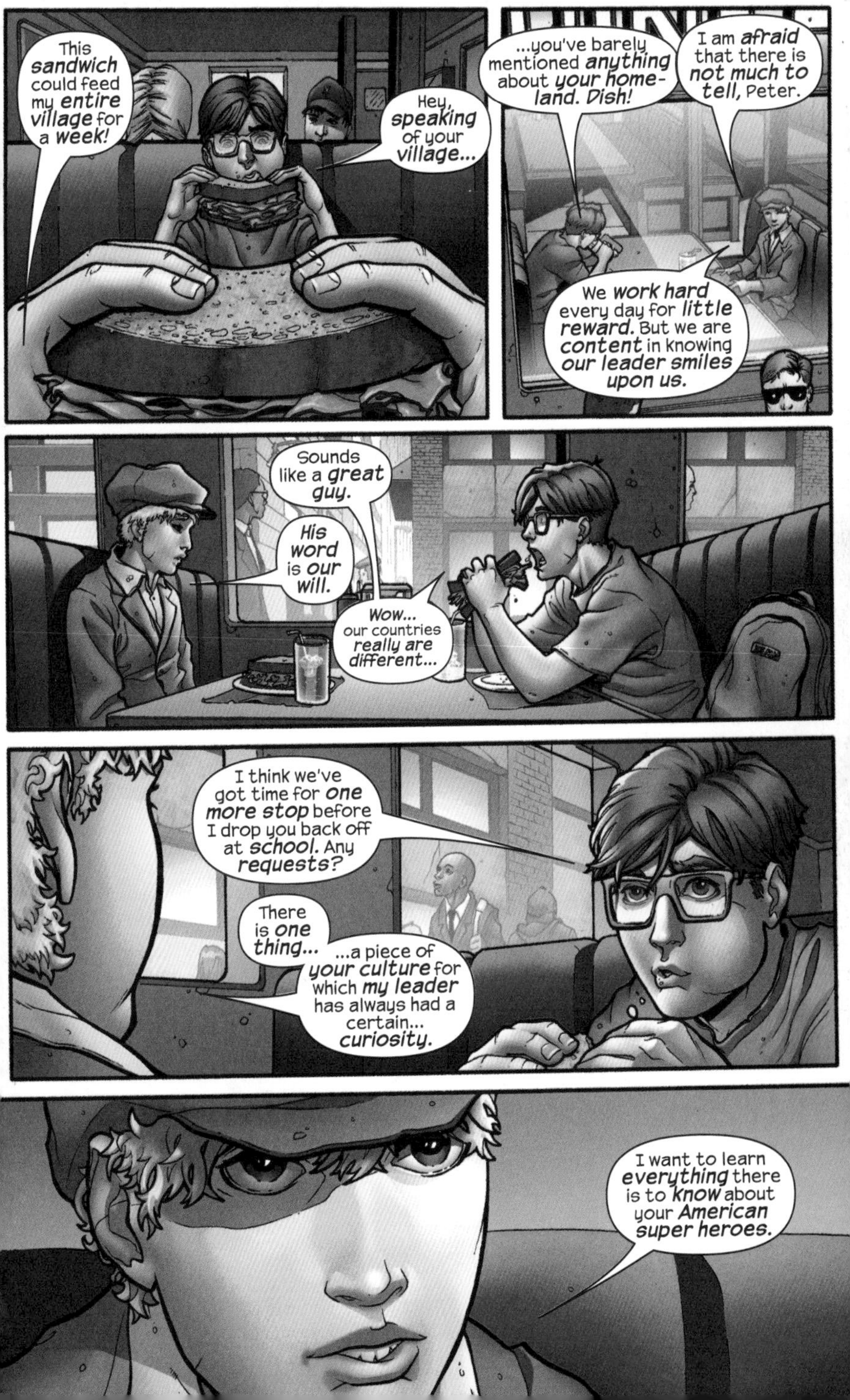
This sandwich could feed my entire village for a week!
Hey, speaking of your village...
...you've barely mentioned anything about your home-land. Dish!
I am afraid that there is not much to tell, Peter.
We work hard every day for little reward. But we are content in knowing our leader smiles upon us.
Sounds like a great guy.
His word is our will.
Wow... our countries really are different...
I think we've got time for one more stop before I drop you back off at school. Any requests?
There is one thing...
...a piece of your culture for which my leader has always had a certain... curiosity.
I want to learn everything there is to know about your American super heroes.

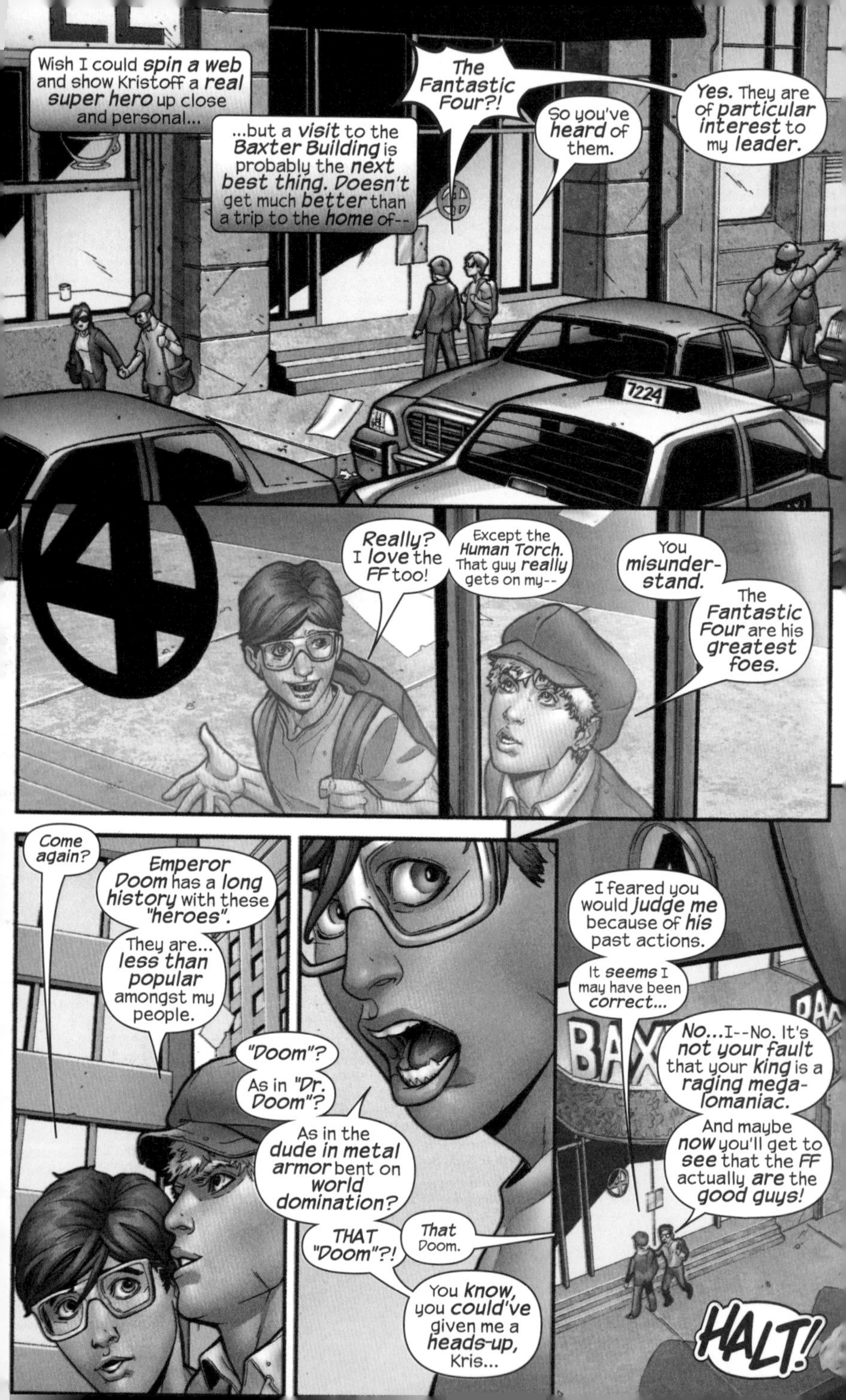
Wish I could spin a web and show Kristoff a real super hero up close and personal...
...but a visit to the Baxter Building is probably the next best thing. Doesn't get much better than a trip to the home of--
The Fantastic Four?!
So you've heard of them.
Yes. They are of particular interest to my leader.
7224
Really? I love the FF too!
Except the Human Torch. That guy really gets on my--
You misunder-stand.
The Fantastic Four are his greatest foes.
Come again?
Emperor Doom has a long history with these "heroes".
They are... less than popular amongst my people.
"Doom"?
As in "Dr. Doom"?
As in the dude in metal armor bent on world domination?
THAT "Doom"?!
That Doom.
You know, you could've given me a heads-up, Kris...
I feared you would judge me because of his past actions.
It seems I may have been correct...
No...I--No. It's not your fault that your king is a raging mega-lomaniac.
And maybe now you'll get to see that the FF actually are the good guys!
HALT!

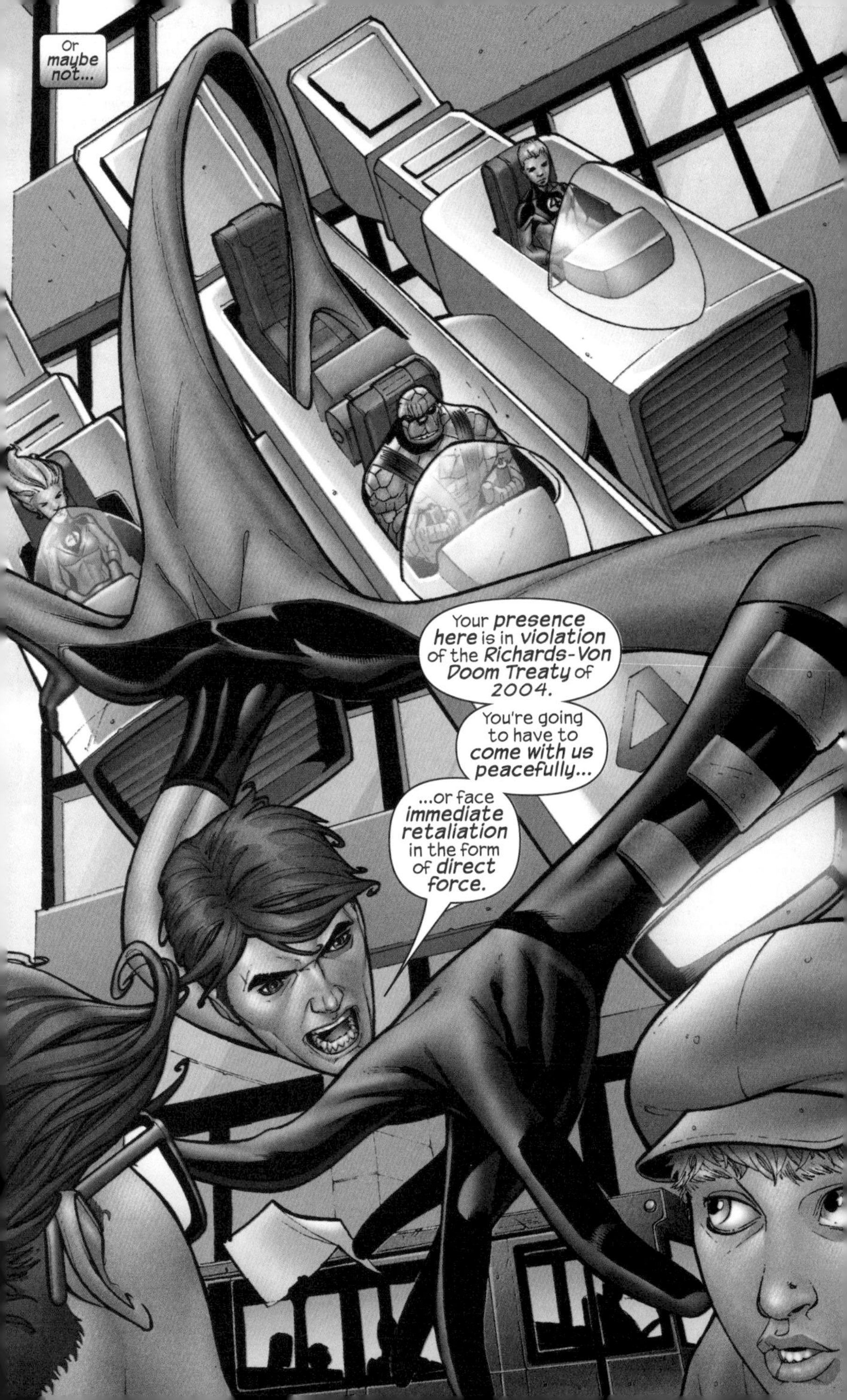
Or maybe not...
Your presence here is in violation of the Richards-Von Doom Treaty of 2004.
You're going to have to come with us peacefully...
...or face immediate retaliation in the form of direct force.

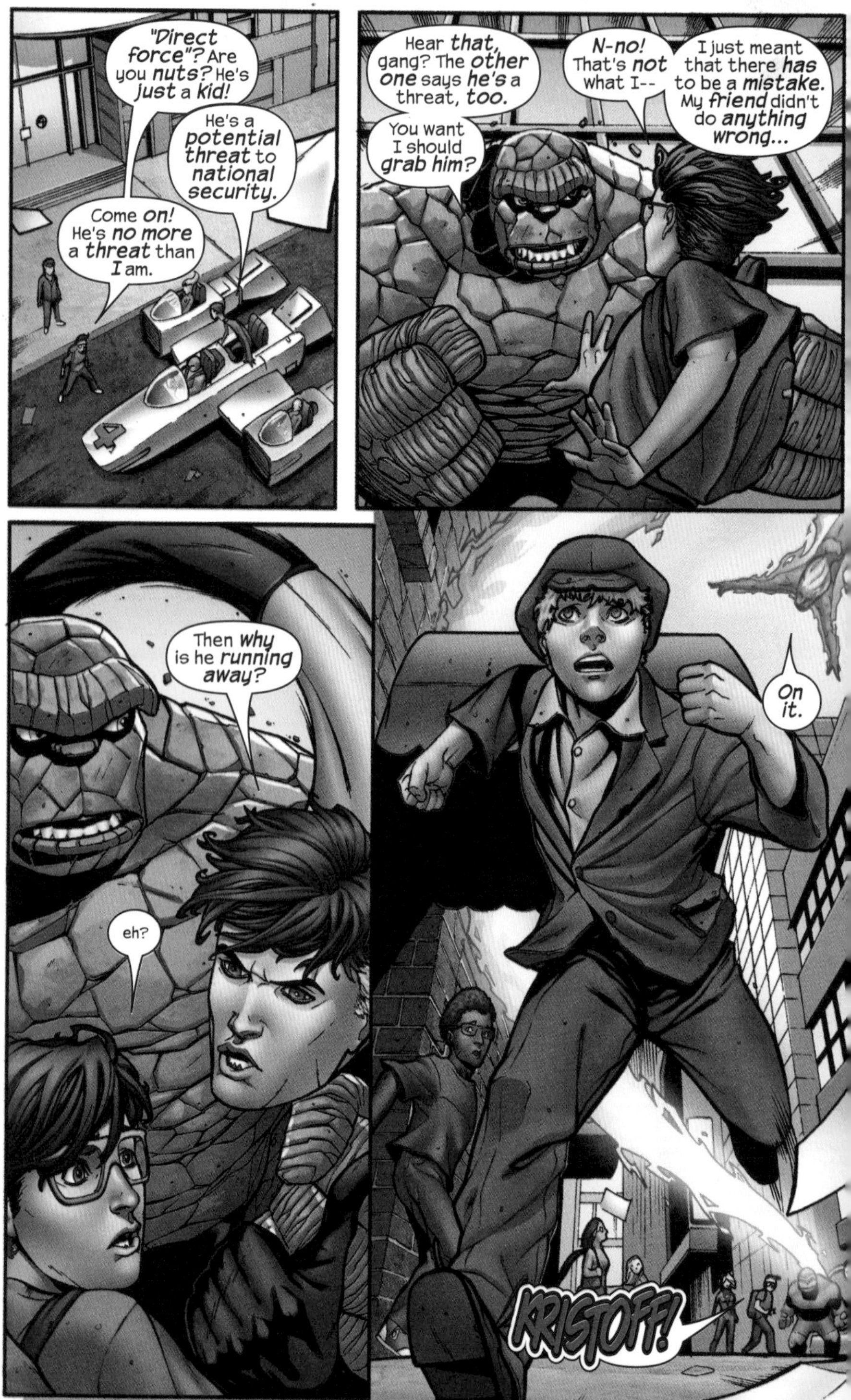
"Direct force"? Are you nuts? He's just a kid!
He's a potential threat to national security.
Come on! He's no more a threat than I am.
Hear that, gang? The other one says he's a threat, too.
You want I should grab him?
N-no! That's not what I--
I just meant that there has to be a mistake. My friend didn't do anything wrong...
Then why is he running away?
eh?
On it.
KRISTOFF!

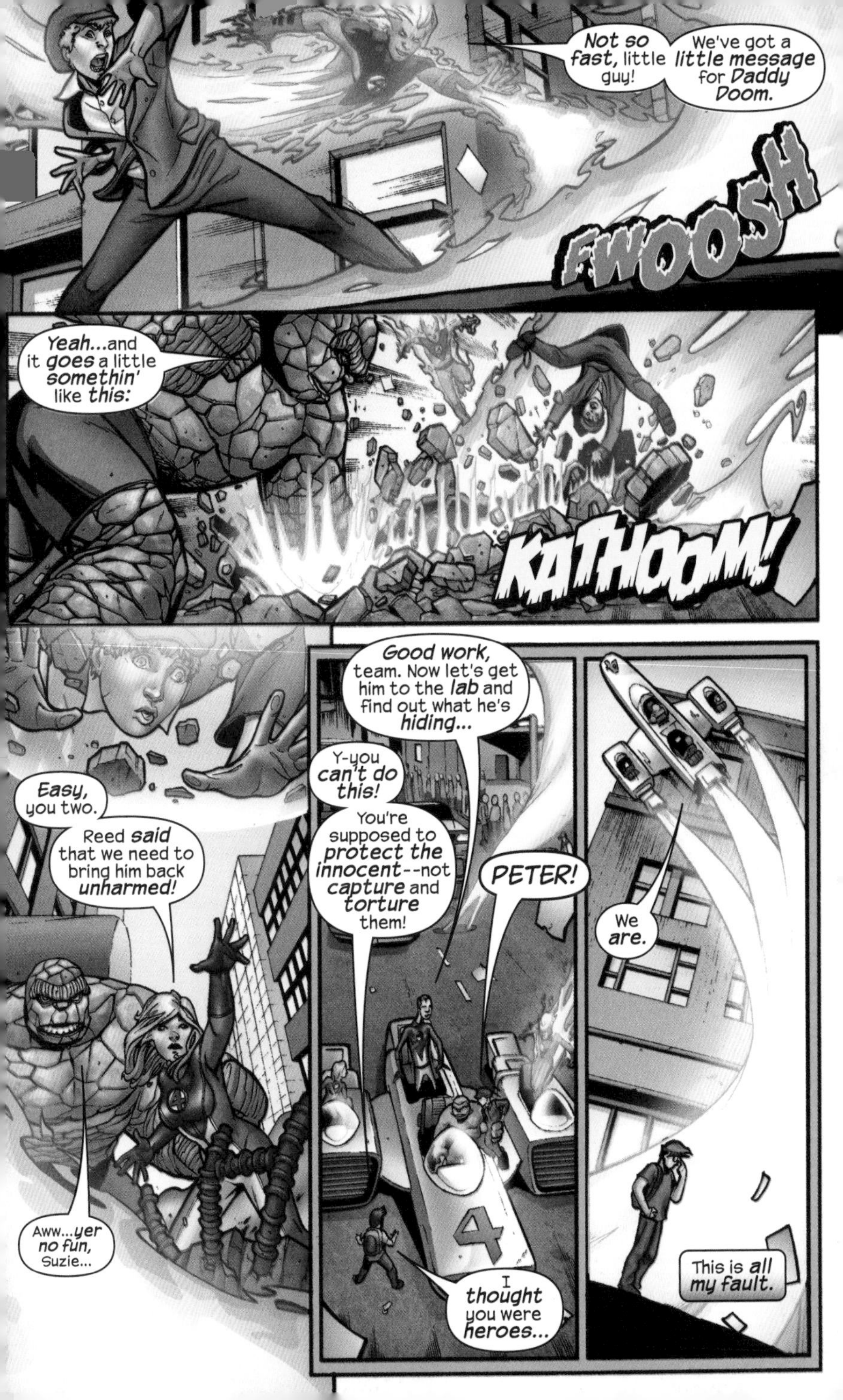

Not so fast, little guy!
We've got a little message for Daddy Doom.
FWOOSH
Yeah...and it goes a little somethin' like this:
KATHOOM!
Easy, you two.
Reed said that we need to bring him back unharmed!
Aww...yer no fun, Suzie...
Good work, team. Now let's get him to the lab and find out what he's hiding...
Y-you can't do this!
You're supposed to protect the innocent--not capture and torture them!
PETER!
I thought you were heroes...
We are.
This is all my fault.

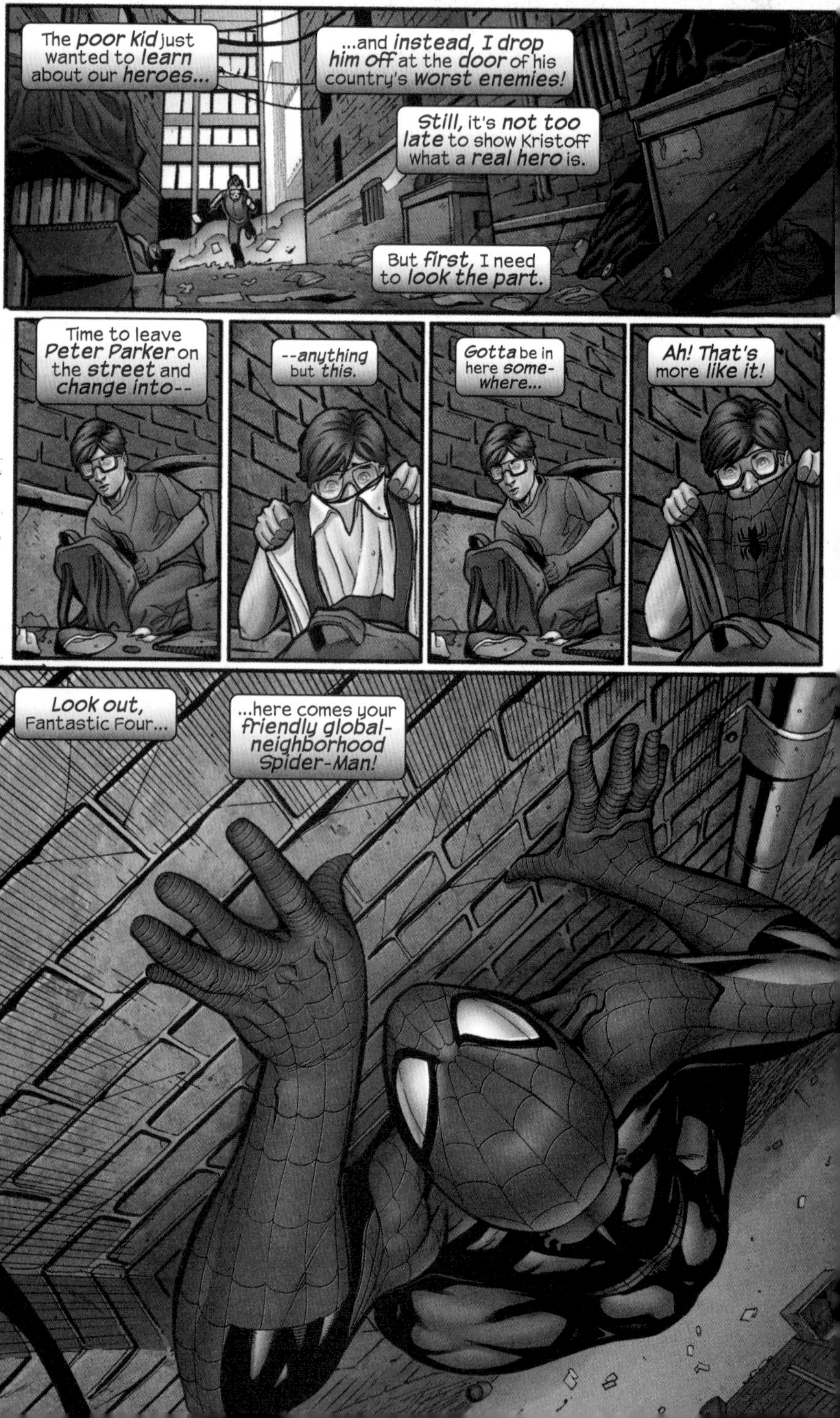
The poor kid just wanted to learn about our heroes...
...and instead, I drop him off at the door of his country's worst enemies!
Still, it's not too late to show Kristoff what a real hero is.
But first, I need to look the part.
Time to leave Peter Parker on the street and change into--
--anything but this.
Gotta be in here some-where...
Ah! That's more like it!
Look out, Fantastic Four...
...here comes your friendly global-neighborhood Spider-Man!

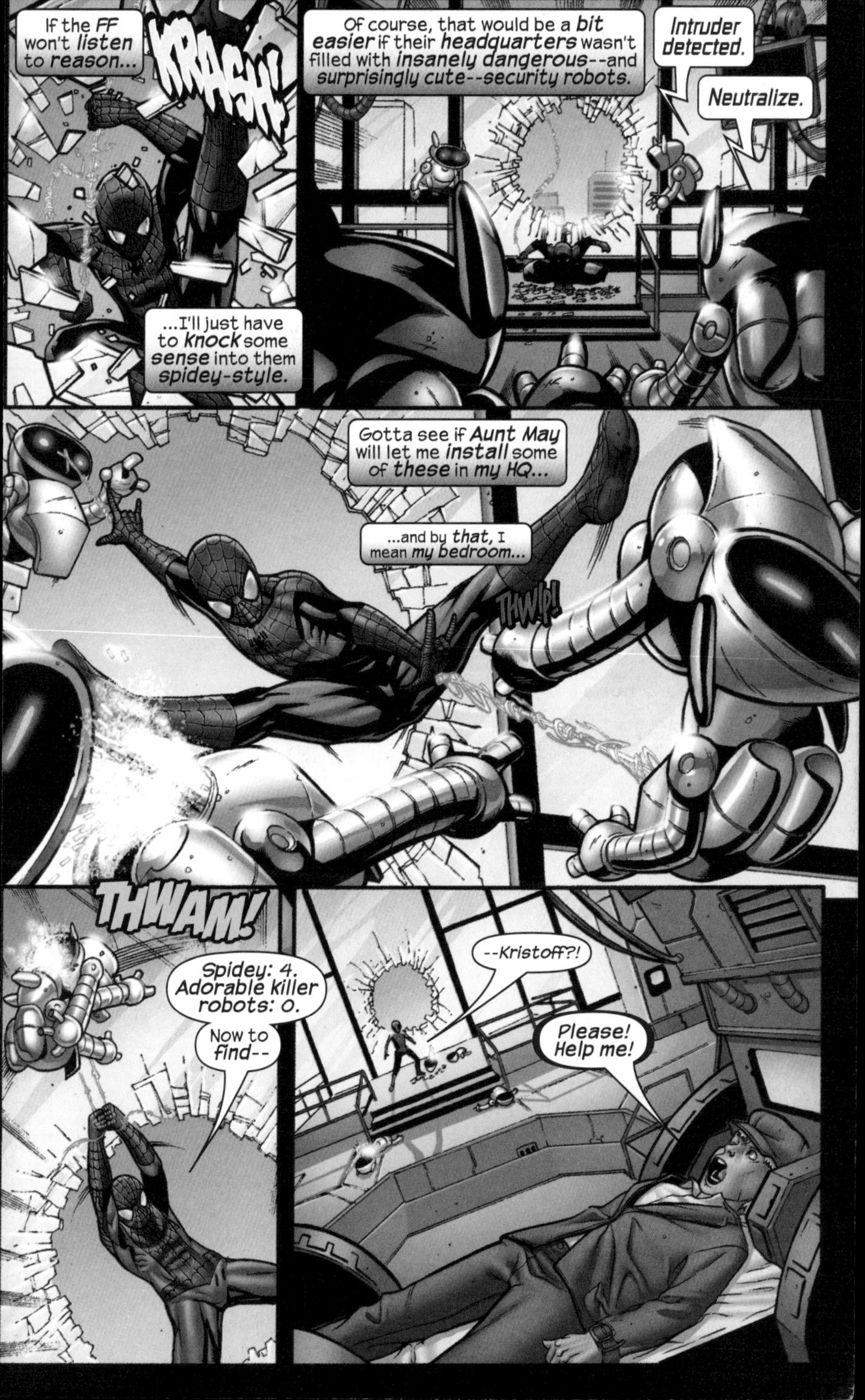
If the FF won't listen to reason...
KRASH!
...I'll just have to knock some sense into them spidey-style.
Of course, that would be a bit easier if their headquarters wasn't filled with insanely dangerous--and surprisingly cute--security robots.
Intruder detected.
Neutralize.
Gotta see if Aunt May will let me install some of these in my HQ...
...and by that, I mean my bedroom...
THWIP!
THWAM!
Spidey: 4. Adorable killer robots: 0.
Now to find--
--Kristoff?!
Please! Help me!

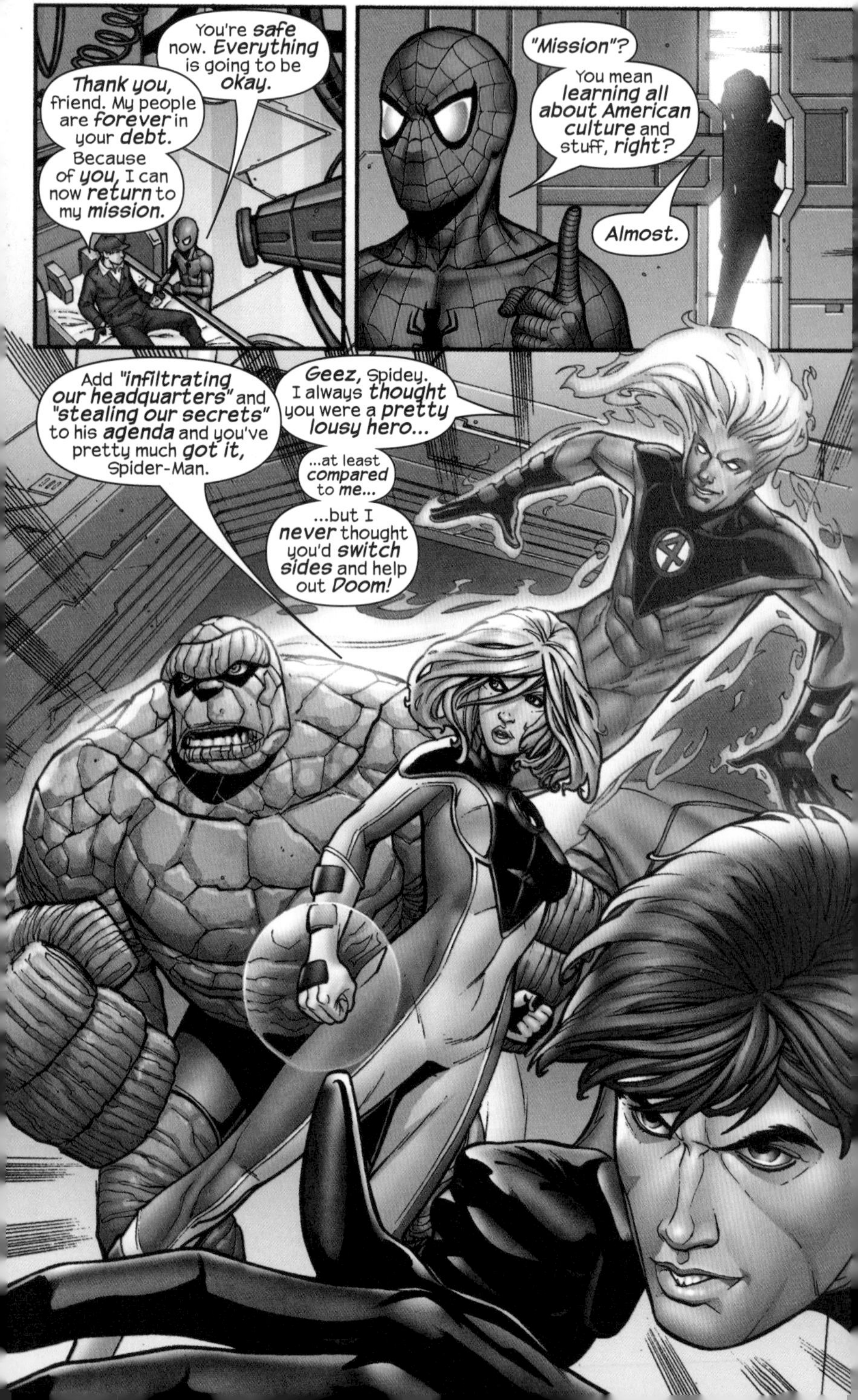
You're safe now. Everything is going to be okay.
Thank you, friend. My people are forever in your debt.
Because of you, I can now return to my mission.
"Mission"?
You mean learning all about American culture and stuff, right?
Almost.
Add "infiltrating our headquarters" and "stealing our secrets" to his agenda and you've pretty much got it, Spider-Man.
Geez, Spidey. I always thought you were a pretty lousy hero...
...at least compared to me...
...but I never thought you'd switch sides and help out Doom!

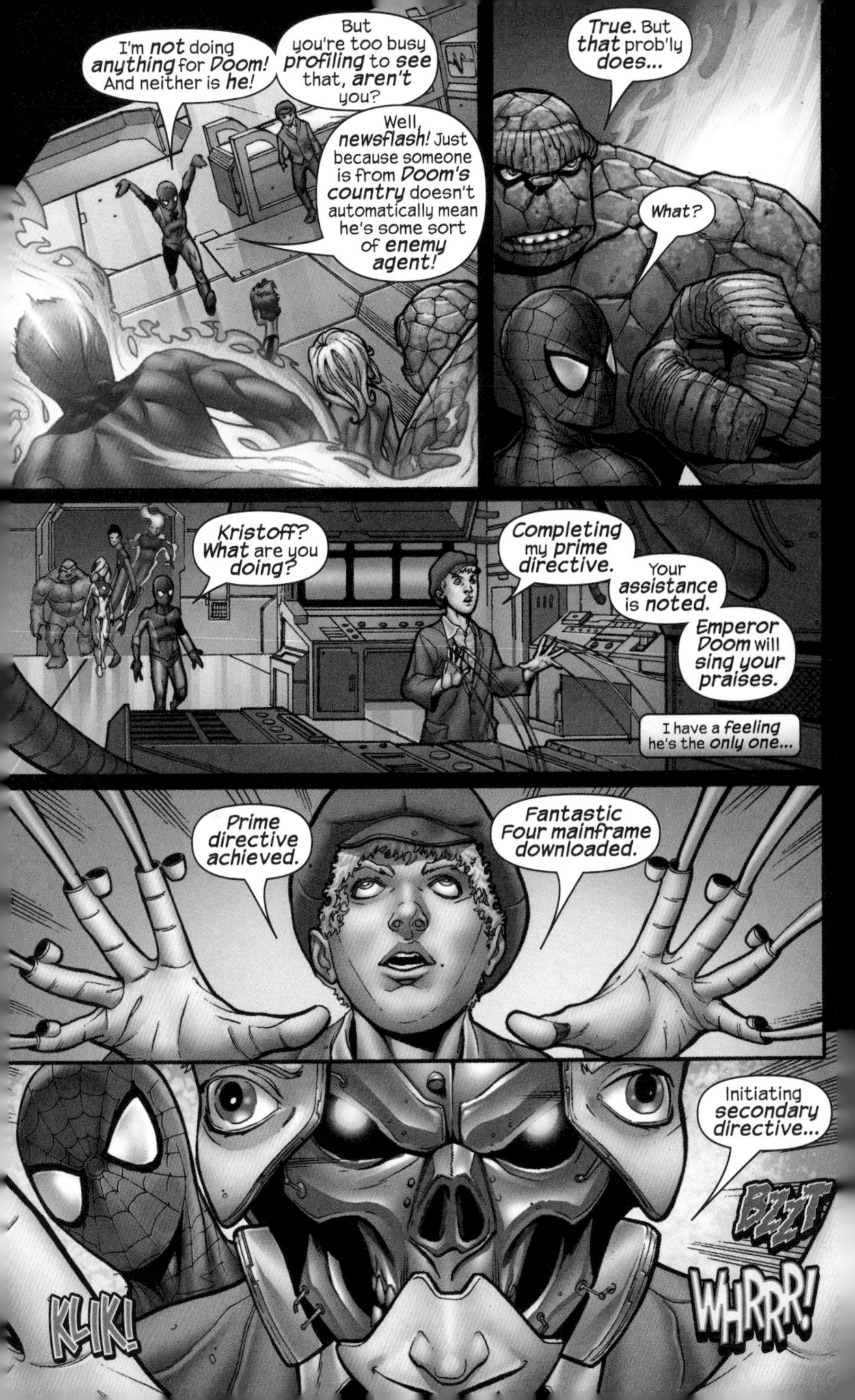
I'm not doing anything for Doom! And neither is he!
But you're too busy profiling to see that, aren't you?
Well, newsflash! Just because someone is from Doom's country doesn't automatically mean he's some sort of enemy agent!
True. But that prob'ly does...
What?
Kristoff? What are you doing?
Completing my prime directive.
Your assistance is noted.
Emperor Doom will sing your praises.
I have a feeling he's the only one...
Prime directive achieved.
Fantastic Four mainframe downloaded.
Initiating secondary directive...
BZZT
KLIK!
WHRRR!

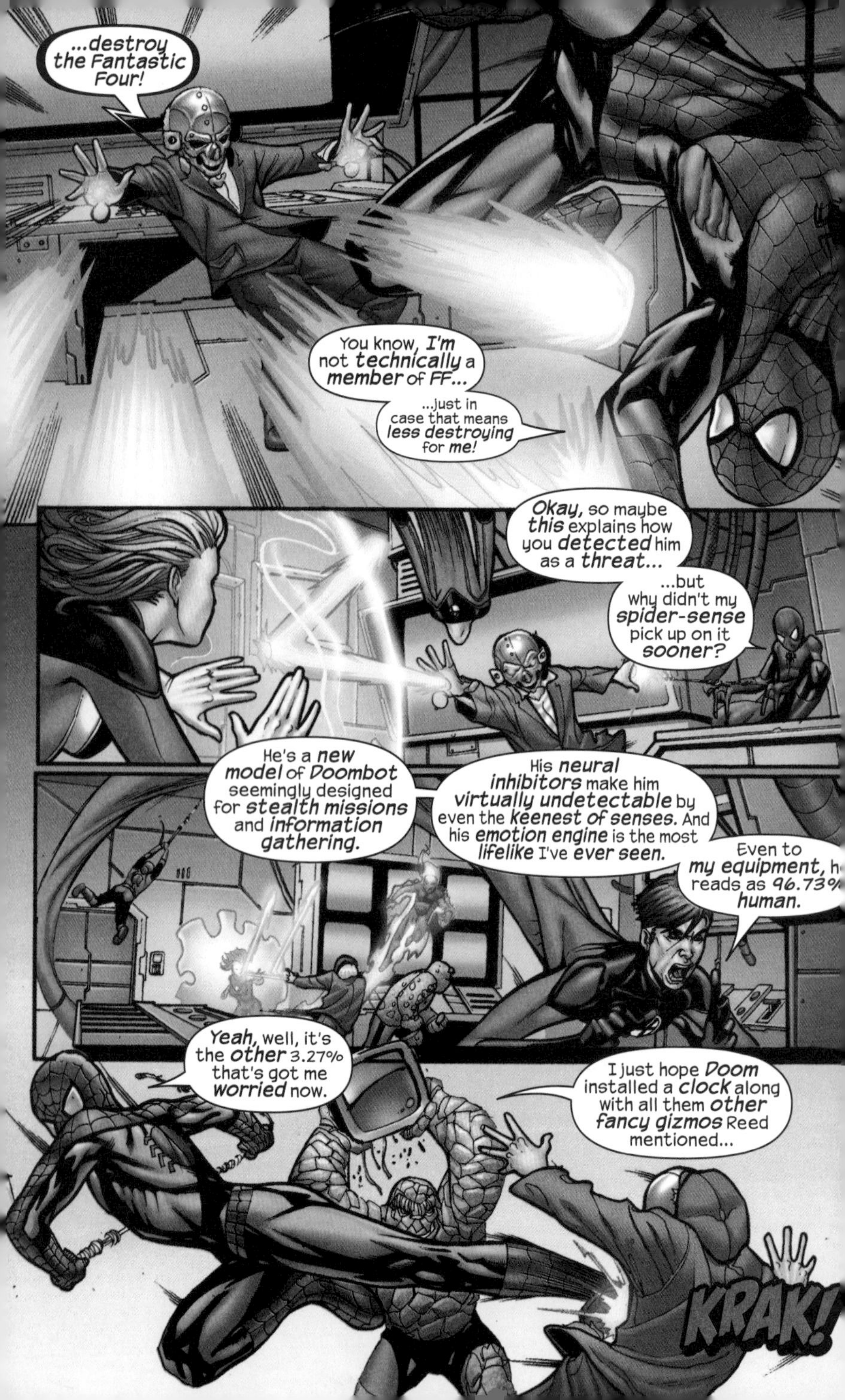
...destroy the Fantastic Four!
You know, I'm not technically a member of FF...
...just in case that means less destroying for me!
Okay, so maybe this explains how you detected him as a threat...
...but why didn't my spider-sense pick up on it sooner?
He's a new model of Doombot seemingly designed for stealth missions and information gathering.
His neural inhibitors make him virtually undetectable by even the keenest of senses. And his emotion engine is the most lifelike I've ever seen.
Even to my equipment, he reads as 96.73% human.
Yeah, well, it's the other 3.27% that's got me worried now.
I just hope Doom installed a clock along with all them other fancy gizmos Reed mentioned...
KRAK!

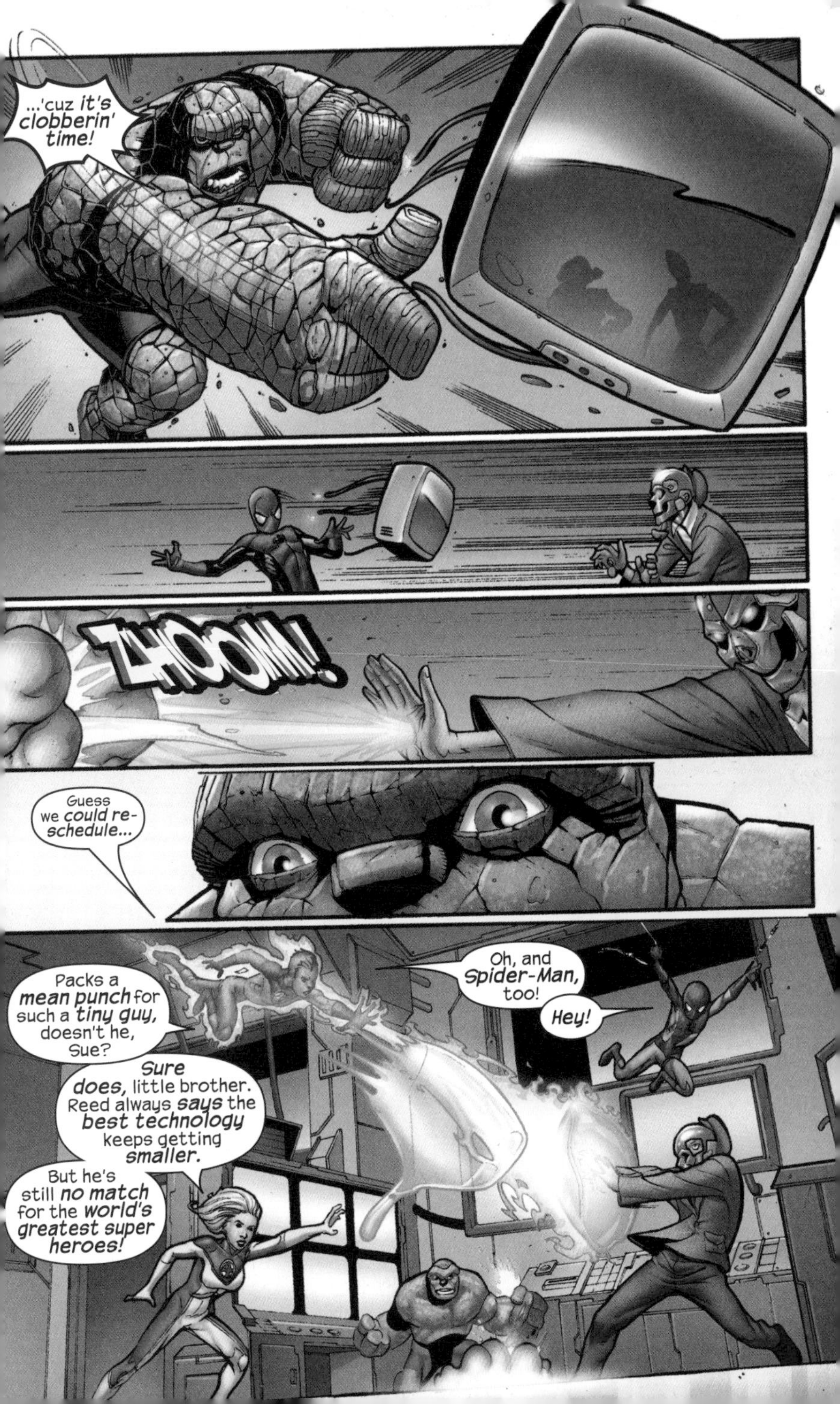
...'cuz it's clobberin' time!
ZHOOM!
Guess we could re-schedule...
Packs a mean punch for such a tiny guy, doesn't he, Sue?
Oh, and Spider-Man, too!
Hey!
Sure does, little brother. Reed always says the best technology keeps getting smaller.
But he's still no match for the world's greatest super heroes!

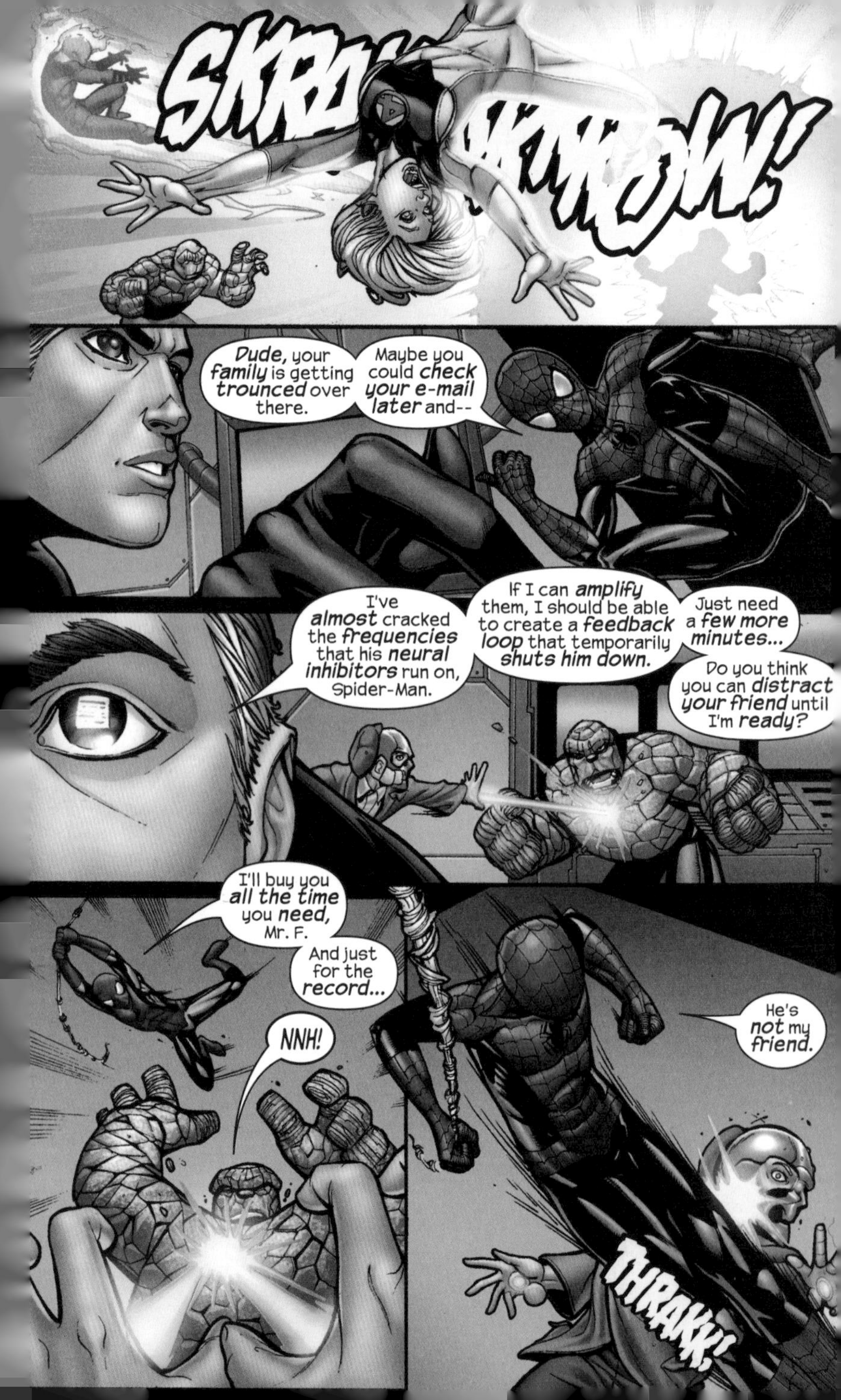

SKROOOWWW!
Dude, your family is getting trounced over there.
Maybe you could check your e-mail later and--
I've almost cracked the frequencies that his neural inhibitors run on, Spider-Man.
If I can amplify them, I should be able to create a feedback loop that temporarily shuts him down.
Just need a few more minutes...
Do you think you can distract your friend until I'm ready?
I'll buy you all the time you need, Mr. F.
And just for the record...
NNH!
He's not my friend.
THRAKK!

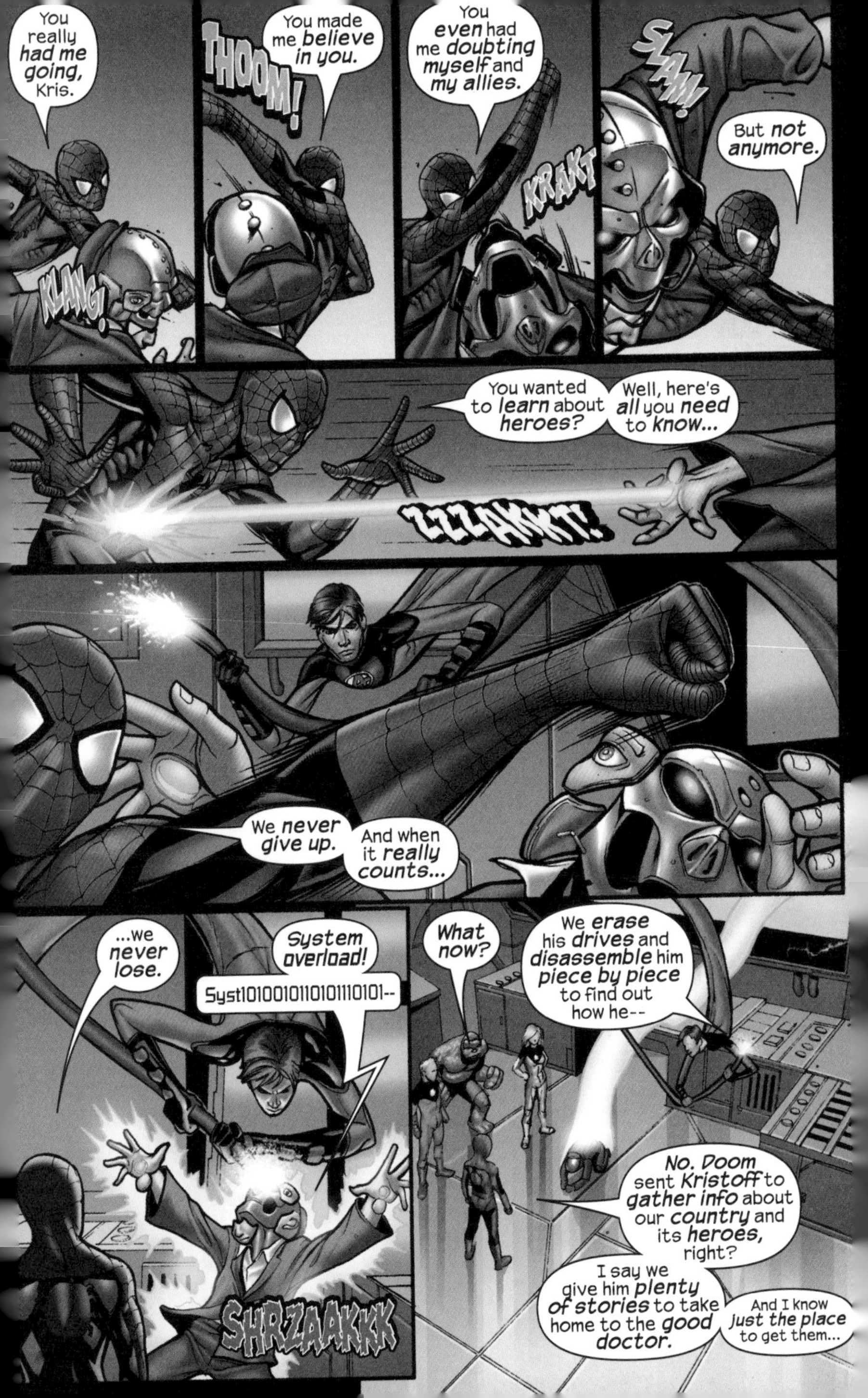
You really had me going, Kris.
KLANG!
THOOM!
You made me believe in you.
You even had me doubting myself and my allies.
KRAKT
SLAM!
But not anymore.
You wanted to learn about heroes?
Well, here's all you need to know...
ZZZAKKT!
We never give up.
And when it really counts...
...we never lose.
System overload!
Syst1010010110101110101--
SHRZAAKKK
What now?
We erase his drives and disassemble him piece by piece to find out how he--
No. Doom sent Kristoff to gather info about our country and its heroes, right?
I say we give him plenty of stories to take home to the good doctor.
And I know just the place to get them...

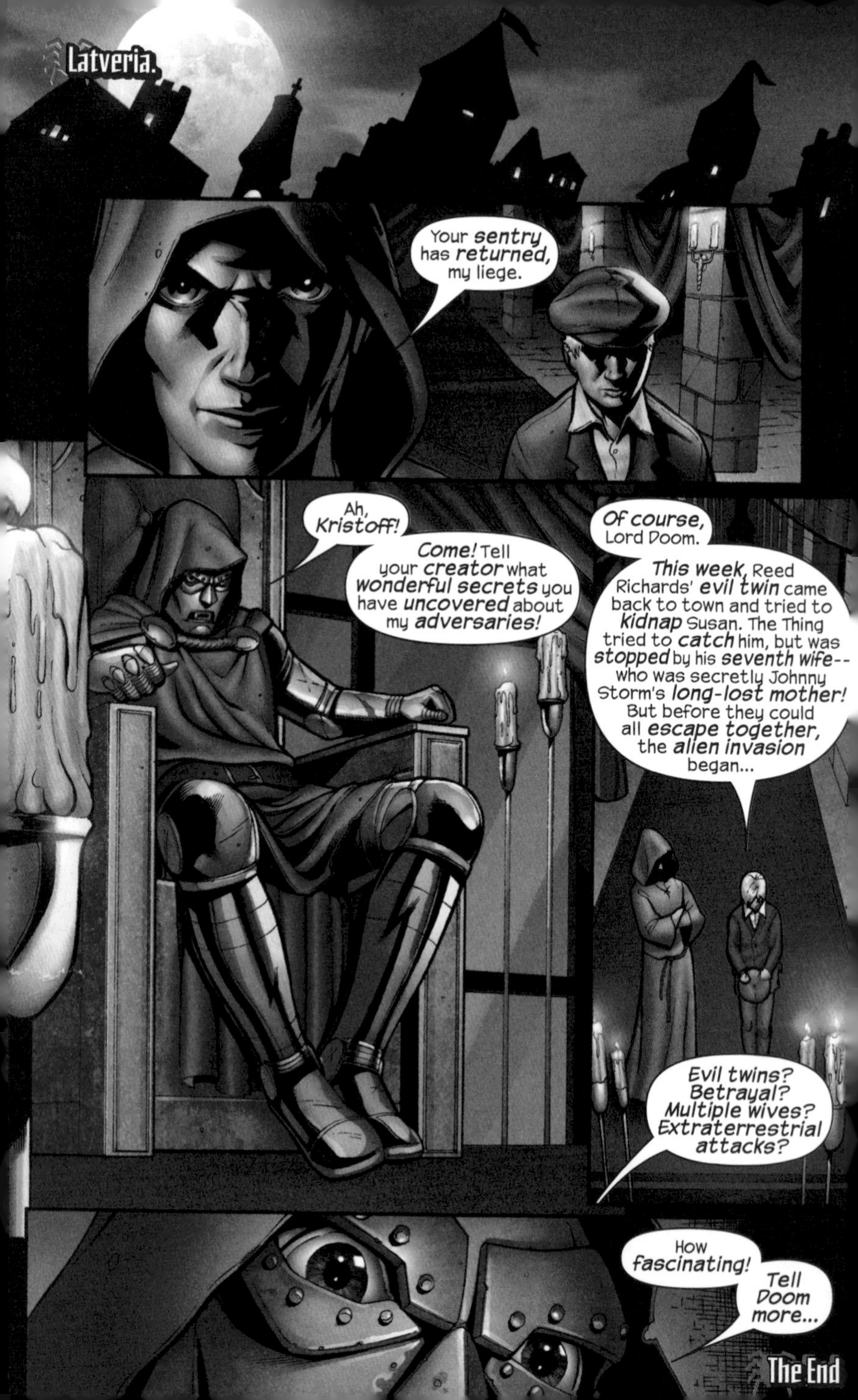
Latveria.
Your sentry has returned, my liege.
Ah, Kristoff!
Come! Tell your creator what wonderful secrets you have uncovered about my adversaries!
Of course, Lord Doom.
This week, Reed Richards' evil twin came back to town and tried to kidnap Susan. The Thing tried to catch him, but was stopped by his seventh wife--who was secretly Johnny Storm's long-lost mother! But before they could all escape together, the alien invasion began...
Evil twins? Betrayal? Multiple wives? Extraterrestrial attacks?
How fascinating!
Tell Doom more...
The End

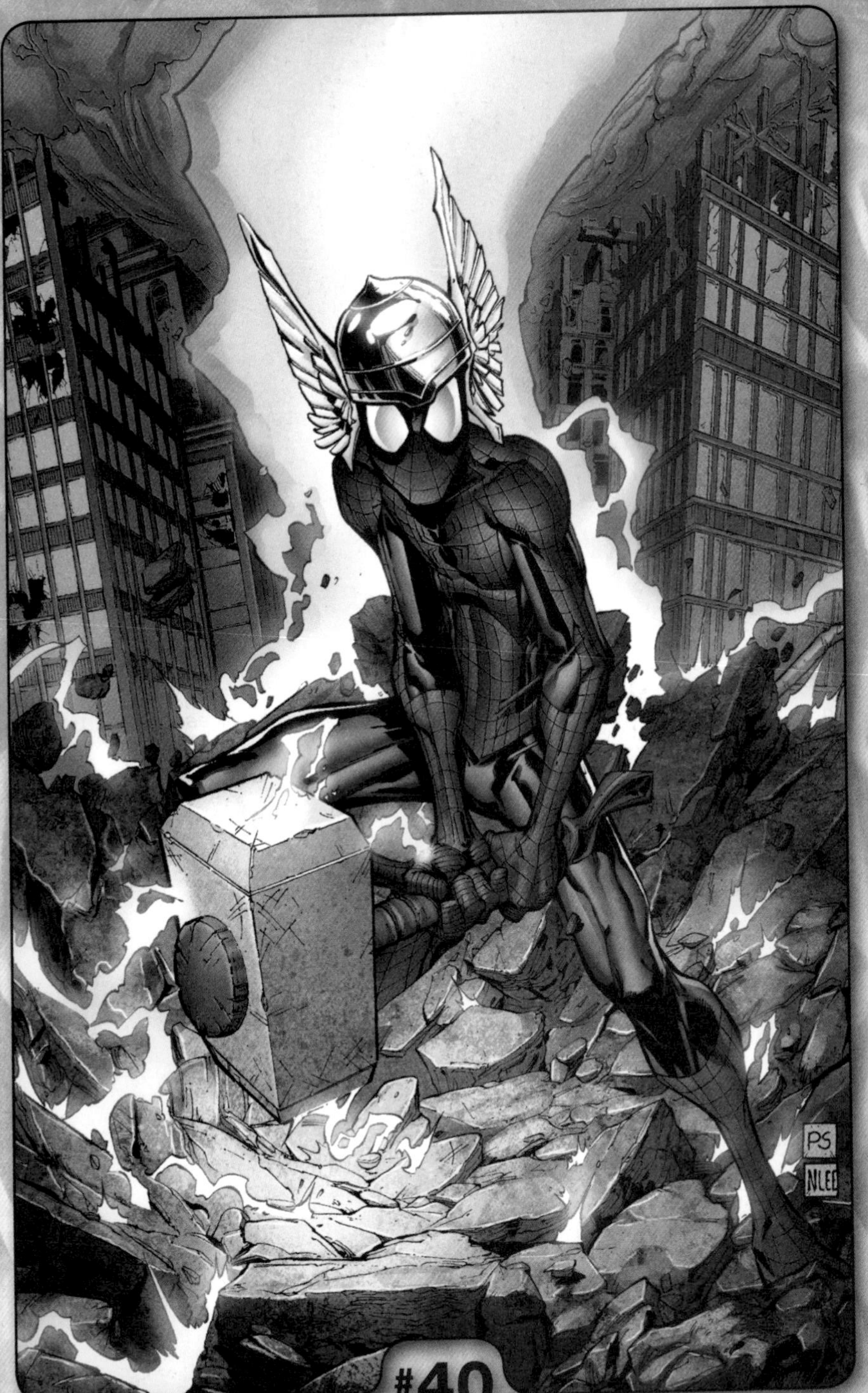

#40

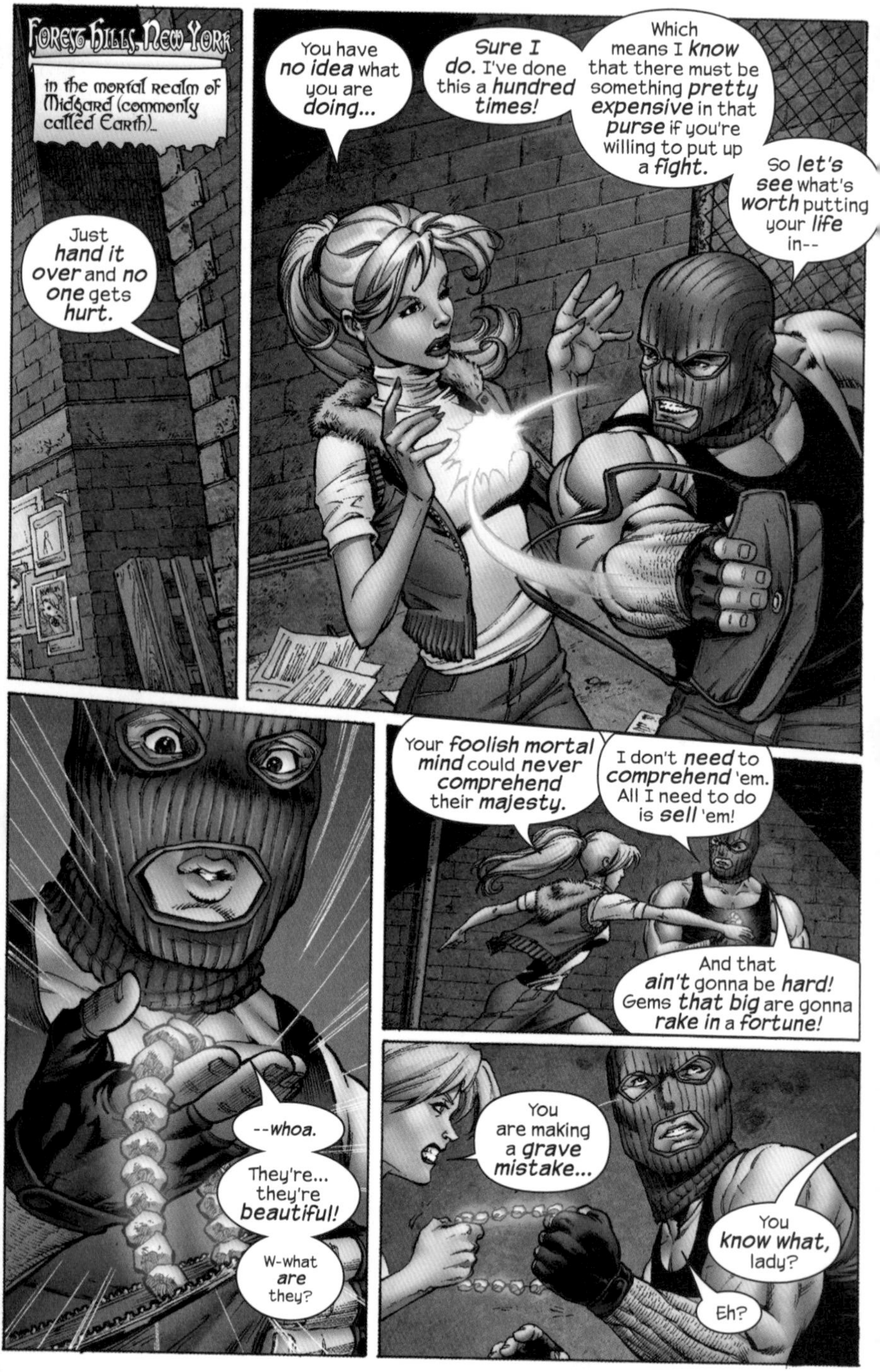
Forest Hills, New York
in the mortal realm of Midgard (commonly called Earth)...
Just hand it over and no one gets hurt.
You have no idea what you are doing...
Sure I do. I've done this a hundred times!
Which means I know that there must be something pretty expensive in that purse if you're willing to put up a fight.
So let's see what's worth putting your life in--
--whoa.
They're... they're beautiful!
W-what are they?
Your foolish mortal mind could never comprehend their majesty.
I don't need to comprehend 'em. All I need to do is sell 'em!
And that ain't gonna be hard! Gems that big are gonna rake in a fortune!
You are making a grave mistake...
You know what, lady?
Eh?

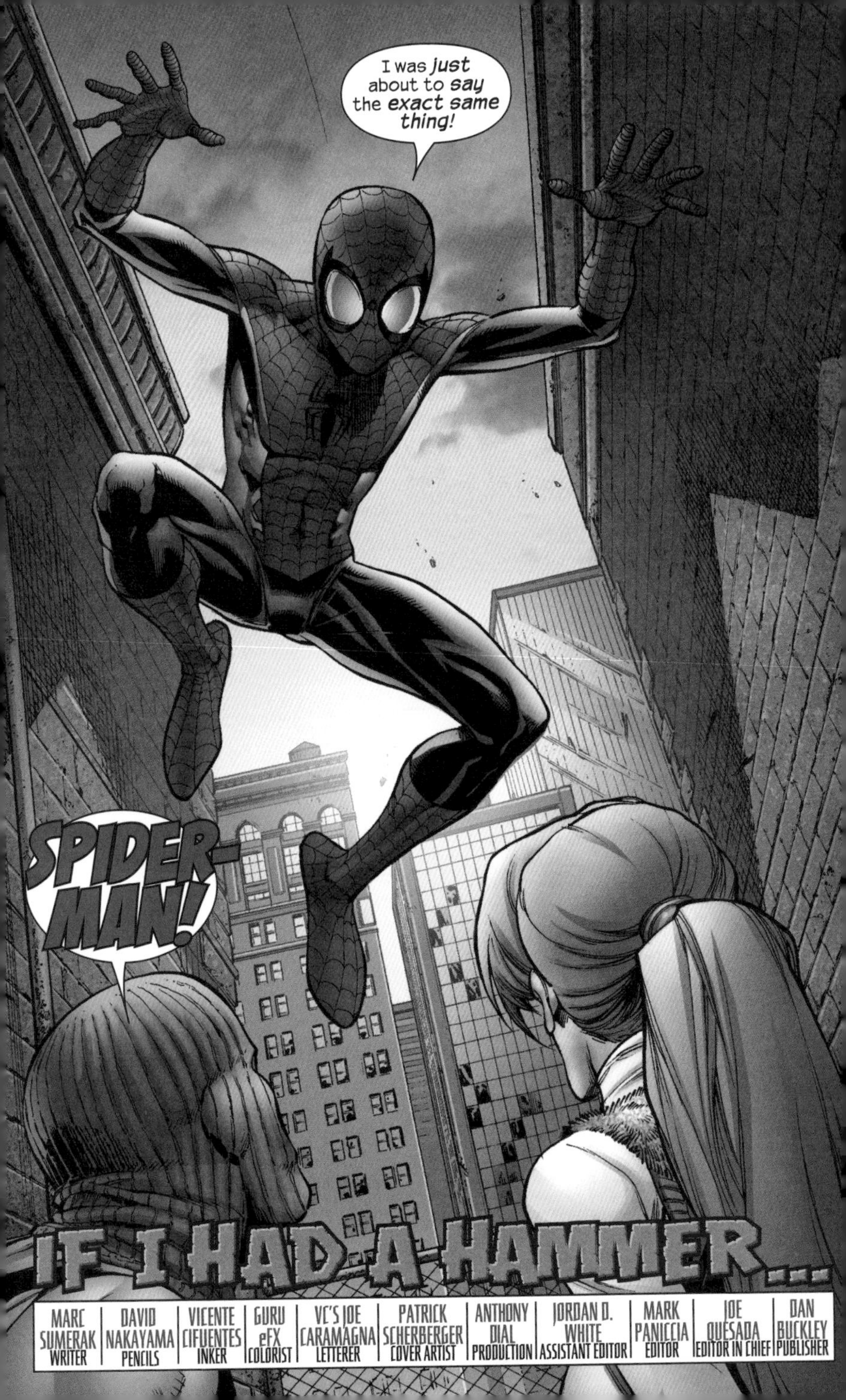

I was just about to say the exact same thing!
SPIDER-MAN!
IF I HAD A HAMMER...
MARC SUMERAK WRITER
DAVID NAKAYAMA PENCILS
VICENTE CIFUENTES INKER
GURU eFX COLORIST
VC'S JOE CARAMAGNA LETTERER
PATRICK SCHERBERGER COVER ARTIST
ANTHONY DIAL PRODUCTION
JORDAN D. WHITE ASSISTANT EDITOR
MARK PANICCIA EDITOR
JOE QUESADA EDITOR IN CHIEF
DAN BUCKLEY PUBLISHER

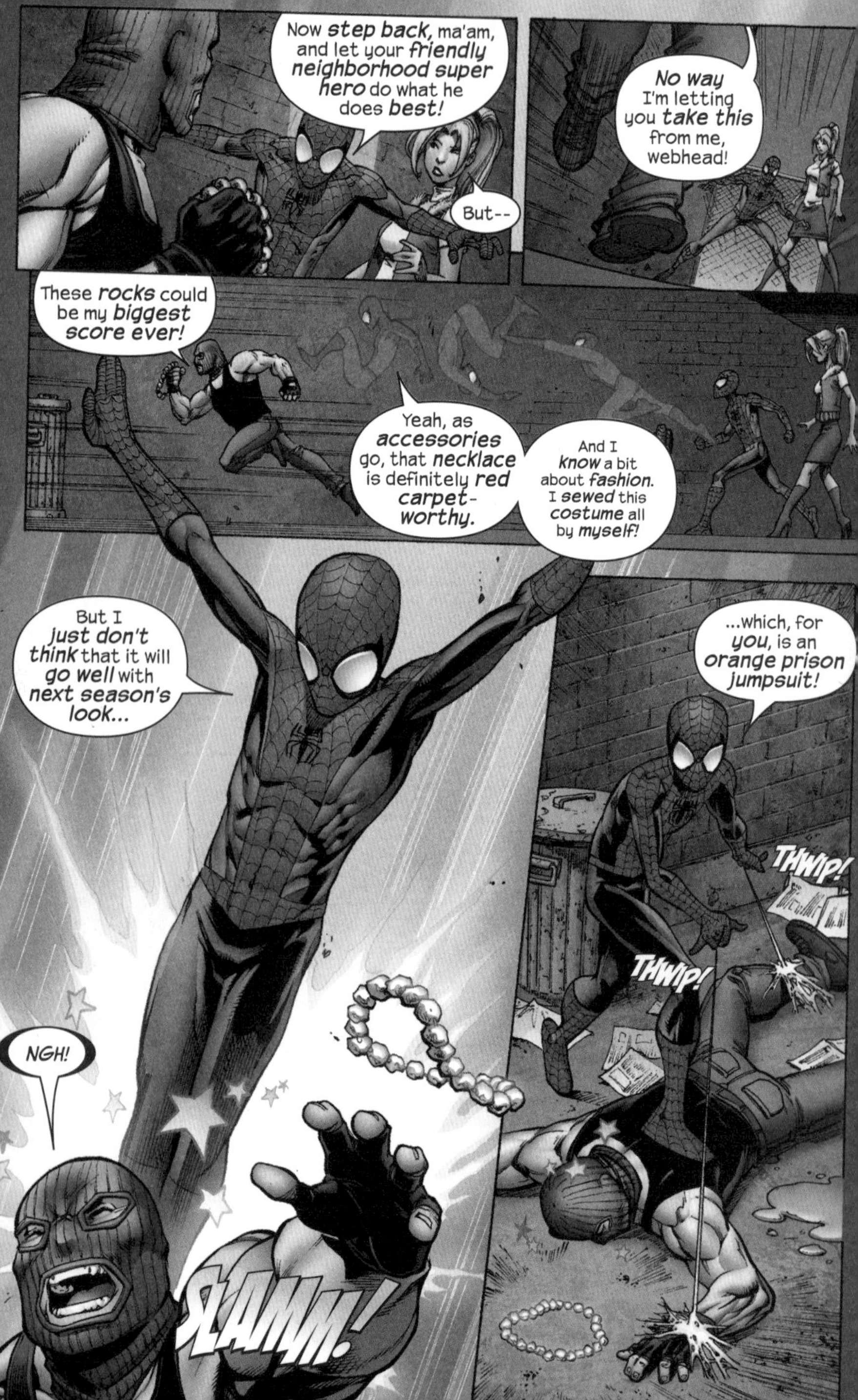

Now step back, ma'am, and let your friendly neighborhood super hero do what he does best!
But--
No way I'm letting you take this from me, webhead!
These rocks could be my biggest score ever!
Yeah, as accessories go, that necklace is definitely red carpet-worthy.
And I know a bit about fashion. I sewed this costume all by myself!
But I just don't think that it will go well with next season's look...
NGH!
SLAMM!
...which, for you, is an orange prison jumpsuit!
THWIP!
THWIP!

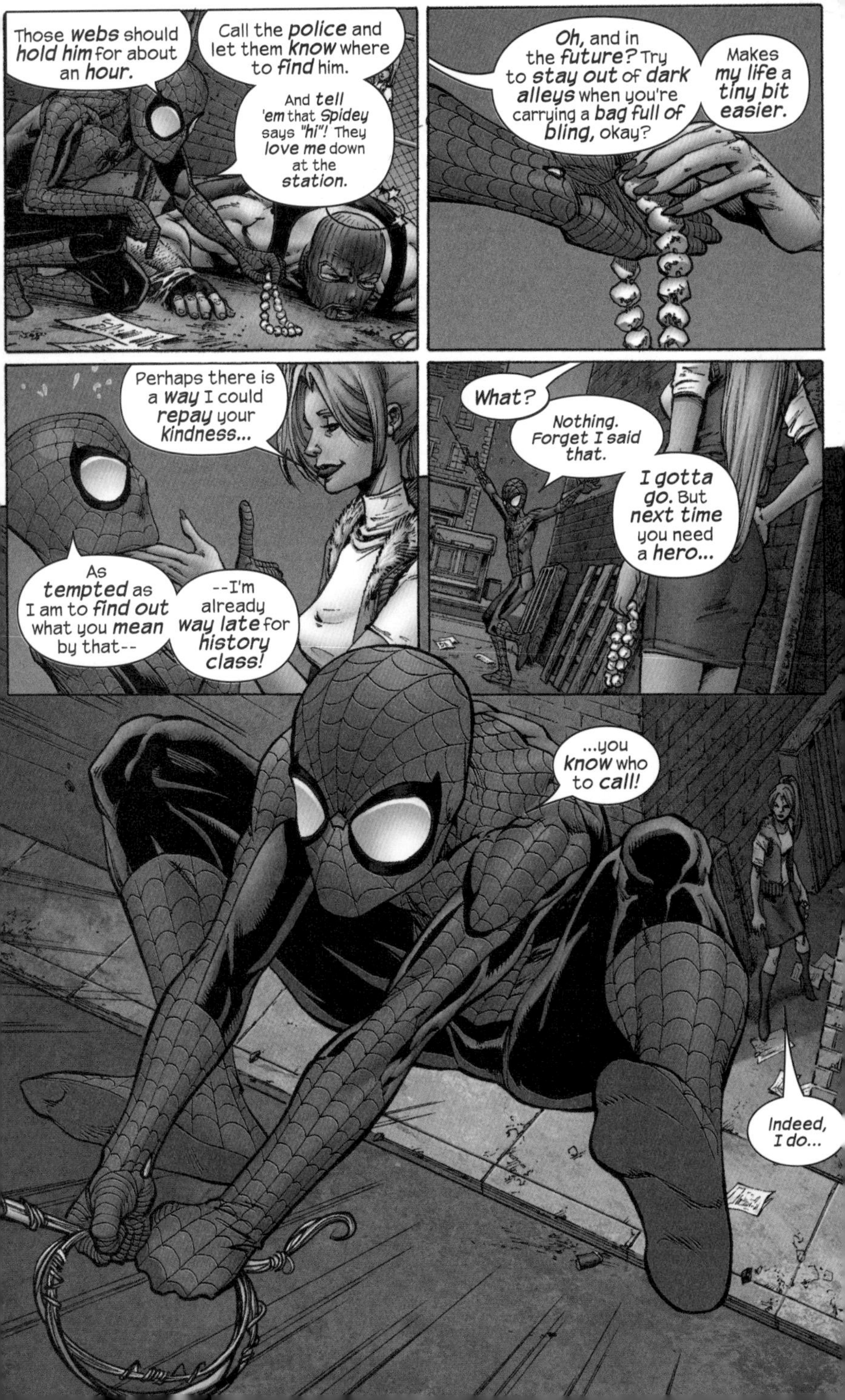

Those webs should hold him for about an hour.
Call the police and let them know where to find him.
And tell 'em that Spidey says "hi"! They love me down at the station.
Oh, and in the future? Try to stay out of dark alleys when you're carrying a bag full of bling, okay?
Makes my life a tiny bit easier.
Perhaps there is a way I could repay your kindness...
As tempted as I am to find out what you mean by that--
--I'm already way late for history class!
What?
Nothing. Forget I said that.
I gotta go. But next time you need a hero...
...you know who to call!
Indeed, I do...

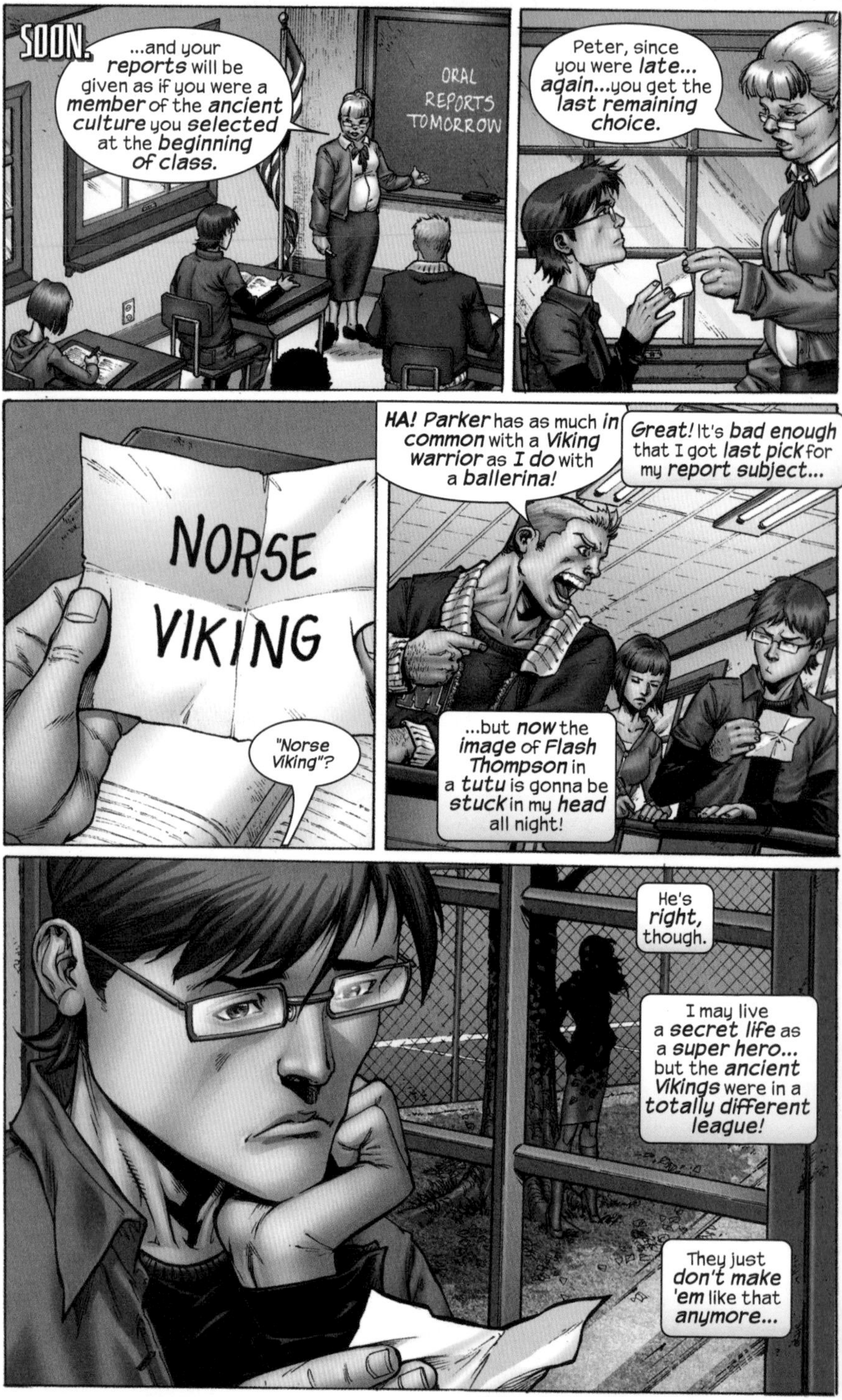
SOON.
...and your reports will be given as if you were a member of the ancient culture you selected at the beginning of class.
ORAL REPORTS TOMORROW
Peter, since you were late... again...you get the last remaining choice.
NORSE VIKING
"Norse Viking"?
HA! Parker has as much in common with a Viking warrior as I do with a ballerina!
Great! It's bad enough that I got last pick for my report subject...
...but now the image of Flash Thompson in a tutu is gonna be stuck in my head all night!
He's right, though.
I may live a secret life as a super hero... but the ancient Vikings were in a totally different league!
They just don't make 'em like that anymore...

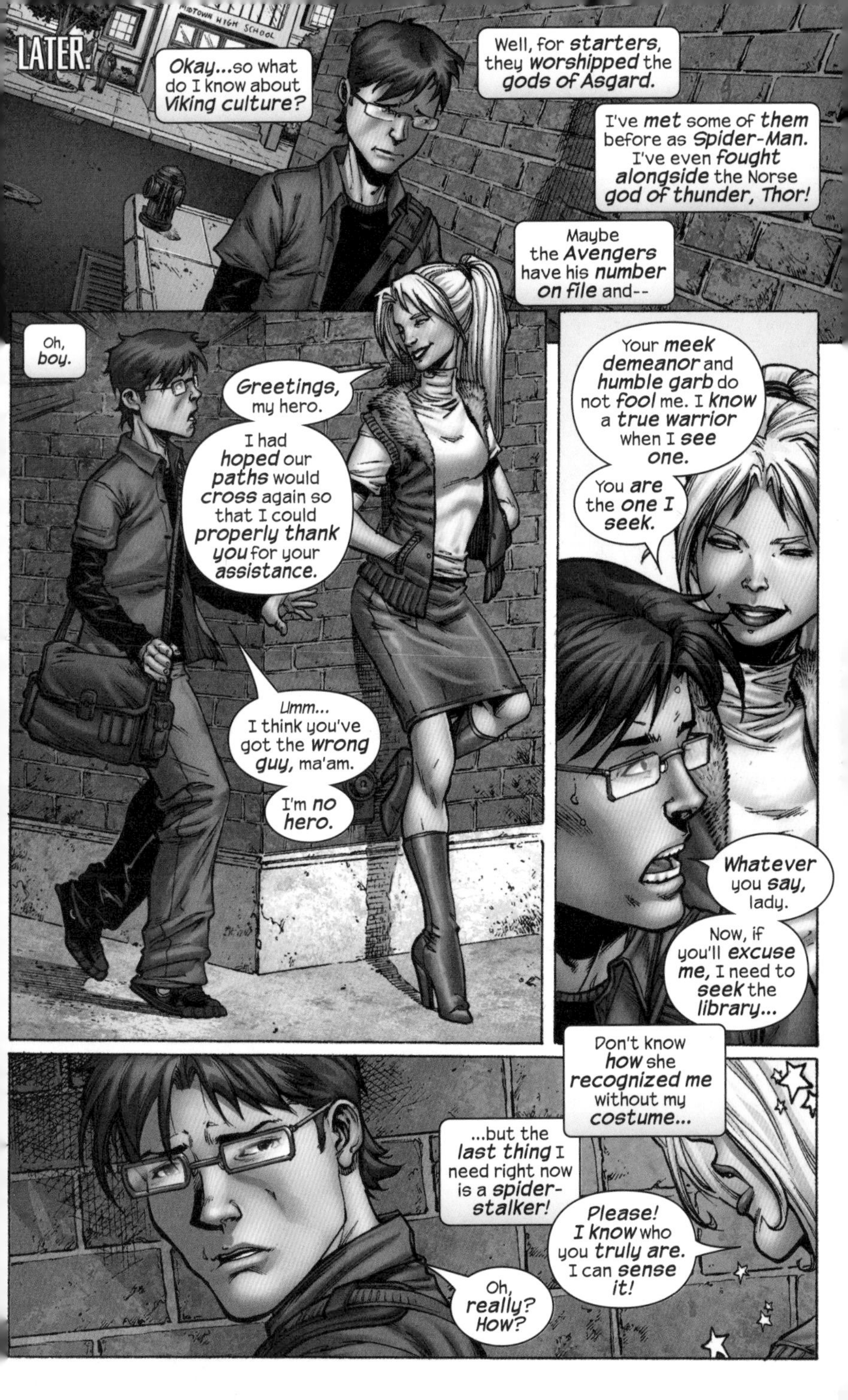
LATER.
MIDTOWN HIGH SCHOOL
Okay...so what do I know about Viking culture?
Well, for starters, they worshipped the gods of Asgard.
I've met some of them before as Spider-Man. I've even fought alongside the Norse god of thunder, Thor!
Maybe the Avengers have his number on file and--
Oh, boy.
Greetings, my hero.
I had hoped our paths would cross again so that I could properly thank you for your assistance.
Umm... I think you've got the wrong guy, ma'am.
I'm no hero.
Your meek demeanor and humble garb do not fool me. I know a true warrior when I see one.
You are the one I seek.
Whatever you say, lady.
Now, if you'll excuse me, I need to seek the library...
Don't know how she recognized me without my costume...
...but the last thing I need right now is a spider-stalker!
Please! I know who you truly are. I can sense it!
Oh, really? How?

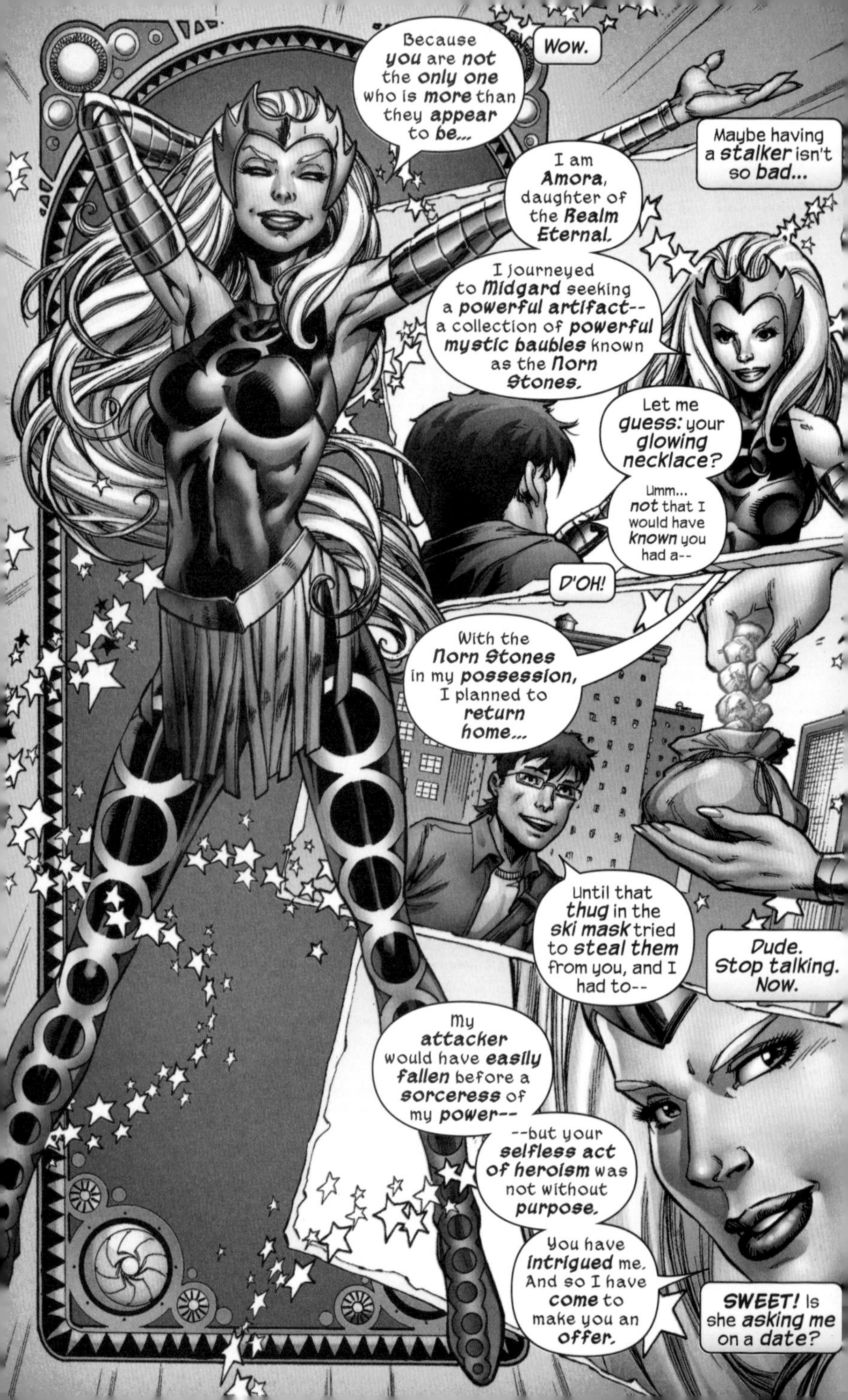
Because you are not the only one who is more than they appear to be...
WOW.
Maybe having a stalker isn't so bad...
I am Amora, daughter of the Realm Eternal.
I journeyed to Midgard seeking a powerful artifact-- a collection of powerful mystic baubles known as the Norn Stones.
Let me guess: your glowing necklace?
Umm... not that I would have known you had a--
D'OH!
With the Norn Stones in my possession, I planned to return home...
Until that thug in the ski mask tried to steal them from you, and I had to--
Dude. Stop talking. Now.
My attacker would have easily fallen before a sorceress of my power--
--but your selfless act of heroism was not without purpose.
You have intrigued me. And so I have come to make you an offer.
SWEET! Is she asking me on a date?

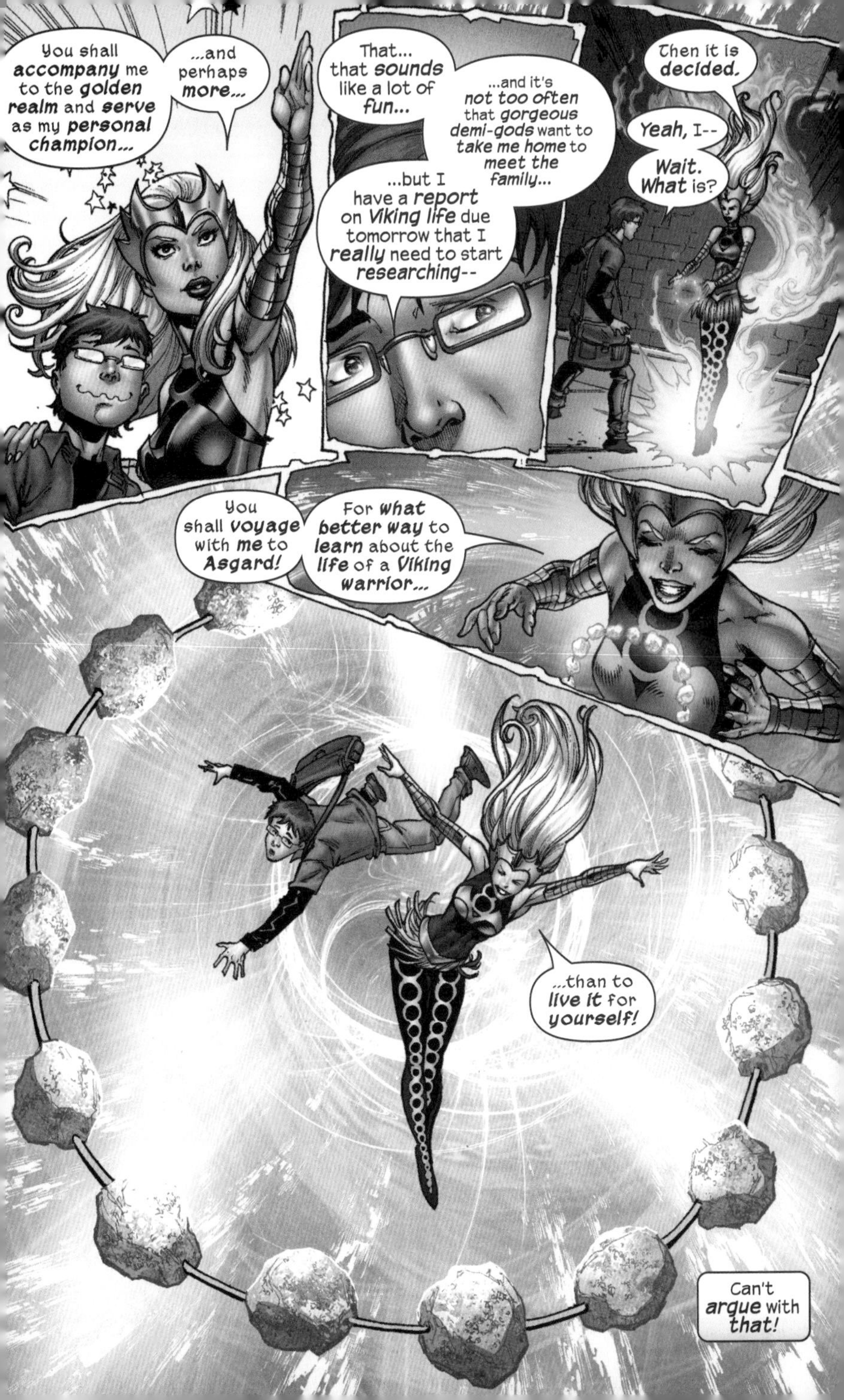

You shall accompany me to the golden realm and serve as my personal champion...
...and perhaps more...
That... that sounds like a lot of fun...
...and it's not too often that gorgeous demi-gods want to take me home to meet the family...
...but I have a report on Viking life due tomorrow that I really need to start researching--
Then it is decided.
Yeah, I--
Wait. What is?
You shall voyage with me to Asgard!
For what better way to learn about the life of a Viking warrior...
...than to live it for yourself!
Can't argue with that!

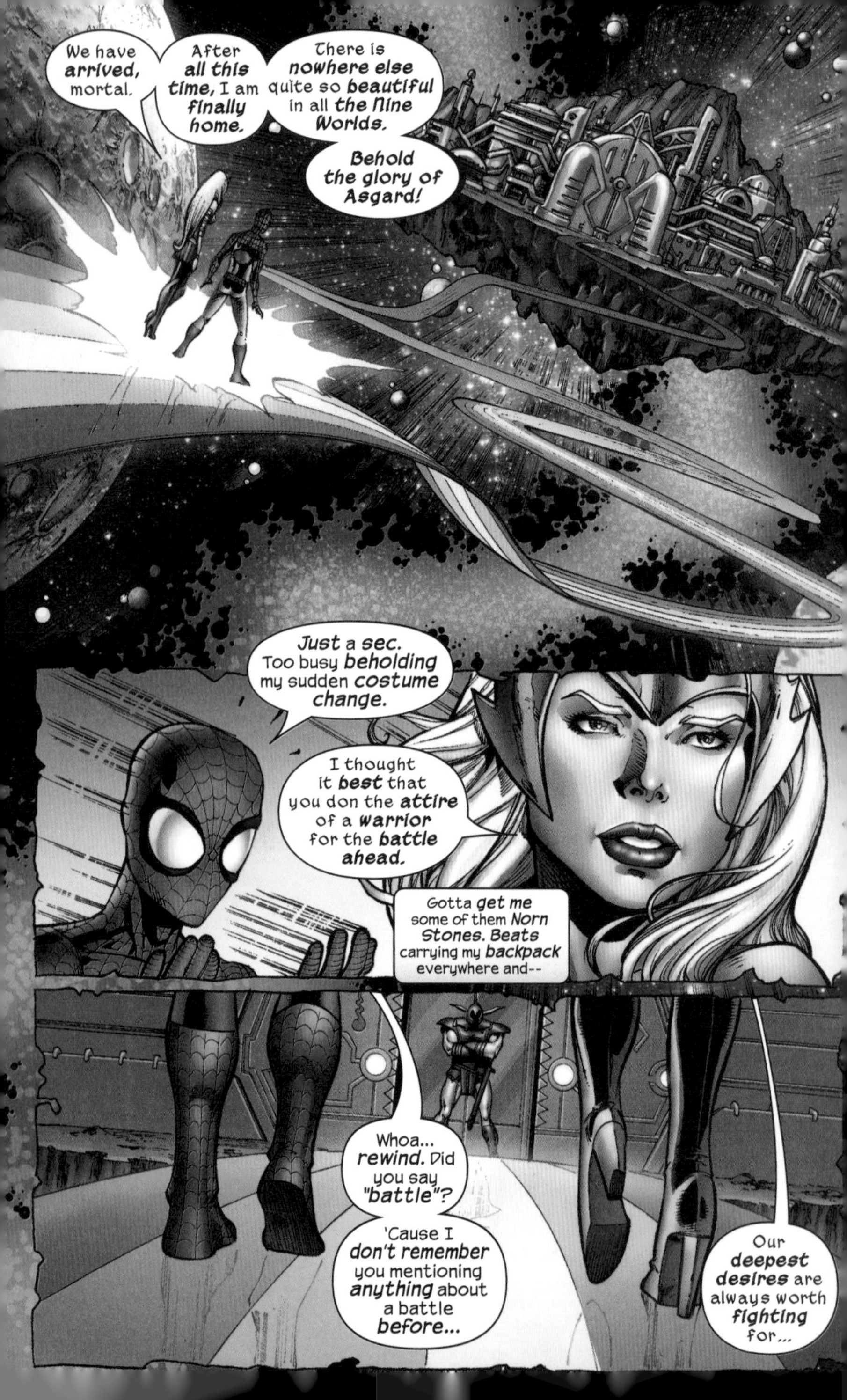
We have arrived, mortal.
After all this time, I am finally home.
There is nowhere else quite so beautiful in all the Nine Worlds.
Behold the glory of Asgard!
Just a sec. Too busy beholding my sudden costume change.
I thought it best that you don the attire of a warrior for the battle ahead.
Gotta get me some of them Norn Stones. Beats carrying my backpack everywhere and--
Whoa... rewind. Did you say "battle"?
'Cause I don't remember you mentioning anything about a battle before...
Our deepest desires are always worth fighting for...

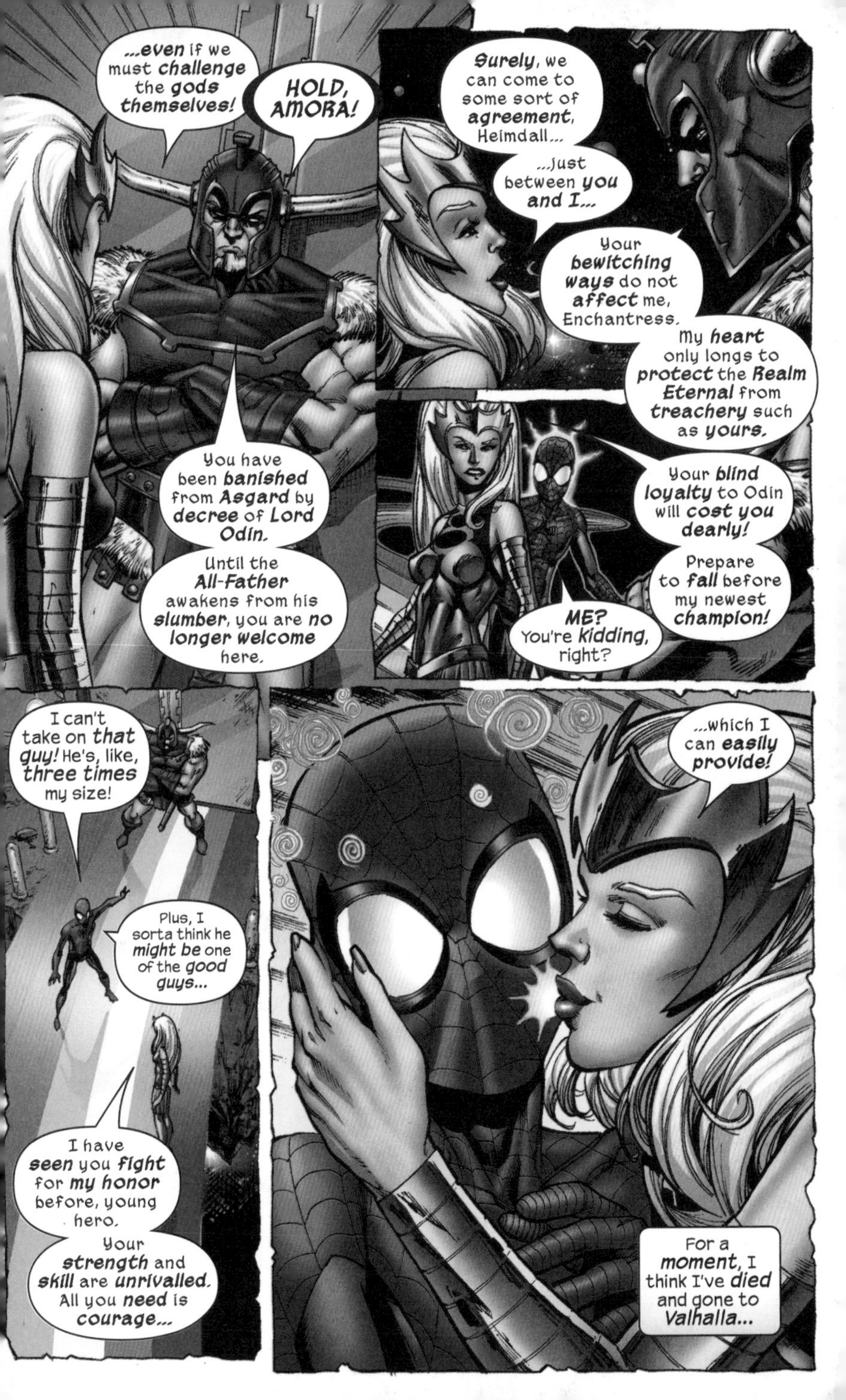
...even if we must challenge the gods themselves!
HOLD, AMORA!
You have been banished from Asgard by decree of Lord Odin.
Until the All-Father awakens from his slumber, you are no longer welcome here.
Surely, we can come to some sort of agreement, Heimdall...
...just between you and I...
Your bewitching ways do not affect me, Enchantress.
My heart only longs to protect the Realm Eternal from treachery such as yours.
Your blind loyalty to Odin will cost you dearly!
Prepare to fall before my newest champion!
ME? You're kidding, right?
I can't take on that guy! He's, like, three times my size!
Plus, I sorta think he might be one of the good guys...
I have seen you fight for my honor before, young hero.
Your strength and skill are unrivalled. All you need is courage...
...which I can easily provide!
For a moment, I think I've died and gone to Valhalla...

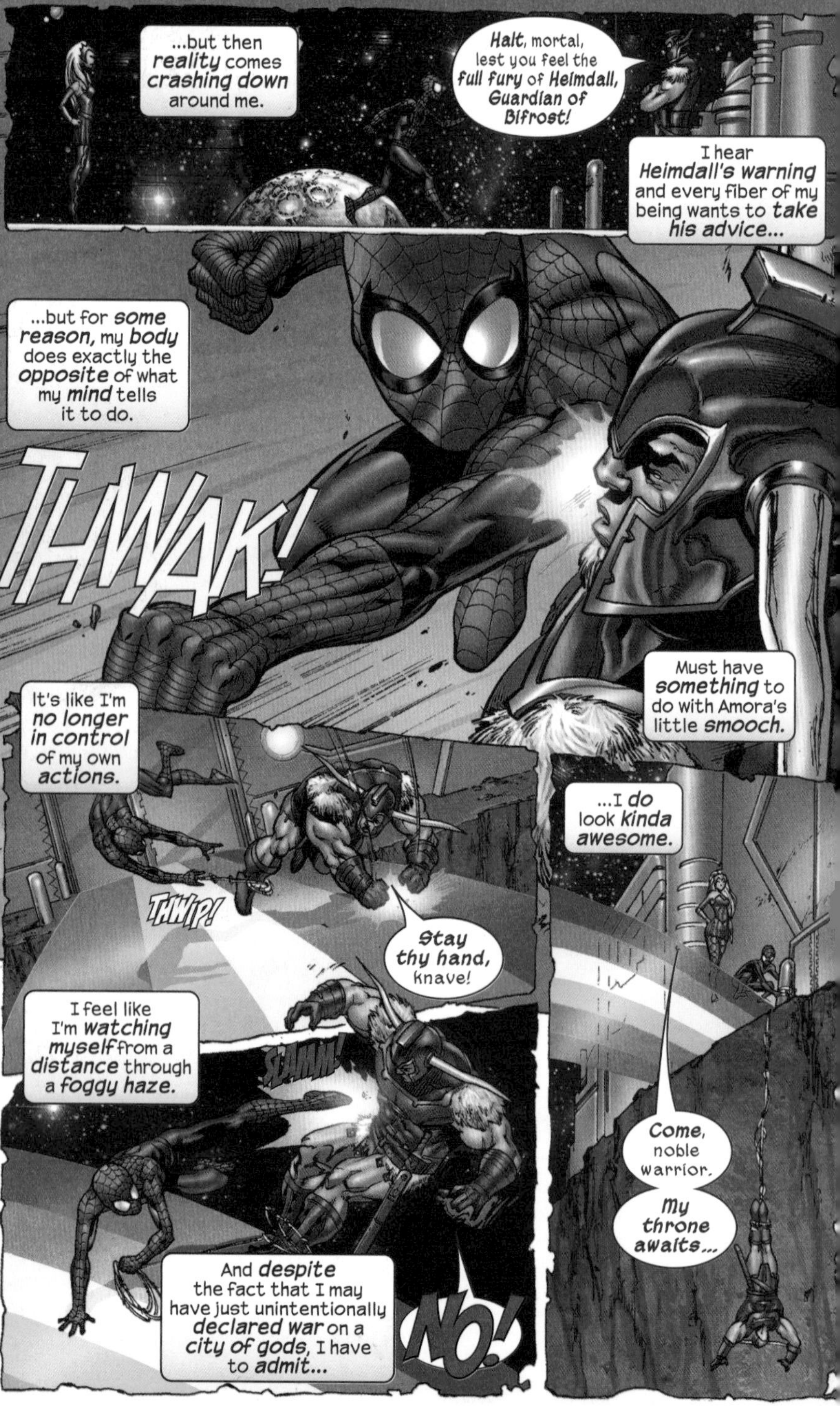
...but then reality comes crashing down around me.
Halt, mortal, lest you feel the full fury of Heimdall, Guardian of Bifrost!
I hear Heimdall's warning and every fiber of my being wants to take his advice...
...but for some reason, my body does exactly the opposite of what my mind tells it to do.
THWAK!
Must have something to do with Amora's little smooch.
It's like I'm no longer in control of my own actions.
THWIP!
Stay thy hand, knave!
I feel like I'm watching myself from a distance through a foggy haze.
SLAMM!
And despite the fact that I may have just unintentionally declared war on a city of gods, I have to admit...
NO!
...I do look kinda awesome.
Come, noble warrior.
My throne awaits...

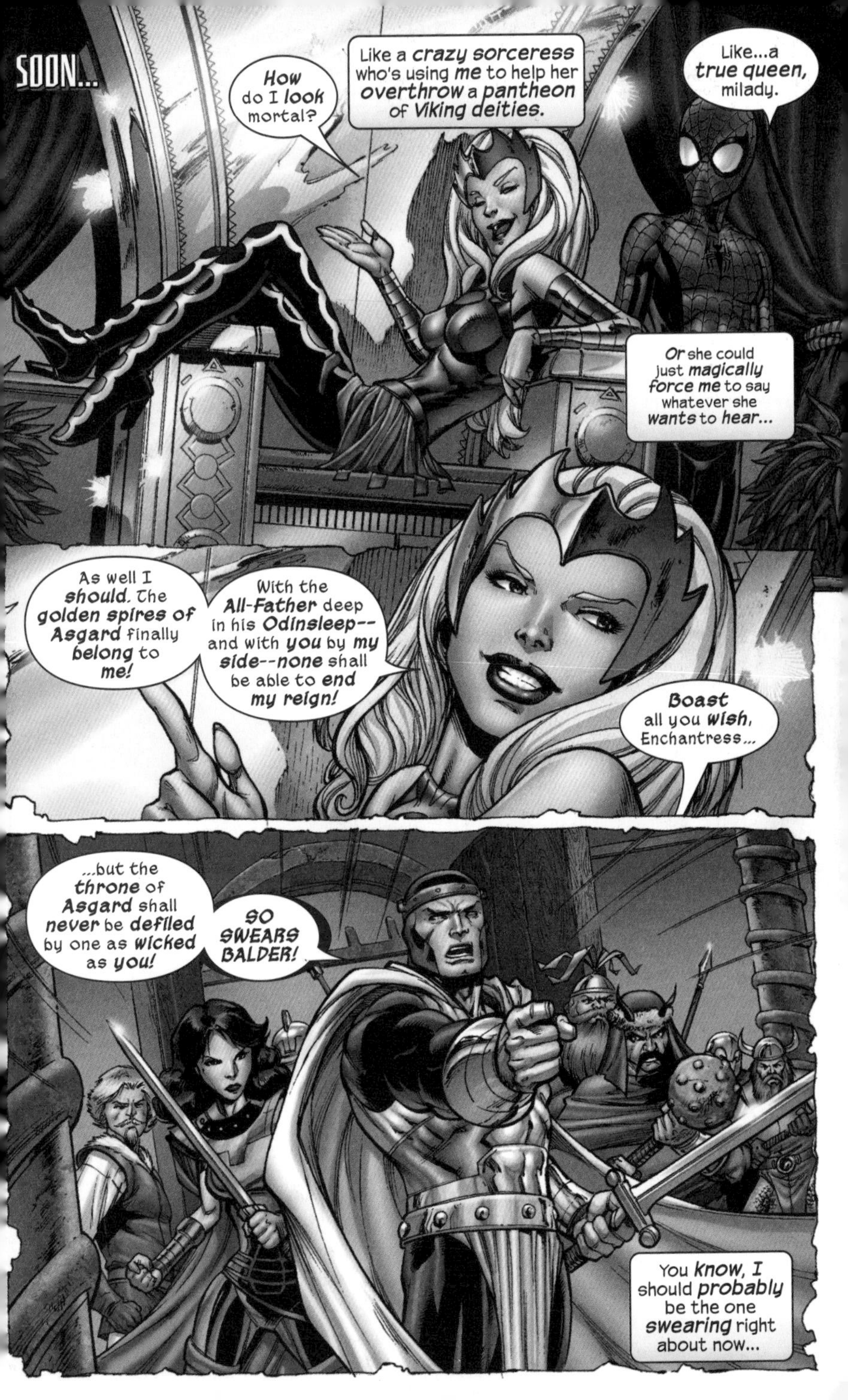
SOON...
How do I look mortal?
Like a crazy sorceress who's using me to help her overthrow a pantheon of Viking deities.
Like...a true queen, milady.
Or she could just magically force me to say whatever she wants to hear...
As well I should. The golden spires of Asgard finally belong to me!
With the All-Father deep in his Odinsleep-- and with you by my side--none shall be able to end my reign!
Boast all you wish, Enchantress...
...but the throne of Asgard shall never be defiled by one as wicked as you!
SO SWEARS BALDER!
You know, I should probably be the one swearing right about now...

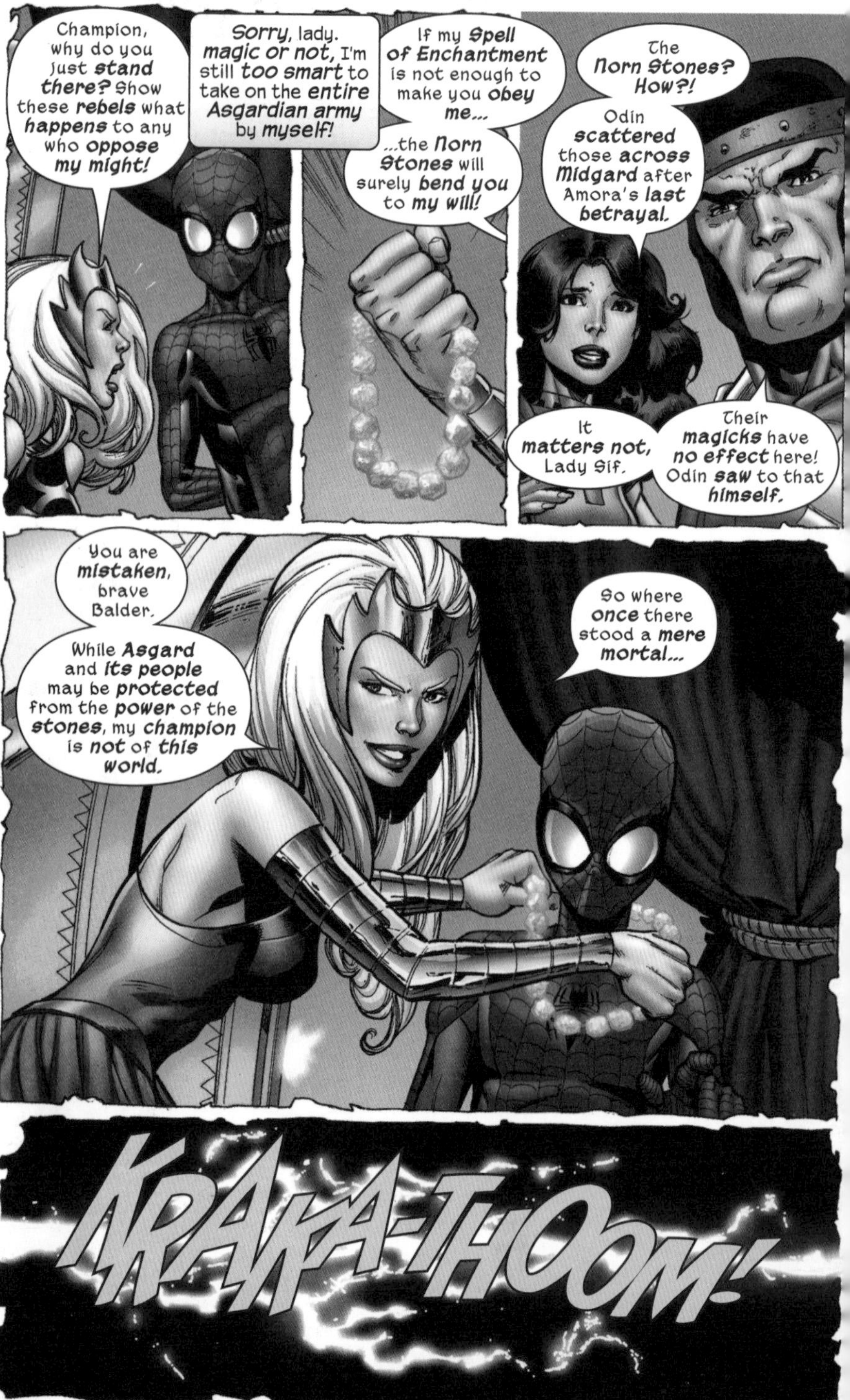

Champion, why do you just stand there? Show these rebels what happens to any who oppose my might!
Sorry, lady. magic or not, I'm still too smart to take on the entire Asgardian army by myself!
If my Spell of Enchantment is not enough to make you obey me...
...the Norn Stones will surely bend you to my will!
The Norn Stones? How?!
Odin scattered those across Midgard after Amora's last betrayal.
It matters not, Lady Sif.
Their magicks have no effect here! Odin saw to that himself.
You are mistaken, brave Balder.
While Asgard and its people may be protected from the power of the stones, my champion is not of this world.
So where once there stood a mere mortal...
KRAKA-THOOM!

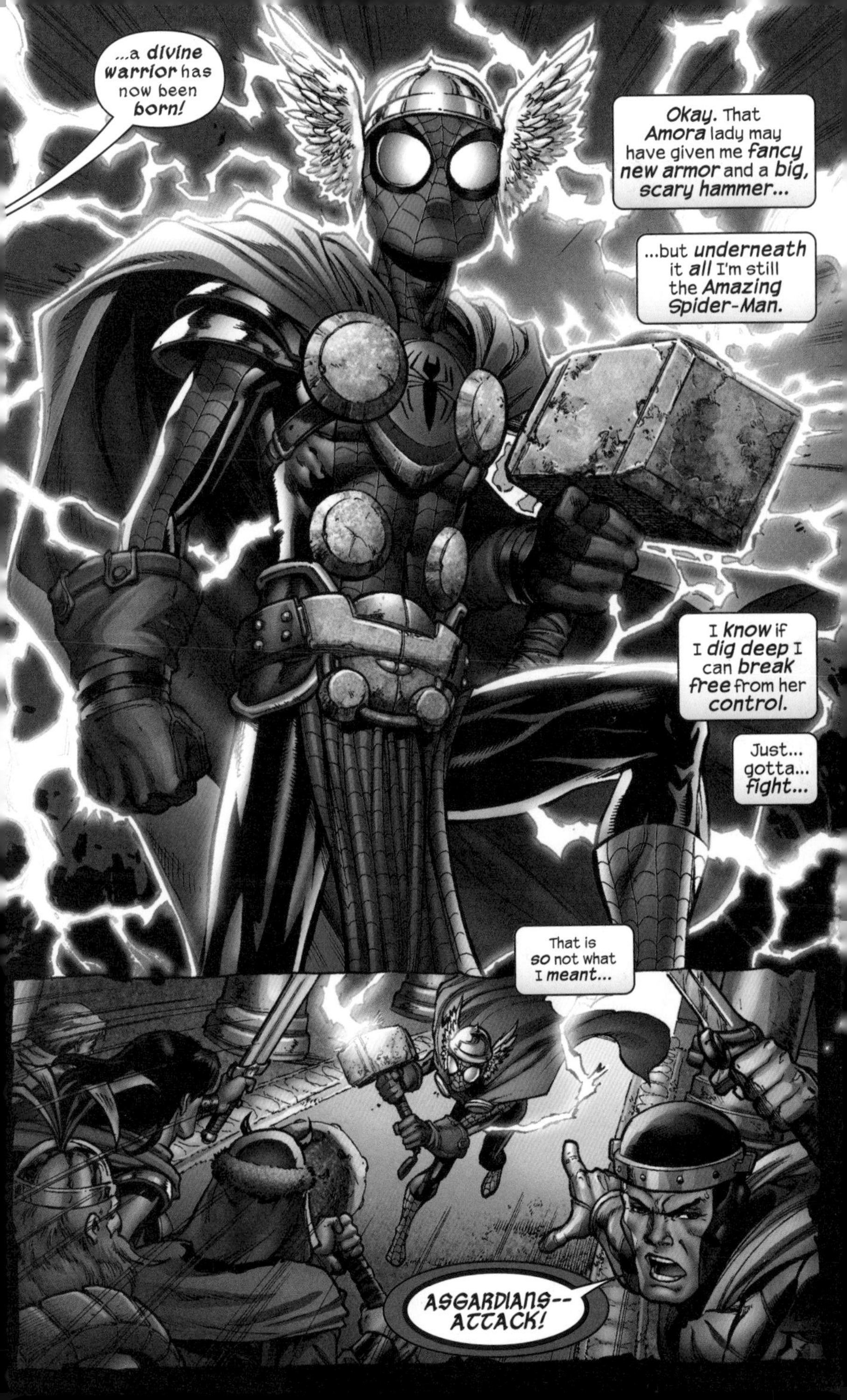
...a divine warrior has now been born!
Okay. That Amora lady may have given me fancy new armor and a big, scary hammer...
...but underneath it all I'm still the Amazing Spider-Man.
I know if I dig deep I can break free from her control.
Just... gotta... fight...
That is so not what I meant...
ASGARDIANS-- ATTACK!

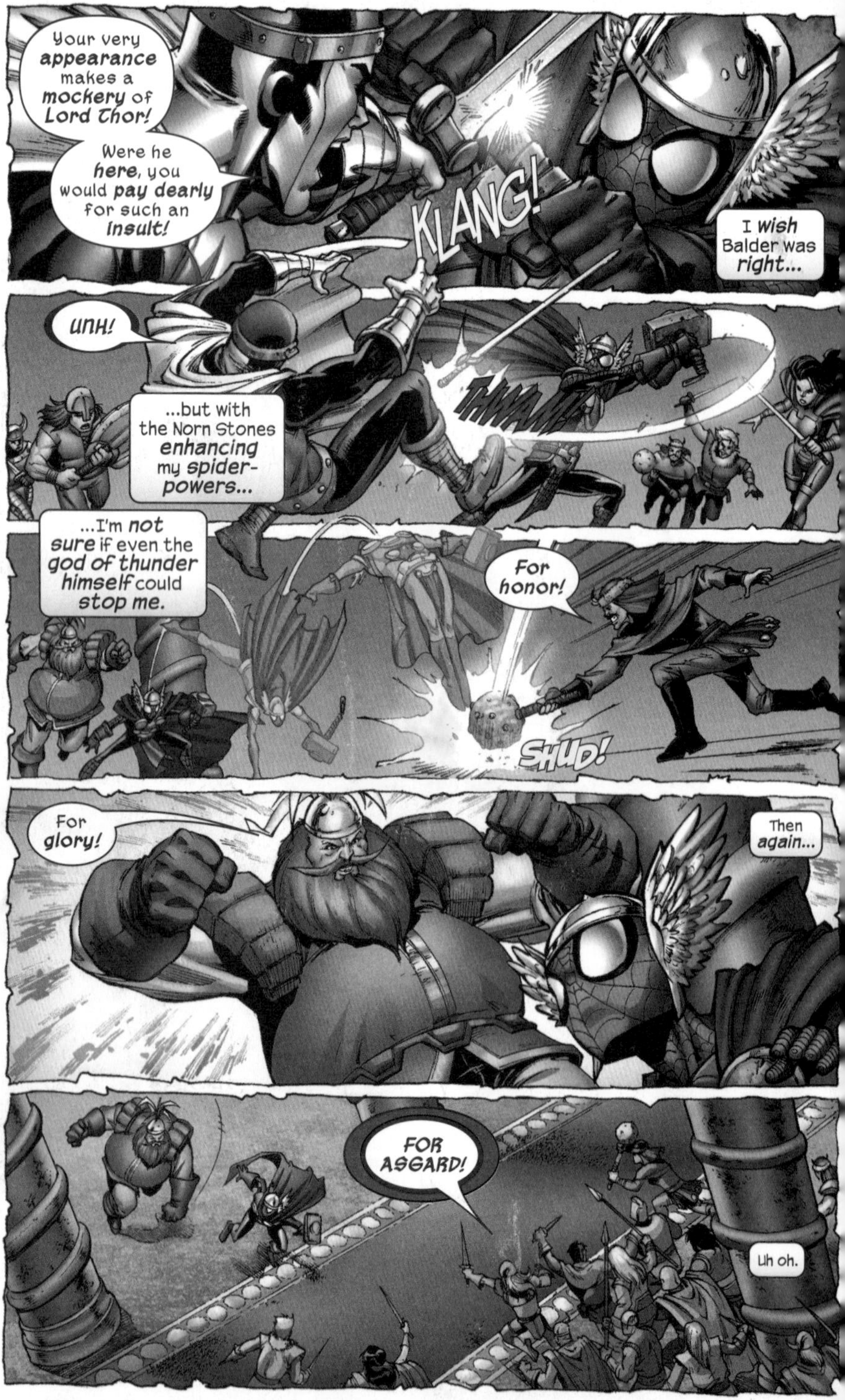
Your very appearance makes a mockery of Lord Thor!
Were he here, you would pay dearly for such an insult!
KLANG!
I wish Balder was right...
UNH!
THWAM!
...but with the Norn Stones enhancing my spider-powers...
...I'm not sure if even the god of thunder himself could stop me.
For honor!
SHUD!
For glory!
Then again...
FOR ASGARD!
Uh oh.

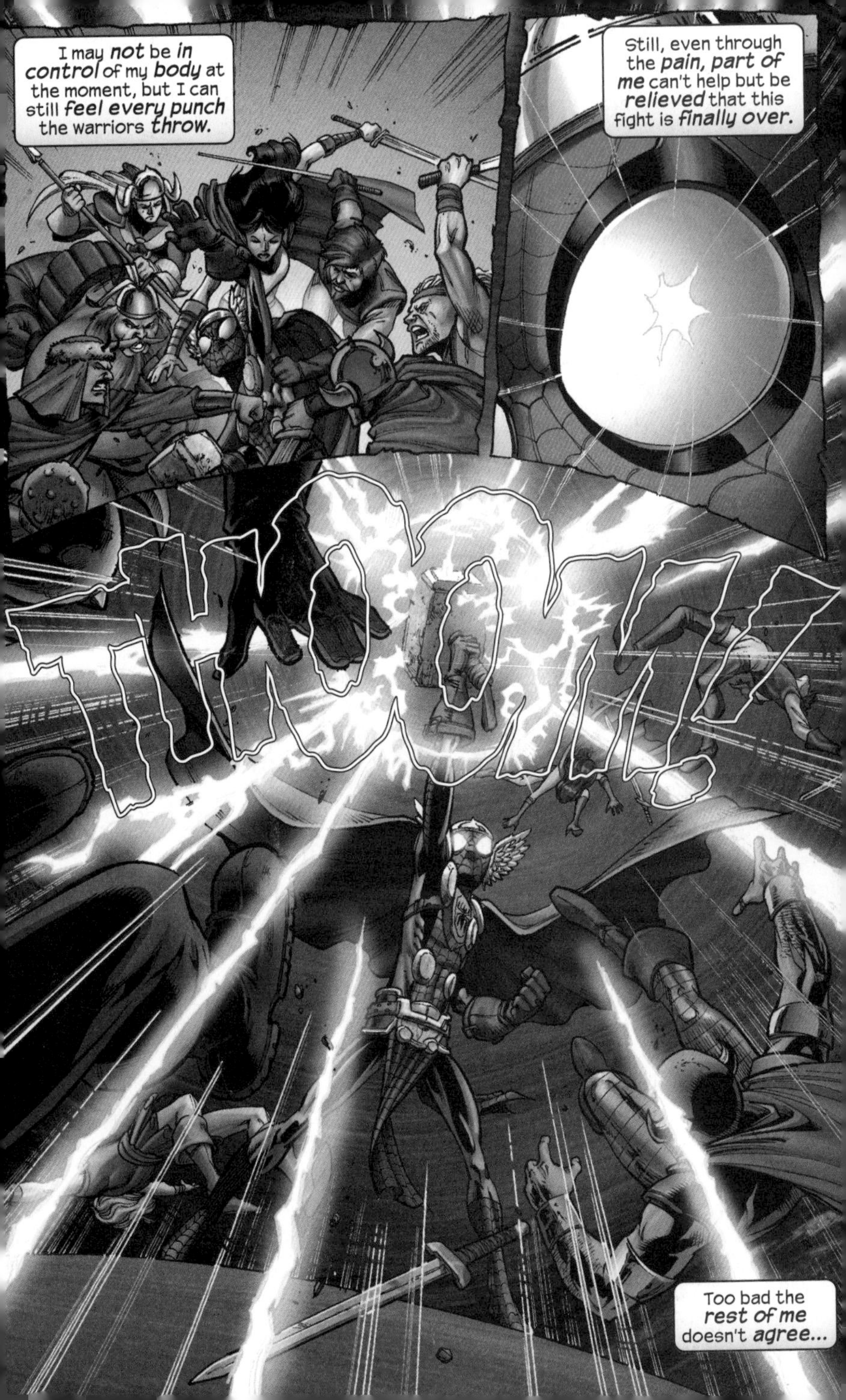
I may not be in control of my body at the moment, but I can still feel every punch the warriors throw.
Still, even through the pain, part of me can't help but be relieved that this fight is finally over.
THOOM!!
Too bad the rest of me doesn't agree...

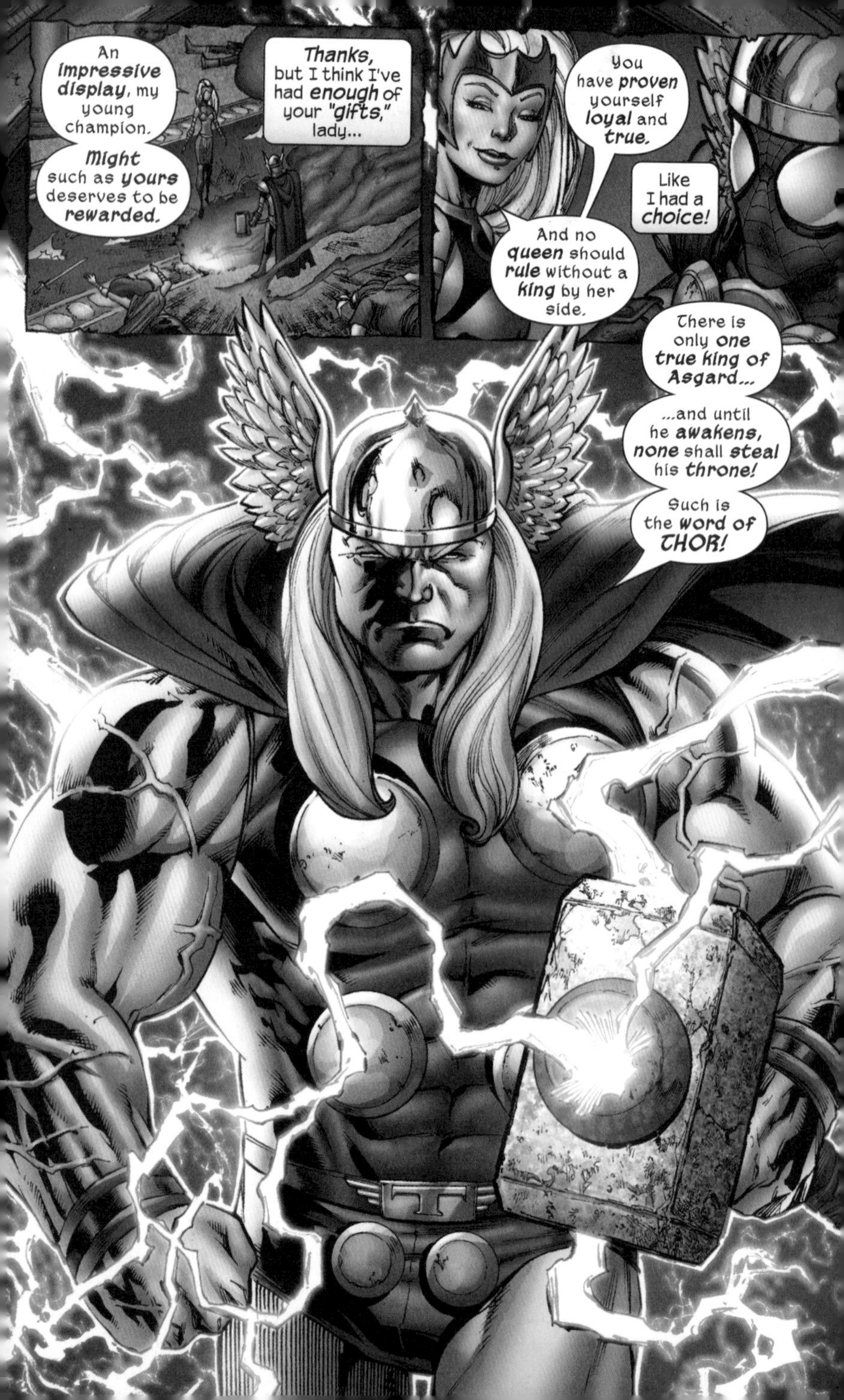

An impressive display, my young champion.
Might such as yours deserves to be rewarded.
Thanks, but I think I've had enough of your "gifts," lady...
You have proven yourself loyal and true.
And no queen should rule without a king by her side.
Like I had a choice!
There is only one true king of Asgard...
...and until he awakens, none shall steal his throne!
Such is the word of THOR!

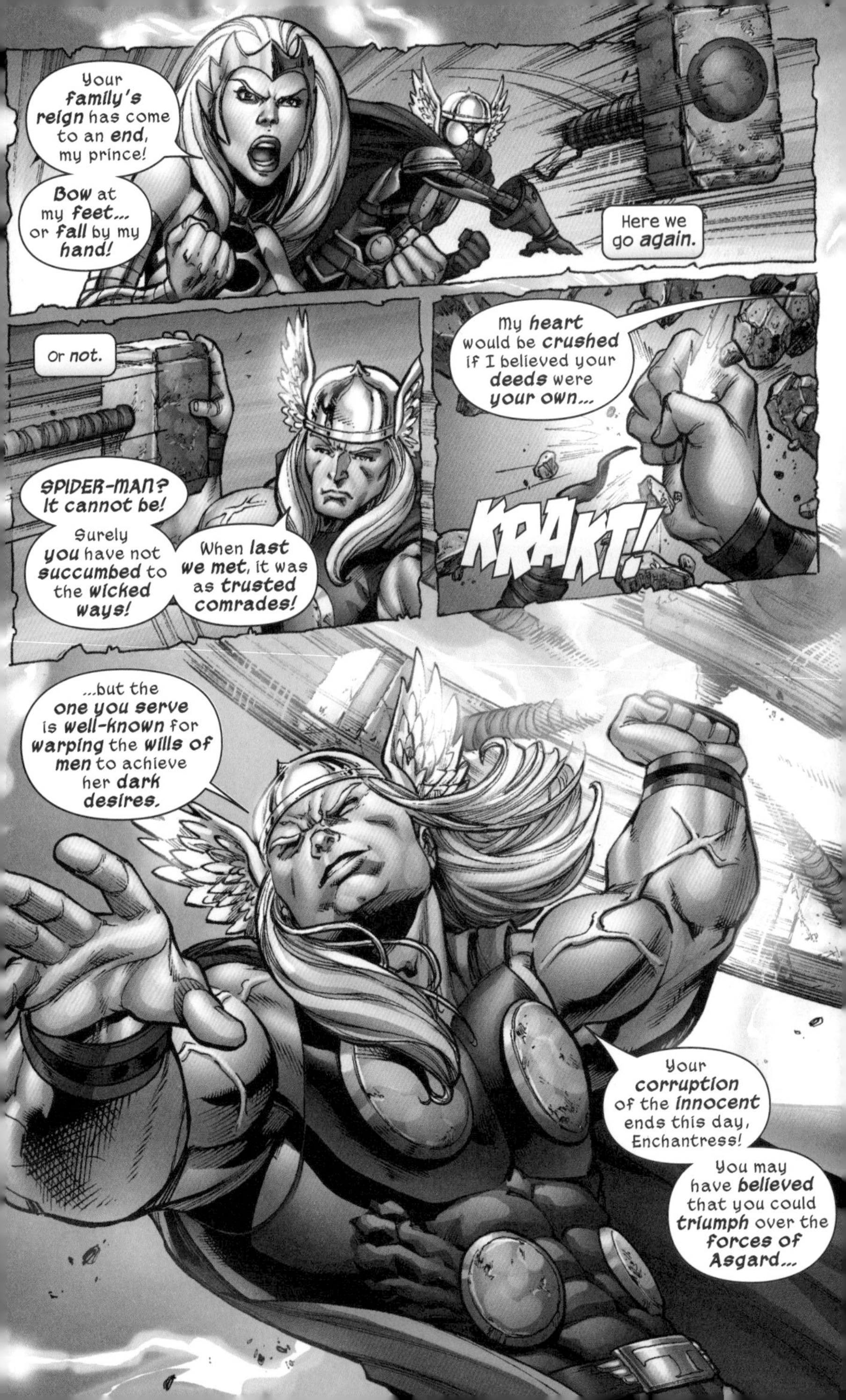
Your family's reign has come to an end, my prince!
Bow at my feet... or fall by my hand!
Here we go again.
Or not.
SPIDER-MAN? It cannot be!
Surely you have not succumbed to the wicked ways!
When last we met, it was as trusted comrades!
My heart would be crushed if I believed your deeds were your own...
KRAKT!!
...but the one you serve is well-known for warping the wills of men to achieve her dark desires.
Your corruption of the innocent ends this day, Enchantress!
You may have believed that you could triumph over the forces of Asgard...

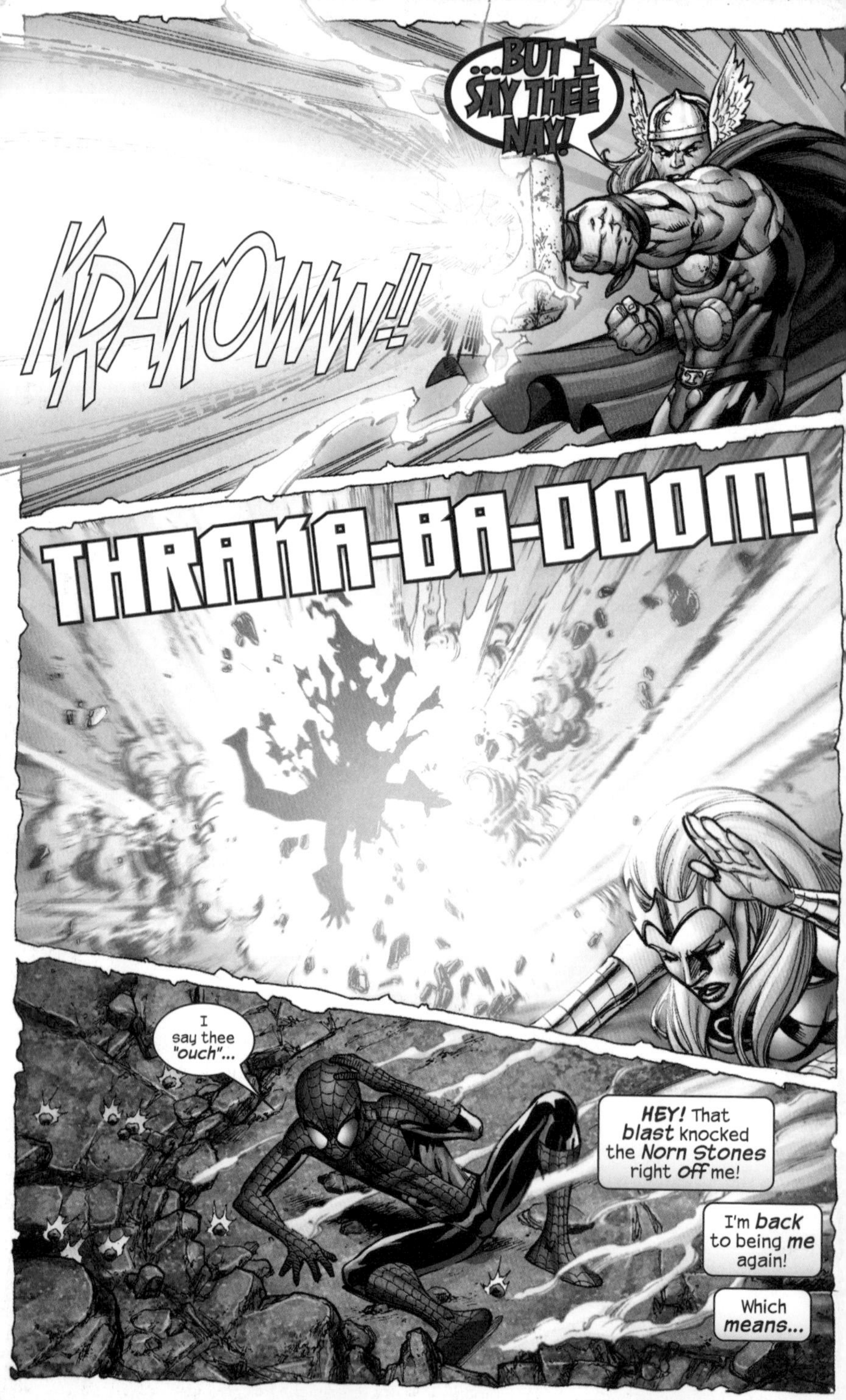
...BUT I SAY THEE NAY!
KRAKOWW!!
THRAKA-BA-DOOM!
I say thee "ouch"...
HEY! That blast knocked the Norn Stones right off me!
I'm back to being me again!
Which means...

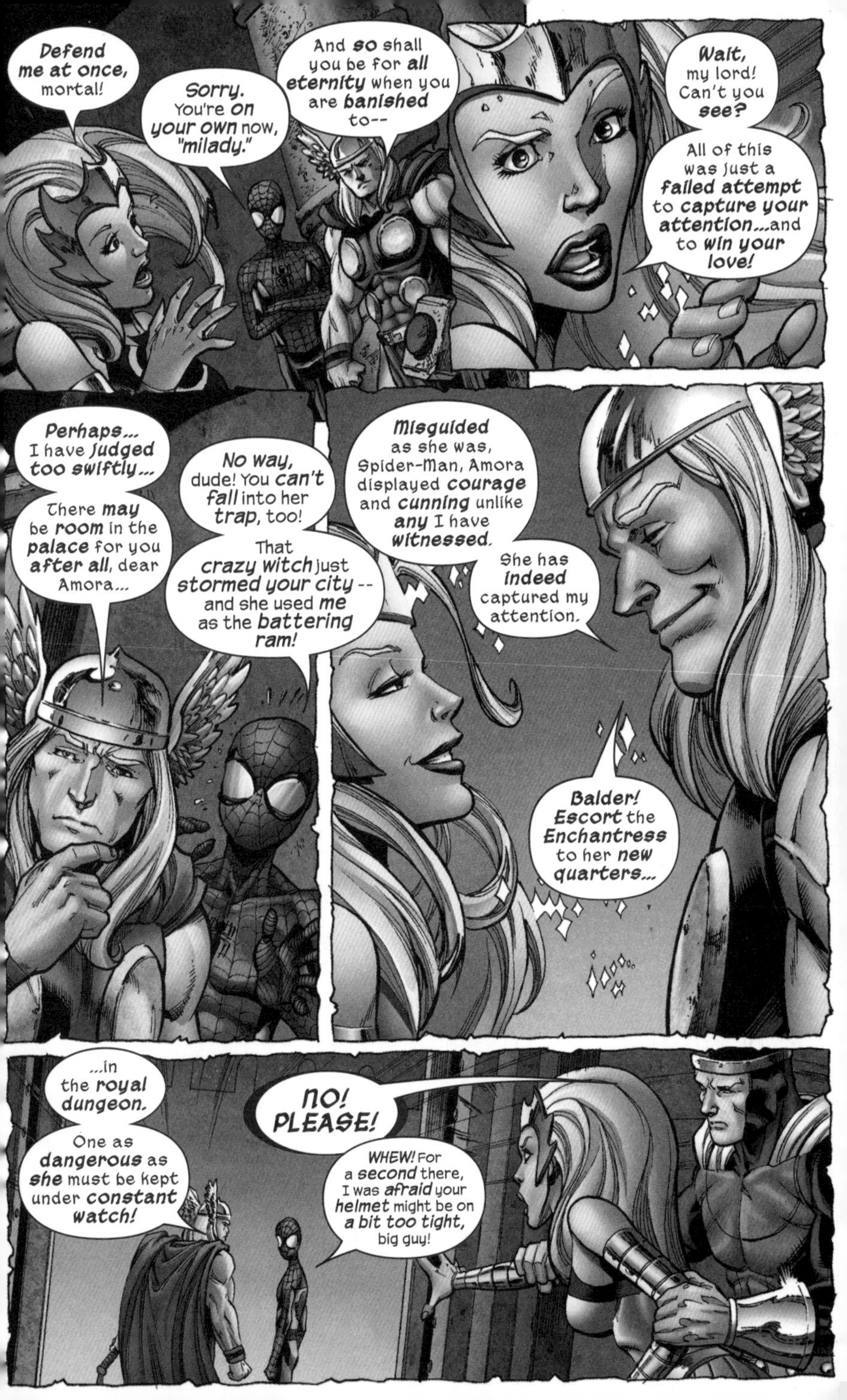
Defend me at once, mortal!
Sorry. You're on your own now, "milady."
And so shall you be for all eternity when you are banished to--
Wait, my lord! Can't you see?
All of this was just a failed attempt to capture your attention...and to win your love!
Perhaps... I have judged too swiftly...
There may be room in the palace for you after all, dear Amora...
No way, dude! You can't fall into her trap, too!
That crazy witch just stormed your city -- and she used me as the battering ram!
Misguided as she was, Spider-Man, Amora displayed courage and cunning unlike any I have witnessed.
She has indeed captured my attention.
Balder! Escort the Enchantress to her new quarters...
...in the royal dungeon.
One as dangerous as she must be kept under constant watch!
NO! PLEASE!
WHEW! For a second there, I was afraid your helmet might be on a bit too tight, big guy!

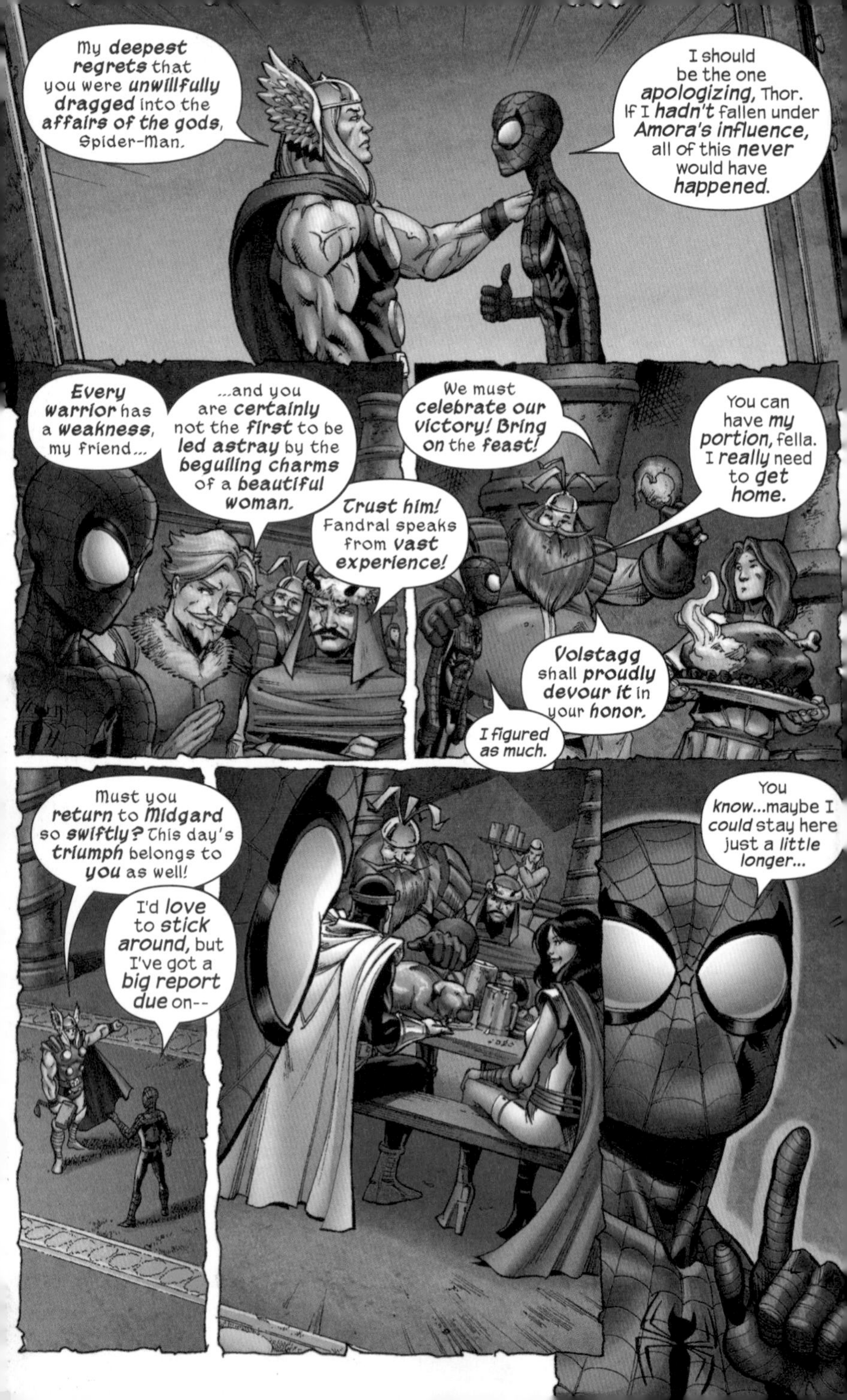
My deepest regrets that you were unwillfully dragged into the affairs of the gods, Spider-Man.
I should be the one apologizing, Thor. If I hadn't fallen under Amora's influence, all of this never would have happened.
Every warrior has a weakness, my friend...
...and you are certainly not the first to be led astray by the beguiling charms of a beautiful woman.
Trust him! Fandral speaks from vast experience!
We must celebrate our victory! Bring on the feast!
You can have my portion, fella. I really need to get home.
Volstagg shall proudly devour it in your honor.
I figured as much.
Must you return to Midgard so swiftly? This day's triumph belongs to you as well!
I'd love to stick around, but I've got a big report due on--
You know...maybe I could stay here just a little longer...

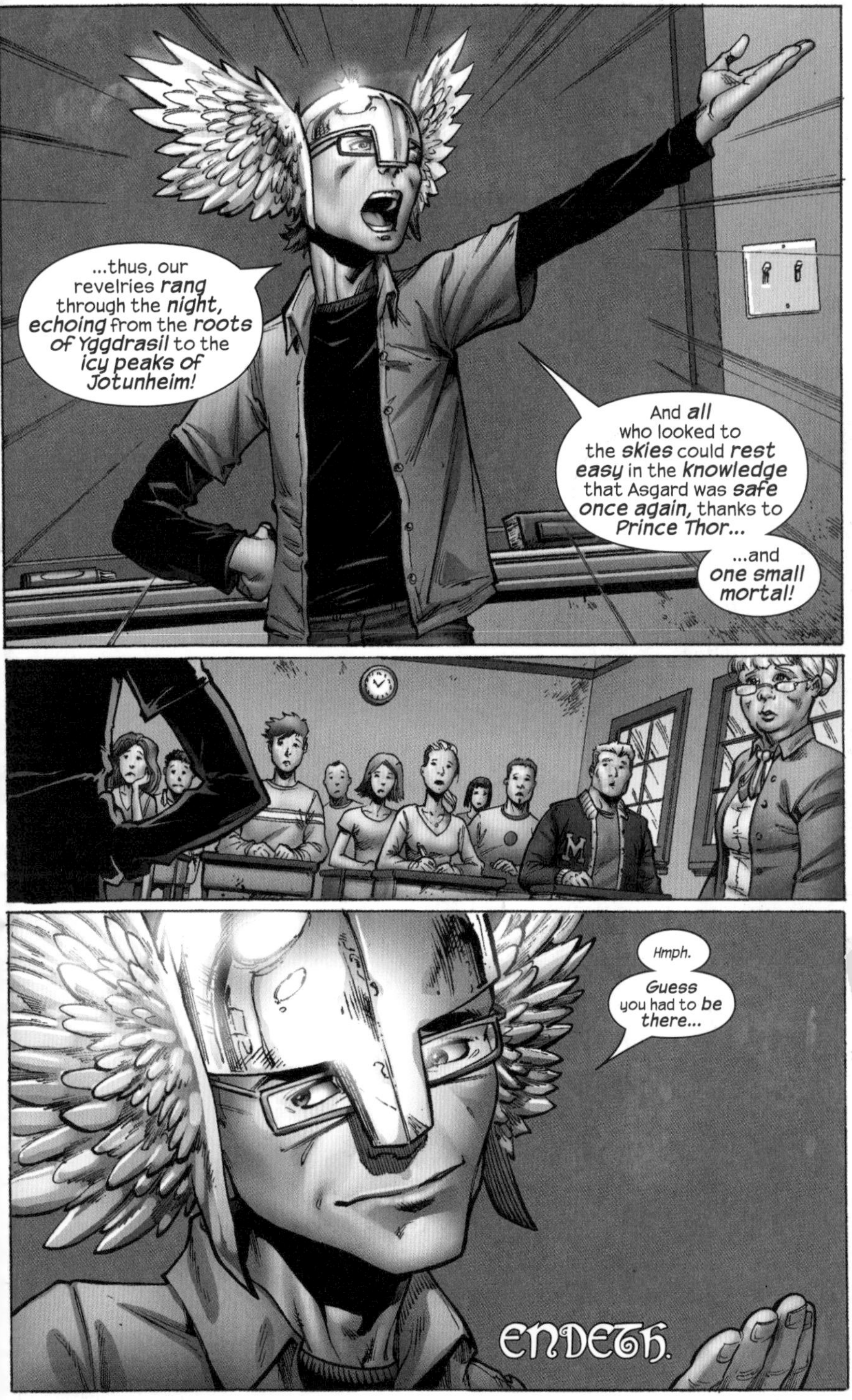
...thus, our revelries rang through the night, echoing from the roots of Yggdrasil to the icy peaks of Jotunheim!
And all who looked to the skies could rest easy in the knowledge that Asgard was safe once again, thanks to Prince Thor...
...and one small mortal!
Hmph.
Guess you had to be there...
ENDETH.

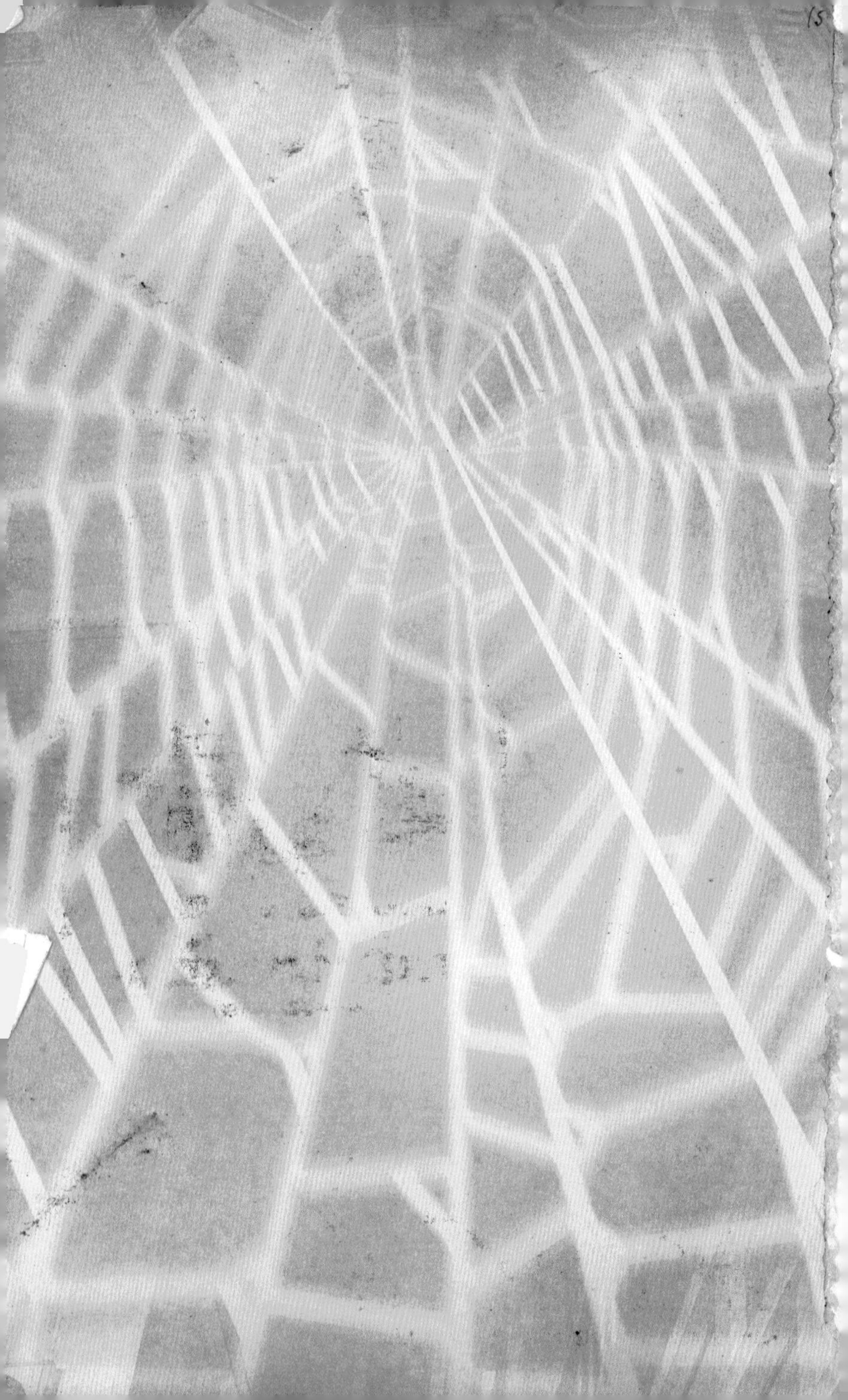